"*I want you.* I think I wanted you the moment I saw you," Tyler murmured.

His fingers continued to stroke, featherlight, up and down her arms. He drew in a slow, rough breath, then molded his hands over her shoulders, holding her. His lips caressed the nape of her neck.

"I want you," he repeated. "Stay with me."

Only in her wildest dreams had Carlie ever considered Tyler saying such a thing to her. It was unbelievable. It was unimaginable.

It was her own private fantasy.

She swallowed hard, squeezed her eyes shut, then whispered, "I want you, too."

LORI
FOSTER

impetuous

BONUS: An original story by JULIE ELIZABETH LETO

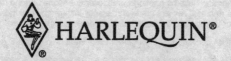

HARLEQUIN®

TORONTO • NEW YORK • LONDON
AMSTERDAM • PARIS • SYDNEY • HAMBURG
STOCKHOLM • ATHENS • TOKYO • MILAN • MADRID
PRAGUE • WARSAW • BUDAPEST • AUCKLAND

ISBN 0-373-83551-5

IMPETUOUS

Copyright © 2003 by Harlequin Books S.A.

The publisher acknowledges the copyright holders of the individual works as follows:

IMPETUOUS
Copyright © 1996 by Lori Foster

ONE WICKED WEEKEND
Copyright © 2001 by Harlequin Books S.A.

CONTENTS

Books by Lori Foster

IMPETUOUS

Lori Foster

To Patti Fischer,
Thank you for being a great cyber friend,
a poster of reviews, a listener of woes
and a loyal bookjunkie. The list
wouldn't be the same without you.

CHAPTER ONE

"YOU CAN'T BE a coward forever."

Carlie chuckled, despite her nervousness. "Quit pushing, Bren. You're not going to provoke me into rushing out into the party dressed like this."

"Rushing? You're already ten minutes late." She had parked in the back of the house, away from the main flow of human traffic entering the party. Small, twinkling lights surrounded the pool and pool house, even though the weather was too brisk for swimming.

"And that's *your* fault. What were you thinking, to pick me a costume that was so…so…" Carlie couldn't quite find the words to describe the skimpy harem outfit her best friend had chosen for her. If she had to go to Brenda's stupid Halloween party at all, she would have preferred to be a pumpkin or a witch. Anything that was less revealing.

"So…what? You look fantastic. What's wrong with that? I want you to have fun tonight. I want you to loosen up a little and try socializing. Talk to people."

"You mean men, don't you?" Carlie shook her head. "I'm not a hermit, Bren. I have my students and more than enough school activities to keep me busy.'' Then she glanced down at herself. ''What *were* you thinking?''

''You said you didn't have time to pick out an outfit yourself.'' Brenda lifted one shoulder in a half-hearted shrug. ''Besides, you make a very sexy harem girl. All the single men here tonight will drool. It'll do you good to realize how attractive you can be when you aren't hiding behind those hideous suits.''

Carlie winced. She was feeling far from attractive. Exhibited, displayed and downright exposed was more accurate. She was pretty certain she looked ridiculous more than anything else. ''Which single men, exactly, did you invite?''

Brenda waved her hand in dismissal. ''You've met almost everyone, I think. Some of Jason's associates, a few neighbors, friends…Tyler.''

Carlie went perfectly still for a heartbeat, then frowned at Brenda. ''Tyler Ramsey at a costume party? I didn't think your notorious brother-in-law would bother with something so—''

''Don't make fun of my party, Carlie.''

''I wasn't. I just thought fancy banquets were more his speed.'' Carlie couldn't imagine Tyler dressed in a costume. He always seemed so…suave. And he always had a very sophisticated, very elegant woman on his arm.

''Tyler came because Jason asked him, and he would never let his brother down. You know how close they are." Brenda shook her head and added, "You know, you and Tyler actually have a few things in common."

Carlie turned away. "You're dreaming, Bren. We live in different worlds."

"You just don't understand Tyler. He had it pretty rough growing up, too." Then she touched Carlie's arm. "But at least Jason was always there for him."

"My brother had his own life," Carlie said. "And he was right, my problems were my own."

"Jason would never turn Tyler away if he needed help."

"Jason's a terrific guy. But he and Tyler are nothing alike."

"Not now, maybe, but they used to be," Brenda said with a grin. "But then, Jason met me. I think Tyler will be the same. When he finds someone he cares about…"

Carlie narrowed her eyes and stiffened her shoulders. "That will be a little hard for him to do when his relationships rarely last long enough to get to know a woman."

Brenda stared at Carlie, her eyebrows raised. "You seem to be keeping pretty close track of my young brother-in-law."

"He's not that young." But Carlie flushed at being caught. "I mean, he's a grown man. He must be in his early thirties…oh, never mind."

"Tyler's a good guy, Carlie. He may change dates

a lot, but that's because the women he usually hooks up with are only impressed by his status in the community and his expanding financial portfolio. Tyler *thinks* he wants a no-strings attachment, but he's never satisfied with it.''

Carlie had a feeling it was Tyler's looks and outrageous charm that really attracted women, but she kept her mouth shut. She certainly didn't want Brenda to get the idea she had a crush on Tyler Ramsey.

Good grief. A *crush!* No, she didn't. Certainly not.

Carlie was shaking her head at her errant thoughts, even as she said, ''You don't have to defend Tyler to me, Bren. What he does is no concern of mine.''

''Fine. Then if you're done stalling, can we get back to the party now? I think it's about to rain.''

Carlie glanced up at the dark sky and smelled the moisture thick in the air. ''You go on, Bren. I think I'll just wait a few more minutes.''

Brenda hesitated, then she nodded. ''Don't be too long.''

Too long? Carlie wondered if another hour or so would be too long. She truly didn't relish the idea of going inside, not that anyone would recognize her. Dressed so differently, no one would see her as Carlie McDaniels, grade-school teacher and spinster extraordinaire. Her persona this evening was as far from her usual self as a woman could get. Even her hair and eyes were different, thanks to the wig that came with the costume, and the colored contacts she was wearing.

She was a coward, true, but it had been two long years since her divorce, and though that had been enough time for her to gain her independence and put some order to her life, it hadn't been time enough to repair her confidence in herself as a woman. Brenda claimed Carlie was attractive and appealing. Carlie's ex had made an entirely different claim.

Shivering, she forced her mind away from the disturbing memories, mustered her courage and started toward the door. She could make Brenda happy by mingling for an hour or so, then she could make her escape. The thought of her small, tidy, *empty* house seemed very nice all of a sudden.

TYLER RAMSEY HATED parties.

Looking around in mild amusement, he tried not to appear bored. Everything was the same—the ritual, the games. There were several women, alone and obviously on the hunt, who had been eyeing him since he'd entered. A Cleopatra, an elf, an Indian maiden— they all were playing their phoney roles to the hilt. They were drawn to his reputation, he knew. The funny part was, most of it wasn't even true.

Turning away, he wondered why he'd allowed Brenda to talk him into coming. True, he'd been bored for a while, at loose ends with himself. He needed a spark; he needed someone who could make him laugh.

His brother laughed a lot these days.

Not that Tyler wanted to settle down. He hadn't met a woman yet with whom he could consider spending the rest of his life. Jason was lucky to have found Brenda; she was the best. But women like her were rare. Glancing around the room again, Tyler realized just what a find Brenda was. The house was filled with females, but none of them held his attention. They were all...the same. Laughing, flirting, drinking. They stood poised to best advantage, their gestures predictable.

He'd been told more than once now how dashing he looked in his pirate costume. Everyone knew it was him. He wasn't wearing makeup as some of the other guests did. His only concession was an eye patch, worn rakishly over his left eye. A billowing white shirt that he found extremely comfortable, and tight black trousers completed the costume. His belt, wide, with a huge brass buckle, held a scabbard, with a sword resting inside it. His black boots came to his knees.

He sat in a chair, observing the crowd dispassionately. Immediately, a blond Valkyrie, brass breastplate shining in the glow of party lights, came to perch on his knee, and gave him a sly smile. He recognized that smile. It belonged to his ex-companion, Valerie. It was a smile that signaled her intent, and he used to respond to it appropriately. All he felt now was irritation. She leaned close, and he forced a polite expression to his features. They'd shared something brief, and by her insistence, with no strings attached. The outcome had been predictable.

She'd wanted a man who knew the score, who could afford the best, who moved in certain circles— her circles. She liked his sports car, his professional connections, and sex. In that order.

And he'd needed someone to help him fill his time, to give him something to think about other than his legal cases and the fact that his personal life was basically...empty. But it was over.

He knew it. Why didn't she?

"Don't you recognize me, Tyler?"

There was no place to put his hands, so he rested one on her back, the other on her naked thigh. "Of course. You're a beautiful Norse goddess." His legendary innate charm surfaced through his impatience.

Valerie chuckled throatily. "You make a very believable pirate. Have you made any plans to plunder the party and steal away with female captives?"

He didn't feel like playing, so he conjured the lie without hesitation. "Actually, sweetheart, I have."

She pouted, and ran her fingers through his hair. "You look so dashing, Tyler."

He barely restrained himself from rolling his eyes. He thought of going home to his empty house—and the thought no longer seemed so unappealing.

He glanced up, and saw his sister-in-law, Brenda, standing by the kitchen door, talking with a man dressed as a Roman general. Tyler was just deciding to go home and nurse his discontent in the privacy of his own home, when Brenda turned toward the kitchen with an expectant look on her face. She gave a wide smile, and the Roman nearly dropped his glass of liquor.

Tyler felt anticipation for the first time that night. He stared, waiting. Brenda suddenly appeared to be very delighted, and he wondered why. She seemed every bit as impish as the fairy she was dressed to be.

Slowly disengaging himself from Valerie's clinging hold, Tyler stood, his curiosity swelling. He was so intent on watching Brenda, he didn't hear Valerie's complaints. His eyes were glued to the kitchen doorway.

And then he saw her.

His knees locked and he felt his thighs tense. The woman stood uncertainly by Brenda, apparently oblivious to the stares she was drawing. She was magnificent.

Long, dark curly hair fell to her shoulders, and her costume left little to the imagination. Lush, was the first thought to come to mind.

She wasn't slim, but her curves were in all the right places. Her long legs were beautifully shaped, lightly muscled, teasingly displayed in the wispy, transparent harem pants. Her waist was trim, her navel a soft shadow in the gentle swell of her belly. Her shoulders, straight and broad for a woman, were held proudly, despite her obvious reluctance, and her pale breasts were very full, firm and high. She was wearing an ornate mask, that covered her face from her nose to her hairline. He didn't care.

She bent and whispered something in Brenda's ear. Brenda lost her smile, and looked around the room as if seeking encouragement. Her eyes passed over Tyler, then seeing his rapt stare, she turned to the harem girl. *Her eyes* soon followed.

He caught her gaze, literally. Even from the distance that separated them, Tyler could feel her nervousness. She seemed startled by his awareness, and displeased. She was poised for flight.

He didn't smile. He pulled off his eye patch and started toward her. She seemed unable to move, her eyes widening. As he came closer, he saw that she was very pale and that her eyes were a startling, unnatural shade of vivid blue. Contacts? As part of her costume?

He was intrigued.

With only a few feet separating them, he was pulled to an abrupt stop by Valerie.

He glanced at Valerie with stark impatience. "I have to go."

"Tyler, wait! I wanted to talk to you." Her hand slid up his arm to grip his shirt. Her voice lowered to a purr. "I need a date tomorrow. For a banquet. It will be...fun."

He didn't have time for this. Valerie always came around when she wanted something from him. He had no doubt she needed him to gain entrée into the charity banquet. With plates going at a thousand dollars apiece, she knew there would be influential people there.

He wasn't interested.

Shaking his head, he turned back toward the woman in the harem costume...but she was gone. He moved to the kitchen in time to see her ducking out the back door. A hundred thoughts flew through his mind.

She was exquisite, exciting, and she was evidently running. From him?

He didn't want to lose sight of her, didn't want to take the chance that he wouldn't be able to find her again later. It was ridiculous, really, the urgency he felt, but he acted on it, anyway.

Brenda caught his arm as he tried to go past her.

"Tyler!" Her grip was firm, effectively stopping him. "Aren't you going to say hi?"

"What?" His question was a bark, filled with impatience.

Brenda stared at him. "What's the matter with you?"

"Who was she?"

Her eyebrows arching, Brenda looked behind her. "Oh…just one of the guests."

Tyler narrowed his eyes. "She's leaving already?"

"No, she…" Brenda shook her head. "She's a little shy. I had to talk her into coming tonight and now she's having second thoughts."

"I think I'll go get some fresh air."

Her smile slipping, Brenda seemed startled by his abrupt statement. "It's starting to rain, Tyler. Why would you…?"

Starting to walk away, but at a more reasonable pace, he said, "Don't worry about it, Brenda. I promise not to track in any mud." Then he stepped out the back door and peered through the cloudy night, trying to catch sight of her. A lighted path led to the pool house, and more lights, in an array of party colors, circled the small building. Through the smattering of raindrops falling on his face, Tyler was able to see a flash of movement. Ignoring the rain, he followed.

His heart was hammering heavily, his stride rapid on the wet flagstone walk. His muscles were so tight, his movements seemed rough and jerky. He couldn't remember the last time he'd felt so anxious to meet a woman.

Impatience and anticipation were riding him, and he forced himself to stop outside the door of the small house. He tilted his head back, letting the rain cool his face. He was overreacting. She was only a woman, after all, he told himself.

But then he remembered her wide, startled eyes and felt his stomach clench.

He put his hand on the doorknob, half expecting it to be locked. It opened silently, allowing the muted sounds of the party to intrude.

Colored light filtered through the windows in diminished shades, elongating shadows and playing over various forms and furnishings. He gave his eyes a moment to adjust to the dim interior, and then he saw her.

She had been standing turned away from him, one hand pressed to her forehead, the other knotted at her side. But when the door closed with a soft click behind him, she jerked, then swung around to face him. Her hand fluttered to her chest and she took a hasty step backward, then halted, staring.

Tyler swallowed heavily. He could *feel* her nervousness, her uncertainty, and something very basic, very male, erupted inside him. He'd never known a woman to be this way, had never before felt the overwhelming urge to offer comfort, to ease a woman with assurances. He wanted—right this minute—to hold her, to touch her...to make love to her. He sucked in a deep breath, leaned back against the closed door and forced a gentle smile. "Hello."

CARLIE FELT FROZEN in place. She could feel his eyes drifting over her body, could hear every breath he took. She didn't know what to do. He couldn't have recognized her, yet he obviously liked what he saw. She'd never seen a man react that way—not to her. She couldn't speak, her voice was trapped in her throat.

He whispered softly, "You're beautiful."

Her eyes shifted nervously with the racing of her heart. Brenda had said men would find her attractive, but…. She hadn't believed her, not really. Usually, Tyler never looked at her twice, but then, he'd never seen her dressed like this.

The costume was definitely a mistake.

Tyler was still watching her, and she inhaled. She had to say something. "You look…dangerous."

His teeth flashed in a quick grin. "Not dashing?"

Confused, she shook her head. In an even lower tone, sounding of accusation and anticipation, she asked, "What happened to your date?"

He tipped his head, as if he was straining to hear her, then carefully stepped away from the door. "She wasn't my date."

Liar, she thought. A man like him wouldn't come to a party alone. He attracted beautiful women without even trying. And Valerie Rush was certainly that; beautiful, chic, sophisticated and very sure of her own appeal. She was everything Carlie was not.

So why was Tyler here now? She'd always been aware of him; he was impossible to ignore. Dark, charming, a devastating man. But completely unattainable. At least for her.

Of course, after her disastrous marriage, she didn't want any man, not even Tyler Ramsey.

He took another step forward when she remained silent, and she went back one, bumping into the wall.

He was watching her so very closely, almost stalking her, and she could feel her chest shuddering, straining for air. She trembled inside, feeling lightheaded and so conscious of him as a male. She didn't dare take her eyes off him.

He took another step.

The rain was coming down more heavily now, tapping against the windows and the wind had begun to whistle. Carlie was glad for the darkness. She didn't want reality to intrude too quickly. She didn't want him to recognize her. Not yet.

Maybe not ever.

He started to reach for her, then dropped his hand. "Do you know who I am?"

She shook her head. "No." She didn't know this man at all, so intense and attentive, exuding raw sexuality. The air was filled with his scent, his purpose.

His eyes drifted over her body again, then he stared intently into hers.

She didn't dare say anything. What was there to say? He wasn't reacting to Carlie McDaniels. He was reacting to the night; to the atmosphere and the mystery of a masquerade. If he knew who she was, he'd lose interest quickly enough. He'd give her that same polite nod she'd always received from him, then go on his way.

Tyler stepped toward her and she balked, feeling her back against the wall. It would be mortifying for him to realize her identity now, with her acting like such a ninny. She was a professional woman, a teacher, mature and capable. And here she was, behaving like a coward. A virgin coward.

She knew in that instant, she wouldn't tell him. He would never find out who she was. She had to leave, had to…

His hand caught her arm. "Wait. Please."

She trembled, trying to pull loose, stunned by the strength of his grasp.

He released her instantly. Holding his hands out to the sides, he tried to softly reassure her. "It's okay. I'm sorry." She trembled again, and he said, "You're cold."

Swamped with uncertainty, wanting to do one thing, but knowing she should do another, Carlie turned away. Then Tyler was behind her, not touching her, but the warmth of his body surrounded her. She felt a pulse beat of heat run through her, swirling in her belly. The feeling was unfamiliar…and exciting. As his breath brushed her nape, she shivered with growing sensation.

His palms grazed her shoulders, smoothing away the chills and the dampness from the rain, warming her. She was surrounded by him, by his scent.

His touch was tentative, careful, and when she didn't move, he leaned closer, his chest barely touching her back, his thighs brushing her own. She shuddered.

His fingers continued to stroke, feather-light, up and down her arms. He drew in a slow, rough breath, then molded his hands over her shoulders, holding her. She felt his suspended breathing, his hesitation. And when he finally spoke, his voice was low and unsteady.

"*I want you.* I think I wanted you the moment I saw you."

She stilled as his lips very lightly touched the side of her neck. Slowly, he drew her toward him, her back against his chest, then waited, keeping her pressed close to his solid length.

"I want you," he repeated. "*Stay with me.*"

Only in her wildest imaginings had she ever considered Tyler saying such a thing to her. It as unbelievable. It was outrageous.

It was her own private fantasy.

She swallowed hard, squeezed her eyes shut, then whispered, "I want you, too."

CHAPTER TWO

TILTING HIS HEAD BACK, Tyler exhaled slowly, then tried to relax. It was unbelievable how much her answer meant to him. *She was staying.*

He didn't understand his own reaction, or hers, for that matter. He only knew he needed to get closer to her. She'd stood there in the doorway earlier, looking feminine, yet so unsure. Unlike the other women in the room, she hadn't flaunted her assets; she hadn't even seemed aware of them, despite the provocative harem costume that left her more bare than not. Even now, she seemed so vulnerable, so wary.

He leaned down, inhaling her fragrance, then touched his open palm to her soft belly. She jerked and pulled away.

He was surprised by her reaction, and forced himself to go perfectly still. He squeezed her shoulders again. "Shh. I'm not going to hurt you." She remained strangely quiet, her body trembling, and then it hit him just how innocent she truly was. Suddenly, it made sense—the way she'd reacted to his interest. She was wary, and with good reason. He felt confusion first, then the unfamiliar stirring of protectiveness. He didn't want to frighten her, didn't want her to be uncomfortable with him. He closed his eyes and wrapped his arms around her, hugging her carefully.

"I would never hurt you."

Her hands came up to clasp his arms where they crossed her chest, giving him her silent trust.

His chest squeezed tight. It was remarkable how she affected him. Smiling, he rubbed his chin against her temple, then turned her to face him.

He cupped her jaw, tilting her chin toward him. He could see the scant light reflected in her wide eyes. Slowly, tentatively, he bent and put his lips to hers. It wasn't a devouring kiss, but tender and sweet. She seemed unsure of where to put her hands, then laid them lightly on his chest.

He groaned quietly, tugging her closer. "Open your mouth," he urged, continuing to nibble at her lips.

She did, gasping, and he teased her, stroking her mouth, licking carefully at her lips, touching her tongue with his own.

After a few moments, he pulled back. Her fingers had curled tight against him, and she was panting softly. Instinctively, he pressed his arousal, full and hard, against her belly. She seemed stunned by his blatant need, and he relished her reaction to it, watching her eyes slowly close. Nothing had ever made him feel so wild or urgent, so alive with sensation, as her innocent acceptance.

Her mask was in the way and he touched his fingers to it. Instantly, she jerked back, her hand coming up to cover her mouth.

His muscles grew taut. "I didn't..." Tyler hesitated, then shook his head. "I'm sorry. I just...it seems so...right."

She shook her head. "You can't take off my mask."

His eyebrows shot up.

"I don't want you to know...who I am."

He stepped closer to her, feeling the heat build under his skin. She was the most fascinating woman he'd ever met. He tried to get her to look at him, but she turned away. It was unbelievably erotic, a woman appearing so demure, but wearing such an enticing costume. He touched her chin, bringing her face back toward him. "What do you want?"

Swallowing hard, she whispered, "You. This." And she leaned toward him.

Tyler caught his breath, and then he was kissing her again. He stroked his tongue deep in her mouth, drawing her closer, feeling his urgency swell. He was no longer thinking of his own consuming desire, not entirely. Now he was driven by a need to give her everything she asked for, everything she could possibly hope for. He didn't want her to regret trusting him.

He didn't want her to regret anything.

When he lifted his head, she was breathless and

trembling, her small hands clasping his shirt in a death grip. Moving slowly, he touched the buttons on her skimpy jacket, for the moment ignoring her mask. "A mystery lady."

His words were deep and husky and she trembled as he undid the first button. As soon as it slid free, he raised his gaze to her face, judging her reaction.

She flattened her hands on the wall beside her hips, but she didn't protest. Tyler smiled, then looked down to watch the slow unveiling of her breasts.

The second button was undone, and still he didn't touch her in any other way. He was only using one hand, being careful not to startle her. The third button was straining at the material. With one finger, he traced her cleavage, over the swell of each breast, then up her throat. He looked at her lips, then traced the fullness of her mouth, pressing slightly to glide over the inside of her bottom lip.

Her lips parted and she instinctively curled her tongue around the tip of his finger. His eyes closed and he drew a slow, painful breath. When he looked at her again, she was watching him cautiously, her eyes dark in the dim shadows. He leaned forward and kissed her very gently, tenderly, his lips moving over her chin, to her collarbone, then her breasts.

The third button held, and Tyler found her nipple through the cloth. She moaned. Even through the material he could feel the heat of her body as he drew upon her, his teeth carefully nipping.

The last button opened, and he covered each breast with a warm palm, cradling her lush weight, shaping her with his hands. He pressed her breasts together and nuzzled her cleavage before moving his mouth to a nipple, licking and plucking with his lips, then finally taking her inside, suckling strongly. A sound of raw hunger escaped her, and he felt the impact of that small sound deep in his belly.

Her fingers sank into his hair, pulling him away. But he didn't leave her. Instead, he slipped to his knees, his mouth against her ribs. Closing his eyes and locking his arms around her hips, he rubbed his face against her skin, breathing in her heated scent, tasting her.

He savored her, taking his time to explore each facet of his senses; touch and taste and smell. And sight. He enjoyed looking at her; he enjoyed her pleasure and her surprise as he found a particularly sensitive spot.

His hands cupped her buttocks, startling her. Then slowly, he removed her slippers, his fingers lingering on her slim ankles. His palms coasted up her calves, over her thighs, and to her buttocks again, squeezing and cuddling. Then his fingers hooked in the waistband of her harem pants and, still watching her, he started sliding them down.

Tyler saw her embarrassment, and he leaned forward, kissing her navel, dipping his tongue teasingly inside. He wanted to reassure her, wanted her to understand how unique this was for him. But at the moment, words escaped him.

She stepped out of the pants as he directed, then remained silent while he looked his fill.

Oh God, what she did to him.

Gazing at her from his position on his knees, he had to call upon all his restraint to keep from rushing her. He wasn't himself. Feelings he hadn't known existed washed over him in hot, insistent waves.

The small jacket hung from her shoulders, serving more as ornamentation than covering since her breasts were freed. The shadowy room only enhanced her curves and made the moment more intimate. He could see the darkness of her nipples, her navel, the soft feminine curls between her thighs. He lightly brushed his fingers over her, finding her wet and hot. He delved deeper, stroking her, his breaths coming fast and low.

She gasped, and her hand clasped his wrist.

He turned his palm so he was holding hers, then took her other hand also, pinning her arms gently to her sides. He leaned forward, and this time it was his tongue that stroked her. She reacted immediately, pulling away, staring at him in appalled fascination.

Again, he felt that possessiveness, that need to protect her.

Tyler came slowly to his feet, his face flushed, his chest rising and falling quickly. He kept his tone gentle and quiet. "What's wrong?"

Her voice emerged as a dry croak. "It's...you can't."

Since he now understood her innocence, Tyler didn't press her. But he wanted her to realize the depth of her own allure. "I understand, but honey, I want to kiss you there. I want to kiss you everywhere." He held her eyes, refusing to let her look away, then added in a husky whisper, "You taste like a woman should, very sweet and sexy."

She shivered, then pressed her right hand over his chest, near where his heart was thundering. He covered her hand with his own, then began unbuttoning his shirt. He felt her nails as she flexed her fingers into his flesh. He'd never had a woman watch him with such intent curiosity. His body reacted to her interest, tightening and swelling. His gaze never left her face.

He removed his trousers quickly, hearing her low, fast breathing. He found a condom in his wallet, then tossed his pants aside. He laid the protection on the table.

When he turned to her again, he saw her uncertainty, and pulled her close, relishing the feel of her naked skin. Kissing her throat and shoulder, his hands curved around her body, his fingers splayed warm and firm on her sensitive belly.

He was patient and gently persuasive, but he was also very aroused. Deliberately, he nestled his fullness against her buttocks. He needed her to know the effect she had on him.

He kissed her for a few moments, and when he finally slid his fingers down her belly and into the soft curls between her legs, she didn't draw away. His fingers delved deeper, and she moaned.

His heart thundered at the small sound. "That's it. Relax, sweetheart." He slid a finger inside her, and she quivered, letting out a short cry. "You're wet," he said, softly stroking her, bringing his other hand up to hold a heavy breast, idly plying the nipple with his thumb. She leaned back on him, gasping, and he smiled.

She clutched at his hard thighs, her fingers biting deep into his muscles. Her legs stiffened and soft, hungry sounds escaped her throat.

Close to losing what was left of his control, Tyler lifted her into his arms and carried her quickly to the narrow couch. He laid her down, coming over her and pulling her close.

She moaned as his mouth closed over her nipple, then moaned again when he smoothed his hand over her soft belly and into her feminine curls. His fingers stroked, dipped, plucked lightly, making her squirm. He lowered his mouth to her nipple and toyed with it, teasing her with his tongue and teeth.

Her climax took him by surprise. It gripped her body, forcing her to arch wildly, her eyes closed, her mouth open as she gasped and gave low, throaty moans. Enthralled, Tyler watched her, feeling her pleasure and her loss of control. Seeing her shock.

And when the rushing sensations would have ended, Tyler bent to taste her, crushing down on her with renewed urgency, his hand holding her face still for his kiss. She was crying, unable to help herself, and he kissed her jaw, undone by her soft, breathy sighs.

"It's all right now. Shh."

She shook her head. With tears clogging her throat and reflecting in her voice, she whispered brokenly, "I've never…"

"Shh. I know." His mouth skimmed hers, his eyes alight with satisfaction and possession.

He couldn't wait any longer.

Lifting slightly away from her, he reached for the condom and slid it on. She didn't watch him, but he didn't think it was embarrassment now, so much as repletion. Her breasts, heaving still, showed soft and white, reflecting the scant light. Her belly still quivered. But there was a small, awed smile on her lips, a look of wonder that filled him.

Thunder clapped loudly outside, and the storm picked up tempo, mirroring his explosive emotions.

He began kissing her again, light, biting kisses that made her smile and open her eyes. His muscles were taut, straining for release. She laid her palm to his cheek.

He sat back to look at her, running his fingers

through her hair. It was then he realized she was wearing a wig. The hair was too coarse, too dense to be real. The fact that she had taken such pains to conceal herself only added to her intrigue. His mystery woman.

She pulled him closer in silent demand.

He reached down and parted her with his fingers, then gently pushed inside. His groan was long and ragged. Gasping, she twisted against him, her arms tightening, her hips lifting to his. He pressed her knees wider, giving himself more access to her body, then clenched his jaw as he sank deeper. "There we go. All the way."

She shuddered as her body adjusted to his length and thickness. It was pure fantasy, he thought, wishing he could stay like this forever. She squirmed beneath him in delicious sensation.

Tyler shuddered, pressing his hips to hers to still her movements, trying to maintain his barely leashed control, but it was too late. He reared up, his arms stiffened on either side of her, his eyes hot and probing, holding her gaze. Then he began to move.

The friction was exquisite, and she lifted her hips toward him, taking more, her legs wrapping around him. His gaze dropped to her breasts, to her tightened nipples. He was enthralled, watching her full breasts sway as each of his thrusts rocked her body.

He threw his head back, biting off a groan. His jaw

was tense, his words a growled whisper. "I don't believe this!"

He felt her tighten around him, felt the pulsing of
her climax. He groaned heavily, and his body went
rigid as he climaxed. Then he stilled.

His weight was now fully upon her and his heartbeat rocked his body with its uneven cadence. He
stroked her idly, without thought, without even knowing what he was doing. She smelled so good, and he
felt so good.

She stirred beneath him, and he obligingly raised
himself to his elbows. Her mask was askew, and he
smiled at the picture she made, tousled innocence,
sensual lure. He didn't want the night to end.

"Do you have to go anytime soon?"

That surprised her.

Smiling, Tyler stroked her cheek. "Will you stay
with me for a while longer?"

Her smile was shaky, a bit uncertain, but it was a
smile.

Laughing, feeling incredibly lighthearted, he held
her tight as he turned on the couch, putting her on
top of him. She came up on her elbows, her heavy
breasts swaying over his chest.

"Now, this is nice." His hands cupped her, his
thumbs flicking over her soft, dusky nipples until they
drew tight.

"Can you scoot up just a bit," he growled. "I want
you in my mouth."

Her lips parted, but she complied, her breath already thickening. Tyler swept his hands down her back and spread them wide over the buttocks, pressing her close.

"I'm going to make love to you all night, honey. I want to show you all the different ways to enjoy yourself. I'm going to see to it that you're so overwhelmed with pleasure, you won't be able to resist seeing me again." He said the words quietly just before he took her nipple in his mouth, licking and teasing and making her shudder. His hands moved over her bottom to the back of her thighs, then parted her legs so she was draped over him. "You'll wake up at night and think of me touching you." His finger slid inside her and she tensed, her hips pressing hard against him.

"I want you to think of me," he explained, loving her with his fingers until she trembled uncontrollably, "because I know I'll be thinking of you."

TYLER HELD to his promise, exhausting both himself and Carlie with pleasure.

Hours later, long after midnight, he slept, still holding her close. Carlie was stunned by all that had happened, never having imagined that such complete satisfaction was possible.

Tyler lay relaxed beside her, one heavy muscled arm circling her belly, his hand splayed over her hip. He was even beautiful when he slept, she thought, when the lines of his face softened, making him look almost vulnerable.

Of course, he could never know the truth. She would be mortified if Tyler ever discovered he'd made love with his sister-in-law's dumpy best friend. Tyler didn't even *look* at women like her, let alone sleep with them.

Not that she wanted it any other way. She was dumpy by design, choosing her clothes with an eye for concealment, rather than enticement. She didn't want a man, any man—not now, not ever.

Relationships hurt. She'd learned that lesson after her marriage failed. And she'd also learned she could rely on no one but herself. Not on the grandfather who'd raised her after her parents' death, treating her more like a burden than a grandchild, nor on her brother, who'd made it clear she was to deal with her mistakes on her own.

But marriage had been her biggest mistake. One she wasn't likely to forget.

She could never tell Tyler the truth, but at least she'd learned something valuable; she wasn't frigid. Her husband had been wrong, his accusations unjust. Probably, it had just been another of his attempts to destroy her self-confidence. But now she knew the truth, and for that, if nothing else, she was glad she'd stayed with Tyler.

He shifted in his sleep, and she stilled, watching him closely, but he didn't awaken. She leaned down

and very gently kissed him on the corner of his
mouth, then slipped from the couch.

By the time Tyler woke, a smile of anticipation on
his face, Carlie was gone.

CHAPTER THREE

"YOU CAN'T TELL anyone I was at the party."

Brenda tugged Carlie through the kitchen door and then quickly shut it. "I wondered all night what happened to you. Where did you go? Why did you leave so soon? I thought for sure you were going to enjoy yourself."

Wincing, Carlie gave Brenda an apologetic look. She had enjoyed herself, all right, just not the way Brenda had expected. She pulled out a chair at the round wooden table and slumped into it. "I didn't mean to worry you. I'm sorry."

"So what happened? Why did you run off?"

Hesitating, Carlie tried to decide how much to tell her friend. It wouldn't be the whole truth, that was for certain. Somehow, the night seemed…magical, something she could tuck away and keep to herself. She couldn't share it, not even with Brenda. But she had to tell her something.…

"Brenda…I felt really foolish…in the costume. Maybe if I hadn't been wearing something so…"

"Sexy?"

Carlie spared her friend a quick look, and saw

Brenda was smiling. "Yeah, well, maybe. I just couldn't face all those people looking like that."

"I'm sorry I pushed, Carlie. I just wanted you to realize how attractive you are. Those damn baggy suits you wear make you look fat." Brenda pursed her lips, then idly traced the wood grain in the table with a fingertip. "Tyler noticed you."

Carlie felt her heartbeat race. "I... Did he say something to you?"

"He asked who you were."

"You didn't tell him!" Carlie nearly choked on her embarrassment, waiting for Brenda's reply.

"No. I just told him you were a guest." Then she patted Carlie's arm. "Hey, calm down. It wouldn't be the end of the world if Tyler took a liking to you. You have to admit, he's gorgeous."

Oh, yeah, he was gorgeous. Carlie licked her lips, then said carefully, "He, ah, approached me."

"He did?"

"Yes." Carlie cleared her throat, then immediately launched into her rehearsed story. "We talked for a while. In, ah, the pool house."

When Brenda's eyes widened, Carlie reminded her, "It was raining, remember? And we went inside to stay dry. He, well, he was attracted to me."

"No kidding?"

Carlie hated the note of fascination in her friend's tone. She also hated lying to her, but she didn't see any way around it. Brenda leaned forward. "So, what happened?"

Carlie shrugged. "He didn't recognize me."

"Well, of course he didn't! He's used to seeing you looking like this!" Brenda indicated Carlie's dark, frumpy suit. With her honey blond hair in a tight braid and a pair of glasses perched on her nose, she looked nothing like the harem girl of the night before.

"This isn't funny, Brenda!" Carlie felt like strangling her. "And you can't ever tell him, either. I don't want him to know it was me he was…flirting with."

Brenda looked skeptical. "Ah, Carlie, don't you think—"

Whatever Brenda was going to say was cut off by a loud voice from the living room. Seconds later, Jason and Tyler strode into the kitchen. Carlie stiffened, all her defenses jerking into place. But her face remained impassive. Almost painfully so. There was absolutely no way she would let Tyler know she was the woman he'd spent the night with. She didn't even want to think about how mortifying that would be.

Brenda didn't miss a beat after shooting Carlie an I'm-not-responsible-for-this look. "I thought you fellas were going fishing. What happened?"

Tyler reached Brenda first. He leaned down and lifted her from her chair, giving her a tight bear hug and a kiss on the cheek.

Brenda's face turned pink. "What did I do to deserve that?"

Tyler's smile was so warm and sincere, Carlie had to look away. "You invited me to your party." Then he added softly, "Thanks."

Jason shook his head, and Carlie had the horrifying suspicion that Tyler had confided to him what had happened. *Don't blush, don't blush!* She glanced at Jason, but he was looking at his wife.

Leaning down, he kissed Brenda, then nodded briefly to Carlie. "The fish weren't biting and it's damned cold out there. Besides, Tyler can't seem to sit still today."

Tyler pulled out a chair and straddled it, crossing his arms over the chair back. "Could I have some coffee, Bren? Then I need to talk to you." He glanced at Carlie, and smiled. "Hi. Ah, Carlie, isn't it?"

"Hello." Carlie mentally applauded her calm response. She was more than a little surprised Tyler remembered her name. She prayed it was all he remembered. And then she looked at him, and despite herself, she remembered lying beside him in the pool house, remembered that magnificent body of his leaning toward her... She looked away, trying to collect her thoughts. Good looks only took a person so far, and from what she knew of Tyler, his had taken him around the block more than a few times. Last night had been a milestone in her life; to Tyler, it had probably been no more than a good time.

Carlie breathed a sigh of relief when she realized he hadn't connected her to the party. His expression had been friendly, nothing more. Already he was ignoring her, dismissing her easily.

"I'll have the coffee ready in just a minute." Brenda was grinning affectionately at Tyler, obviously more than pleased to cater to him.

Tyler tapped his fingers on the table with an excess of energy. His gaze took a turn around the room, then settled on Carlie again. "So. What are you ladies up to today?"

She felt her heart flutter and color rise to her cheeks. Carlie wanted to smack herself. Enough was enough. She would not be an idiot around this man. She composed her features and met his look squarely. "We were talking about the new sports program I'm working on for the school." She paused, then decided to elaborate. "It's a way to help the kids who have trouble socializing. They're not bad kids but they just aren't sure how to conduct themselves with their peers. They need guidance and a chance to interact, with supervision. If they're playing a sport, they'll be getting exercise, burning off energy and learning to work together. I think the program will go over pretty good. I thought I'd try basketball first. The kids have to play together, but since it's not really a contact sport, tussles ought to be kept to a minimum. Brenda and I were just discussing how great it is that Jason has agreed to be an instructor."

Tyler listened, his eyes intent on Carlie's face, watching her so closely she felt herself near to blushing again. "Sounds like you really care about these kids."

His tone was soft, almost disbelieving, and Carlie stiffened. "Of course I do. I care very much about all my students."

Tyler rubbed his chin, still watching her. "And you really think you can make a difference?"

Carlie leaned back in her chair, forgetting her embarrassment, forgetting last night. The gall of the man, to question her like this! With her hands in fists, she replied, "I'll certainly do my best to. At least *I'm* trying to do something to help."

Jason looked at Carlie, then Tyler. A smile appeared. "I, ah, suppose I should tell you something, Carlie. I won't be able to help you, after all. Some things came up at the office." His grin widened, and he shrugged. "I talked to Tyler this morning, and he agreed to do the project with you, instead."

Carlie closed her eyes for a heartbeat, praying she hadn't heard that. But when she opened her eyes, Tyler was still watching her, his smile now smug.

She cleared her throat and shoved her glasses needlessly up the bridge of her nose. "I don't know, Jason." What excuse could she use after practically challenging the man to help? "Maybe that wouldn't be a good idea."

It was Tyler who answered her. "Why not?"

Floundering, she racked her brain, but couldn't come up with a valid reason. "You understand, it will be three or four nights a week? And we need someone who will set a good example for the kids. Someone patient."

Tyler raised his eyebrow, looking affronted. "I'd be a good example. Hell, I'm a lawyer, same as Jason. I've been to college. I'm articulate."

"You're even housebroken," Brenda added, seeming to enjoy the situation.

He nodded. "Damn right." Then to Carlie, "You see? I'll be perfect for the job."

"But…" The truth was, she simply didn't want to work with Tyler. Not now, not after last night. "I don't know. Have you ever worked with kids? And remember, these kids can be a little…difficult."

Jason interrupted. "Tyler should understand them on a gut level, because he was always damned difficult, too."

Tyler laughed. "So it's settled. When do we start?"

Carlie stood with as much aplomb as she could muster. Tyler's eyes drifted over her body, almost out of habit, it seemed, but there was no sign of recognition in his expression. It rankled, even while she prayed he wouldn't make the connection. She tugged at the bottom of her tailored suit coat, smoothing it over her slacks. Then she used a tactic that had worked with many rebellious students. She deliberately looked down her nose at him. "I'll have to let you know."

Tyler merely nodded. "You do that."

Brenda rushed forward to give Carlie a hug. "Give me a call later. Promise?"

"Of course. And thanks for the company, Bren. See ya' later, Jason." She ignored Tyler, not feeling the least bit guilty about it, and exited the room, her back stiff, her tight braid pulling at her temples. She wasn't entirely out of the house when she heard Tyler say, "That has to be the prickliest woman I've ever met. I got the distinct impression she didn't like me. Can you imagine?"

Jason's laugh was sharp. "Unheard of, isn't it?"

There was a shrug in his tone when Tyler replied, "There's just no figuring some women."

Carlie allowed the door to slam just a bit too hard behind her.

IT WAS A VERY NEAT, utilitarian office. Carlie was surprised at how functional each piece of furniture was, with only a modicum of necessary decorations. The walls were beige, the carpet a swirling mixture of blues and creams. The sofa and two chairs were upholstered in a rough nubby fabric of a deep blue, and the wooden end tables were light oak. It was a comfortable room, without any indication of Tyler's personal style, which she'd assumed to be rather flamboyant.

The office door opened and Tyler stepped out, accompanied by the secretary who had first greeted Carlie. His smile was warm, a natural smile that Carlie knew he bestowed on almost every female he encountered. Beyond him, she could see into his office, and noticed his desk strewn with papers and files. Suddenly, she realized how disruptive, and presumptuous, her visit was, but she also knew if she hadn't come today, she wouldn't have come at all. Brenda had told her he'd been asking about the harem girl from the party. He wanted to know who she was.

Carlie hoped he would eventually give up and forget about that night...but then, she also knew how badly it would hurt her if he was able to do just that.

Lately, she felt awfully confused.

"I'm sorry I kept you waiting, Carlie. I didn't realize it was you. I'm not familiar with the name McDaniels."

Of course, he wouldn't be. Carlie took his hand. Very briefly. "I hope I'm not interrupting. I can see you're busy. I just wanted to stop by and tell you I'd like to accept your offer of assistance for our new sports program." She was rushing through her words, but she couldn't seem to stop herself. She'd spent three days stewing over what to do, and finally decided that her personal embarrassment had to take a back seat to the kids' problems. She was the only one who knew she had reason to be embarrassed, and since no one else had agreed to help, Tyler was her only option.

"We hope to start next week, so I wanted to drop

off the material I've put together. You might want to look it over before meeting the children.''

Tyler accepted the papers she thrust toward him, then motioned her into his office. ''Come on in and have a seat.''

''I don't want to take up too much of your time.'' And she wanted to get away from him as quickly as possible.

He lifted one shoulder in an exaggerated shrug. ''I needed a break, anyway.''

Carlie followed him into his office and sat on the edge of a straight-back, narrow leather chair. Tyler went behind his desk, seating himself with all the officious attitude of any good lawyer.

After skimming through the papers she'd given him, he looked at her again. ''You're very thorough.''

She blushed and she hated herself for it. ''It's just a basic overview of the children who will begin in the program. I thought it would help if you knew what kind of problem each child was having and what their backgrounds were like. The idea is that any child who collects more than three after-school detentions or in-school suspensions will have the choice of joining the team or having their misconduct shown in their grades. Of course, if they choose to join the team, they'll have to contribute wholeheartedly and follow instructions to the letter. In other words, they'll have to work together and get along. They'll have to accept that rules have a purpose, and everyone has to follow them. The program had been used in several schools. So far, it's been very promising.''

Tyler nodded, then gave her another of his intent, probing stares. "How many children will we be starting with?"

Carlie cleared her throat and looked away. She let her eyes roam around his office while she spoke, pretending an interest in his bookshelves, but really trying to avoid his stare. "The list I've given you has nine kids. Of course, that number can change daily. And the children will be released from their obligation whenever they show an improved attitude toward school. But no child will ever be forced to quit the team."

"Will we get to compete against other teams?"

Carlie didn't answer right away. Tyler's genuine interest amazed and confused her. She had half expected him to give only a show of concern. But he was studying the list, all signs of the womanizer gone while he perused her notes. She was looking at the top of his head, at how thick and dark his hair was, how it curled just the tiniest bit. He glanced up and caught her staring. At his *hair* for crying out loud.

He ran his fingers through it negligently. "What's the matter? Have I sprung a streak of gray?"

Carlie folded her arms defensively. "No, I…no. I was just thinking."

Tyler laid the file down, once again giving her his full attention. "About what?"

"About...whether or not we'd be playing other schools, of course," she said quickly. Then, taking a deep breath, she continued. "I don't believe so, at least not at first. If after a time the team shapes up, that would be entirely your decision how far to carry it." Carlie forced herself to stare at him directly, though she felt a faint blush on her cheeks.

Tyler smiled at her again, leaning back in his chair and folding his hands across his stomach. "You have the most unusual eyes. Very intense. Especially now, while we're talking about the children. I don't believe I've ever seen that exact shade of hazel."

She stiffened. "Thank you, but I don't think the color of my eyes has any bearing on this program."

"It was just an observation."

He was still leaning back in his chair, his posture relaxed, his gaze lazy, and Carlie realized he was deliberately provoking her. She decided not to oblige him. She came to her feet, still holding his gaze, and stared down at him. "Personal observations aside, do you have anything else you'd like to discuss?"

Carlie watched as he struggled to stifle his amusement. He stood behind his desk, his dark eyes warm and smiling. Then, leisurely, he began looking her over. She tolerated his perusal, trying to keep her expression blank, even while her pulse raced and her palms grew damp. She was well aware of what she looked like. Her suit was a deep, dark green, almost brown, and it was cut in straight lines, effectively hiding any signs of her figure.

"You're tall for a woman."

What an inane comment. But true. Carlie's head was just about even with his nose, and she was wearing flats. She glanced down at her shoes when he did. They were ugly, round-toed, and extremely comfortable.

She drew on disdain to hide her sudden discomfort. "If you don't have any other questions about the program, I'll be on my way. I wouldn't want to keep you from anything...important." She turned, and headed for the door without another word.

Tyler came around his desk and stepped in front of her, blocking her exit. He wasn't grinning now, but she could still see the humor in his eyes. "Forgive me, Carlie. I didn't mean to be rude." Before she could reply, he lifted the folder in his hand. "May I keep this?"

She watched him warily. His apology sounded genuine, but she still felt he was laughing at her. She gritted her teeth, wishing she could rid her mind of intimate thoughts concerning Tyler Ramsey. She hadn't thought of a man that way in a very long time.

She was determined to stop right now. She didn't return his smile, or acknowledge his apology. "Of course. I have my own copy."

Tyler gave her an amused, mischievous grin, almost as if he'd read her thoughts. "Excellent. When do we start?"

"How soon can you start? I'll send home the notices to the parents as soon as you give me a schedule that suits you."

"Tell you what. Let me check things over and I'll get back to you tomorrow. What time do you leave the school?"

Carlie hesitated. "Around four."

"I'll come by then. Maybe we could go somewhere and work out a schedule that will suit us both." He indicated his cluttered desk. "Unfortunately, I don't have the time right now to take care of it."

"I…" Carlie mentally scurried for excuses. She did not want to go anywhere with Tyler Ramsey. The man had a chaotic effect on her senses. He had only to smile at her, and memories came rushing back, so intense, so powerful, that her stomach clenched and her nerve endings rioted. She hoped her thoughts of him would fade with time; she hoped she could eventually forget him completely.

It wouldn't happen today. Though she hated to admit it, even to herself, he rattled her as few people could. But she refused to be a coward about the situation. The best way to deal with a problem was to face it head-on, she reminded herself. Summoning a bland smile, she nodded. "That would be fine, Tyler. Thank you."

SHE WAS STANDING at her desk, stacking papers, when Tyler walked in. Her door was open, so he took a moment to simply look at her. Dressed in another of her prim, spinsterish outfits, her hair pulled back in a braid, she looked like the epitome of the perfect schoolmarm. And she was humming softly.

He felt something shift inside him. Never in his own school days could he remember a teacher like her, someone who actually wanted to help. He'd always thought of Carlie as simply Brenda's friend, a little odd, a lot frumpy, but nice enough.

Now he had to look at her with new respect.

Raising a hand, he gave two sharp knocks on the open door. She jerked, looking up with wide eyes and peering at him through the lenses of her glasses.

"They told me at the office where I could find you." He stepped in, looking around the room with interest. "Very nice."

She smiled with an obvious touch of pride. "Thank you. I try to make the classroom nice. It should be a comfortable place to be, an *easy* place to be. Do you know what I mean?"

Strangely enough, he did. The room was decorated in bright colors with plenty of the children's artwork hanging on the walls. It was a thought-provoking room. He walked toward a workstation that was filled with hands-on activities. There were dominoes, rubber stamps and numerous math games. The room gave an overall appearance of bustling activity. He smiled at her, seeing that she was watching him cautiously. "You like to teach."

She straightened. "Yes. And I'm good at it. Children respond well to me."

She could be so damned bristly, with no real provocation. "I'm sure you are. You're authoritative, but gently so. Children wouldn't be afraid of you."

Lowering her eyebrows, she gave him a ferocious look, as if she didn't trust the sincerity of his words. He smiled back, and waited.

Finally, she nodded. "No child should ever be afraid. Certainly not of their teacher. I do my best to make sure they're at ease, to let them know they can talk to me if they need to."

Tyler turned away. He didn't want her to see how she affected him. He could still remember being a kid himself, feeling defensive and hurt because his dad wasn't around, and his mother couldn't be bothered. His teachers hadn't cared about a kid with problems. Their idea of understanding was to send him to the office whenever he upset their lessons.

He certainly hadn't had a teacher like Carlie.

"What is it, Tyler? What's wrong?"

Her perception was uncanny. He realized he was holding a math paper one student had left on a desk, and he slowly laid it down and turned to her. "I have the greatest respect for teachers. For anyone having a gift with children. There are too many people out there who don't care about kids, even their own."

He knew he shouldn't have said so much the minute the words were out of his mouth. Carlie was scrutinizing him carefully. He shook his head and wandered around the room, surveying all the desks, laughing when he saw one that was overflowing with old papers. He straightened a chair, centered a book, replaced a pencil that had fallen on the floor.

Carlie began helping him tidy up. "The children may like me, but they're always in a hurry to leave when the bell rings." She indicated the disheveled desks. "They tend to be a little sloppy at times."

Tyler refocused on her. "Do you have children of your own?" He discovered he was suddenly very interested in her.

"No."

Just that one curt word. He crossed his arms over his chest. "You're not married?"

"Mr. Ramsey..."

He smiled. "Do you want children of your own someday?"

Lowering her gaze, she ignored his question and pulled her purse from beneath her desk. "We'd better be going. I have tests to grade tonight and lessons to prepare for the morning."

He accepted her change of subject without comment, and motioned for her to lead the way. They'd be spending a lot of time together, several nights a week. He'd get to know her better, and she would eventually warm up to him.

That thought brought with it images of another woman, a woman who had warmed up to him, only to leave him. He still felt irritated when he thought of how he'd woken up alone, a stupid smile on his face. But even then, he hadn't considered that was the end of it. He'd assumed he'd find out who she was from Brenda, then have the pleasure of getting to know his harem girl better.

But Brenda said the woman didn't want to be identified, and short of telling her *why* he wanted to know, he couldn't very well demand the mystery woman's name. But he hated the thought he might never see her again, and he hated even more that the night had evidently meant so little to her. It had been special to him, a night to cherish.

And the woman didn't want anything to do with him.

Carlie was halfway to the door when Tyler caught up with her, automatically taking her arm. "Let's take my car, and I'll bring you back here when we're finished."

"I'd prefer to drive."

Bristly. She was stiff, her arm rigid in his grasp. He had the distinct notion she resented his touch, though he hadn't a clue why. He was getting a little disgruntled with female rejection, and the question came out a little sharper than he'd intended. "Why?"

She didn't look at him, but he saw her pull her

bottom lip between her teeth. She had a nice profile, he realized, and the lip she was punishing was soft and full. Then she nodded. "Very well. You may drive."

CHAPTER FOUR

TYLER HAD very large hands.

Carlie stared, without meaning to, as he cut into a piece of peach pie, then put the bite in his mouth and chewed. His jaw was strong, lean and hard, with only a slight shadow of dark beard stubble. His nose, straight and high-bridged, would appear aristocratic but for the lump where he had broken it in a fight when he was younger. Bren had told her the story, about how Jason had joined in and the two brothers had ended up defeating four other kids.

His eyebrows were straight and dark. His lashes thick and long. His cheekbones high and sculpted. There was a healthy color to his skin, not a dark-baked tan, but definitely the added color of outdoor activities.

Carlie sipped her coffee, her gaze going again to his hands. She remembered those hands so well, the way they had touched her, their strength, their gentleness. The memory gave her an odd tingle.

"Aren't you going to eat your pie?" he asked.

Carlie pulled her eyes away from his hands. She nodded and took a large mouthful to give her something to do, namely chew, while Tyler filled the silence with questions.

"I could come to the school Friday, around four again, if you want me to do some sort of sign-up, or make a roster. What about you? Can you make it, or is that too soon?"

"Friday would be terrific. I'll put out a few calls tomorrow during lunch to see who can stay over. The ones who can't make it can have a schedule Monday."

Tyler pulled a piece of paper from his pocket. "These are my best times to get together. I tried to make them as regular as possible, so the kids can know what to expect. You can look that over then let me know if you'll have a problem with any of those dates."

She tucked the paper into her purse. "It'll be fine."

"You didn't even look at it. How do you know it won't interrupt your plans."

Carlie gave him a quick smile. "We're glad to have your help. Whatever works for you is fine with me."

Tyler laid his fork by his plate and shook his head. "You know the saying about all work and no play? You have to take time for a social life, too."

"Why don't you let me worry about my social life, all right?" she said, annoyed with his persistence.

"What social life? It doesn't sound to me as if you have one."

That was entirely too close to the truth, and rubbed

Carlie the wrong way. "Look, Mr. Ramsey. You may be the authority on having a good time, but I take my commitments seriously."

She watched Tyler's face go rigid, and then he leaned toward her. "And I don't?"

"Not from what I hear."

Leaning back, Tyler observed Carlie thoughtfully. "You know, if we're going to work together, you'll have to get over your attitude. I don't know why you dislike me so much, but it's not something I'm used to. Nor do I intend to get used to it." He waited a heartbeat, and Carlie felt his annoyance wash over her before he added, "I'd really like to work with you and the kids. But if you would rather find someone else to help you with your project, I'll drop out."

It was plain, by his tone and expression, he didn't want to do that. He wanted to be involved, for whatever reasons, and Carlie *did* need him. She hated to admit the truth, but it was her own personal conflict that was causing the problems. What she needed was an emotional compromise.

After adjusting her glasses, she straightened. "I think we can manage to get along if we keep it on a business level."

Tyler shook his head. "No go. I don't have a 'business level.' You're going to have to get your little nose out of the air and be friendly."

Her compromise exploded into oblivion. Did everything have to be his way? "You're an extremely arrogant person!"

His chuckle was warm and husky. "Bren says the same thing regularly. Funny, it sounds almost affectionate coming from her."

"She's too softhearted."

"Yes, she is. It's amazing you two are friends."

Uh-oh. Dangerous territory. Carlie held his gaze with an effort, the implied insult overlooked entirely. "We've known each other for a long time."

Tyler considered that. "Do you know many of her other friends?"

"A few."

"Who?"

Ah, so that was it. He didn't for one minute suspect her as the mystery woman from the other night; she was too unlikely to even be considered. But he was fishing to find out who the woman was. She hesitated just long enough, pretending deep thought, until he cleared his throat.

Several names came to mind, most of the women quite attractive, and Carlie named them, watching as he pondered each one. She was ready to laugh, when a familiar voice interrupted them.

"Ms. McDaniels! How nice to see you here. And how is my boy doing?"

Carlie smiled, and turned in her seat to face Mr. Briant.

She was totally at ease as a teacher dealing with a

parent, and invited him to join their table. She reassured the anxious father, taking a few minutes to go over things he could do at home that would help his son improve his skills even more. She was specific, but very patient with the man's concerns. She was also aware that Tyler was watching her, sipping his coffee and listening to their conversation intently. He looked almost…impressed by her.

When the father finally left, Tyler lifted his coffee cup in a salute to her. "Does that happen often?"

"Yes. This is a small town, and thankfully the parents are, for the most part, very involved with their children's education."

"Your Mr. Briant seemed to hang on your every word."

Carlie smiled crookedly. "We had a misunderstanding of sorts with the first failing grade I sent home with his son. You see, he decided it was my fault, and came to the school to tell me so."

"Let me guess. You chewed him up and spit him out, right?"

Carlie's smile froze. "I'm not an ogre. He was upset, so I tried to explain. I pulled out all the papers I had been keeping on his son, Brady, and showed them to him. I went over the procedure we used with new materials, and I told him his son was distracted and not paying attention in class."

"Carlie, I didn't mean—"

She shook her head. "It's all right. I know what

you meant.'' Idly stirring her coffee, she whispered, ''It was such a sad situation. Mr. Briant had just lost his wife. He was very withdrawn and angry. He hadn't been able to concentrate on his son yet, who was having his own problems adjusting.'' She sighed, remembering how difficult it had been to see the father and son together, each struggling with his loss. ''We spent a lot of time together after class. Sometimes we worked on lessons, but a lot of the time we just talked. I...I lost my parents when I was young, so I knew how Brady must have felt. At a time like that, school work kind of takes a back seat to trying to survive the emotional pain.''

Tyler was studying his coffee cup. ''It must have been rough for you.''

His quiet words, filled with understanding and sympathy surprised her.

She nodded. ''Everything worked out, though. After Brady started catching up, Mr. Briant joined us in our after-school lessons. I think he was lonely, too, and looking for some direction. He wanted to learn how to help his son study, so for a few weeks I helped him do that. Now they're on their own, and Brady Briant is earning A's.''

Tyler stared at her, and Carlie could feel him looking beneath her calm control, trying to read her thoughts. ''You're very dedicated,'' he said quietly.

''You have to be dedicated, to any job, if you want to do it well.'' Then she smiled, curious over Tyler's distracted expression. "That's no reason to be so solemn, though."

"I was just wondering how dedicated I am to my job, to handling the small load of petty cases that land on my desk each month."

"And?"

"Oh, I'd say...not very."

"That can't be true. Jason says you do a wonderful job."

"I'm a good lawyer." It was a statement of fact, with no fringe of lace to pretty it up. Abruptly, he reached across the table and took her hand.

Carlie tried to pull away, but he held her firm. "I'm sorry if I inadvertently insulted you. I only meant that you're very sure of yourself and you appear to be able to handle any situation. Including irascible fathers."

It was more difficult than she'd expected, because Tyler wasn't what she'd expected. At least, not completely. There were too many facets to his personality, and now he seemed genuinely thoughtful, interested in the children and concerned that he might have hurt her feelings. And he'd been very patient while she'd talked to Mr. Briant.

His hand was warm and strong, feeling exactly as she remembered. But her reaction wasn't dulled by familiarity.

"I'm not invincible, Mr. Ramsey. I simply don't believe in allowing myself to be trod upon."

"You've done that before, you know. Called me

mister when you're agitated. I think we know each other well enough to dispense with mister and Ms., don't you?''

She managed to slip her hand free, but only because Tyler allowed it. She needed to regather her defenses; Tyler was a devastating man when he was being the seducer. But as a caring, considerate man, he was downright potent. ''I don't really know you at all, but I think I know your type, and I'm not all that impressed by it. That's one of the reasons I hesitated to involve you in this program. But I'll be honest with you…Tyler. There was no one else to take Jason's place, and—''

He interrupted her long enough to say facetiously, ''Stop, Carlie. You'll swell my ego with all this praise.''

Carlie heaved a disgruntled sigh, and saw Tyler's eyes go automatically to her breasts as she inhaled. He wouldn't be able to tell a damned thing, though, other than the fact that she did have them. Her shirt was buttoned to the throat and her suit coat was bulky, concealing any dimensions or shape. Carlie glared at him.

Still not looking at her face, he said, ''You've made quite a few assumptions about me, haven't you? Did you ever consider you might be wrong?''

''No. I hadn't considered that.''

''Well maybe you should.''

When he finally looked up, appearing totally unrepentant, she frowned at him in exasperation. "I think it would be better if you kept your hands to yourself."

Tyler did a double take. "All I did was hold your hand. I didn't make an indecent proposal."

His blunt speech could easily rattle her, but still her tone was brisk and confident. "This is a very small town," she said. "People love to gossip. I don't want to give anyone reason to speculate."

Tyler blinked, completely incredulous, a small, uncertain smile playing about his mouth. Then the smile broke, and he indulged in unrestrained laughter. Carlie immediately felt like a fool. Her remark had been totally asinine. No one would ever assume Tyler Ramsey was romantically involved with her. Secret rendezvous in disguise aside, the idea was too absurd.

Tyler shook his head, still chuckling and watching Carlie with an air of expectation, as if he was waiting for another joke. She knew her face was red, and she hated it. She reached into her purse, blindly searching for her wallet, then threw a couple of bills on the table and stood. She slipped her purse over her shoulder and walked away.

"Carlie! Wait a minute."

She ignored him.

Tyler cursed as she walked out the door. When Carlie glanced back, he was hurrying after her.

It was a beautiful autumn day outside, with only a hint of chill in the air to suggest that winter was approaching. The sun was a hazy tangerine glow dipping low on the horizon. And beneath it, her sturdy shoes clapping loudly on the pavement, stomped Carlie. She was intent on marching back to the school to retrieve her car.

She heard Tyler jogging after her.

"Leave me alone," she said succinctly as he reached her side and tried to grasp her arm.

"Be reasonable, Carlie. You can't walk all the way back to the school."

"Of course I can. We didn't go that far."

"I'd rather drive you."

"*I'd* rather walk."

Growling, Tyler grabbed her arms, despite her resistance, then shook her gently. "Will you stop being so contrary? You were worried about causing speculation? Well, what do you think it will do if I carry you back to my car?"

"You wouldn't dare."

"Take one more step and you'll find out what I dare."

It was a standoff, and they glared at each other until finally Carlie did an about-face and, without a word to Tyler, stalked over to his car. She stood by the passenger door, impatiently waiting for him to unlock it. But before he opened the door, he caught her shoulders again.

"Carlie, I didn't mean to…that is… Oh, hell, I'm sorry, all right?"

Carlie faced him, hard as that was to do. She felt thoroughly humiliated and had no problem blaming Tyler for her discomfort. She may have memories to cherish, but Tyler would obviously be appalled to learn the true identity of his mystery woman.

Straightening her shoulders to hide her hurt, she stared at him with cold indifference. "Do a good job with the children. That's all I ask. Beyond that, you don't concern me."

Tyler nodded stiffly, then walked to his own side of the car. His hands flexed on the wheel twice before he started the engine.

"Doesn't anything rattle that damned calm reserve of yours?"

Carlie stared out her window. "Is that what your insult was meant to do? Rattle me?"

"Actually, I didn't mean to insult you at all."

Carlie snorted. "I'm not an idiot, Tyler. I understand how ridiculous I must have sounded. Certainly no one would ever think... I mean, the idea of me and you..."

"That's not why I laughed, Carlie."

She snorted again, and he grinned. "There, you see?" he said. "You just never say or do what I expect. You were sitting back there all prim and proper, your pretty hazel eyes all disapproving, and it just struck me funny. You seem too much a woman of the 90s to be so prudish."

Carlie felt mortified. "I'm not prudish," she mumbled, memories of a few nights ago tumbling about in her mind. Then she told the necessary lie. "Just circumspect."

They stopped at a red light, and he turned toward her, scrutinizing her. She stubbornly ignored him, only briefly glancing his way. But it was enough to see his smile. She had the vague suspicion that he felt challenged. And an even worse suspicion that if it came to a battle of wills, she'd lose. Hands down.

Tyler certainly had more experience sparring words. A thrill of trepidation ran down her spine, and then her reason for that trepidation was verified.

"Your lips are nice. Full and soft, but not a hint of a smile. And I like your small, stubborn chin."

He was teasing, she could tell. And she almost grinned at his underhanded tactics. Almost.

"Does it hurt?"

That gained her reluctant attention, and a quizzical frown. "What?"

"Wearing your hair so tight. It gives me a headache just to look at it."

She should never have looked at him. His dark eyes were shining and his firm lips were tilted in a boyish grin. He appeared totally harmless. But she wasn't buying it.

"How long is it?" Tyler moved when the traffic light turned green and drove smoothly down the uncrowded street. "Shoulder-length? Longer?"

"I can't see where my hair could possibly interest you, Tyler. But to end your juvenile tactics to annoy me, I'll tell you. It reaches my shoulder blades, is a very mousy brownish blond, and I wear it this way because I don't have time to fuss with fancy hairdos. As long as a person's hair is clean, what should it matter to anyone else how it's worn?"

Very softly, but with devastating sincerity, he said, "I don't think your hair is mousy."

Her head swiveled so sharply to look at him, she winced.

"I think it's a nice color, especially with the sun on it. I see shades of red—which suits you—but also blond and dark brown. It's very nice. You should wear it loose."

"I don't know what game you're playing, but I'm not interested. I'm not a teenager to be flattered by comments on my hair or eyes. I want to do a job here, Tyler. I'm very serious about it, even if you aren't."

"You are so damned defensive."

With reason, she wanted to scream. If he found out.... She sucked in a calming breath and stared at his profile. Her voice was patience personified, and filled with sane reasoning. "I'm not defensive. Just realistic. As you already made clear, there's very little about me that would ever entice you. I'm not naive. I'm aware of how I look. Why don't we talk about something important now? Like the students."

"I was only being honest with you, Carlie."

She gave him her patented teacher's look, reserved for students who had pushed her past the line. He shrugged, then returned his attention to the road.

She felt oddly deflated.

As he pulled into the school parking lot a few minutes later, he asked, "Were you at Bren's Halloween party?"

Coming out of left field like that, the question left her temporarily routed. Then she gathered her wits, opened the door and stepped out. Tyler left the car also, the consummate gentleman, and walked her to her own car, opening her door.

Carlie wasn't certain if it was just an innocent question, or if he was guessing at the identity of the masked lady again. She hesitated.

"Carlie?"

She saw no way around the lie. "No, I didn't go. There's always a lot happening at school this time of year. We had our own class party, you know. For the students, I mean. And we've already started practicing for the Thanksgiving play. And then, with the new project I've been working on..." Carlie came to a fast stop, appalled at her rambling. She looked into his eyes as she added truthfully, "I don't go to parties very often."

"Why not? You don't have a steady date?"

Carlie rolled her eyes, leaning back on the car. She adjusted her glasses carefully on the bridge of her nose. "I most certainly don't need a man to take me to a party if I wish to go."

"Of course not. I was only going to say that I didn't have a date, either, but I…well, I had a… terrific time. You should have come. I think you would have enjoyed yourself." He grinned. "I went as a pirate."

"How appropriate. Did you rape and pillage your way through the party?"

It was a lousy jest, and Tyler made certain she instantly regretted it.

"I wouldn't do something as reprehensible as rape, Carlie. As for pillaging, I would never steal from my brother. Now, if it was at your house…do you own anything worth stealing?"

She should have known better than to throw that verbal punch, but she hadn't been able to resist. She didn't have an answer to his facetious question, so she settled for a look of disdain. Tyler only smiled.

Carlie turned away and climbed into her car. She needed to get away. She couldn't remember the last time she'd felt so emotionally drained. Or so invigorated.

That personal acknowledgment angered her even more, and she tried to slam her car door. But Tyler got in her way, gripping the window frame and holding the door open.

"You should go out more, Carlie. It might do you some good to socialize, I think."

"Then you probably shouldn't think. You might damage something vital, and then what would the female population do?" She smiled with false sweetness, slammed the door and immediately pulled away.

She glanced in her rearview mirror and saw Tyler still standing there, watching after her. Even from a distance, she could see he was smiling. And then Carlie realized she was smiling also. She shook her head, bemused. She couldn't recall the last time she'd actually had fun with a man. Even arguing with Tyler was somehow fun.

Maybe she had been missing out and didn't even know it.

ON HER DRIVE HOME, she thought about seeing Tyler again. She was actually anticipating it. He didn't seem to be at all deterred by the cold shoulder she was giving him. In fact, she believed it amused him. He smiled often enough to give her that impression.

The very last thing she wanted to do was amuse Tyler. She had to maintain an emotional distance; she had to keep herself safe. It certainly wouldn't be easy, but she'd just have to try harder not to react to his little provocations. The only problem was, Tyler could be very provoking even when he wasn't trying. All the man had to do was stand there, and women fawned all over him.

But Carlie wouldn't be like other women. He'd find that out soon enough. She'd see to it.

TYLER BOUNCED the basketball, feeling impatient. Where was Carlie? He was anxious to see her again, which surprised him to no end. He'd decided he must be a glutton for punishment, because as much as she seemed to look down on him and his life-style, he still enjoyed every minute he spent with her. Even when they were arguing.

The woman had a real flair for putting him in what she considered his place. She was fun.

He heard a sudden squeaking of gym shoes and looked up, a huge grin spreading across his face when he saw her. Carlie was waltzing onto the gym floor, looking as if she wore the comfortable, baggy sweatpants and thigh-length sweatshirt every day. She couldn't quite stop her nervous hands, however, from tugging on the hem of the shirt, trying to pull it farther over her thighs.

He couldn't resist teasing her. "Well, Ms. Mc-Daniels! You have very long legs. I hadn't realized."

She held his steady gaze and Tyler found himself anticipating what she might say. She never reacted as he expected her to. She never reacted as most other women would.

She was definitely unique.

"There was no need, nor will there ever be a need, for you to notice my legs, Tyler."

His grin never slipped. He enjoyed baiting her, watching her struggle with her temper. "Is every damned thing you own the same shade of mud? Don't you have anything blue or yellow?'' He smacked his forehead, as if struck by a thought. ''Red! You might look...nice, in red.''

Her teeth snapped together in a loud click. ''Watch your language. There are children present, and no, I have no desire...''

''None at all?''

''...*to wear red!* We're only playing basketball, for goodness' sake, and I hardly think the occasion warrants dressing up.''

''It doesn't warrant dressing down, either. Is your body actually in there somewhere?'' He leaned back, his gaze ranging slowly over her. ''There's enough extra material there to clothe three women.''

''Not that it's necessary for me to explain myself to you,'' she told him, starting to lose that steady, rock-solid calm, ''but I thought I should wear clothes that were loose to allow for freedom of movement. I always wore something similar when I was a child and played basketball. I believe in being comfortable.''

Tyler paused with interest. ''You have some experience with the game then?''

''A little.''

He chuckled. Knowing Carlie, and he *was* getting to know her, despite her efforts to remain aloof, ''a little'' probably meant she was very proficient at the game. ''Excellent. We'll start by outlining the rules to the children, then we'll choose sides. I'll lead one team, you can lead the other.''

Carlie nodded, but put in, ''After warm-ups. I don't want to take a chance on anybody getting hurt.''

''Whatever you say. But you'll have to lead those. I don't know any, other than sit-ups and such, and I'm not certain what kids this age are used to.''

Tyler watched Carlie as she rounded up the kids and introduced them to him. As he spoke with each child, taking the time to joke and put them at ease, he caught Carlie staring. He winked at her, and she favored him with a genuine smile.

He wasn't used to her doing that, and for a second there, it threw him. Then he realized she was merely pleased that he was taking the time to really *talk* with the children. What had she thought he'd do? Bark at them?

The exercises she'd chosen were simple, but she challenged the children to keep up, to do each individual stretch properly. Throughout it all, Tyler watched her, and he grew increasingly curious.

Her breasts bounced. He'd never really noticed how amply endowed she was until now, but Mother Nature had treated her generously. And from what he could tell, she was totally unaware of it.

Unfortunately, he wasn't.

After helping a little girl catch the rhythm of the exercise, he wandered between all the children, checking to see if anyone else needed help. But even as he did that, he kept his gaze on Carlie, watching her every move.

When they finally broke up into teams, Carlie taking four girls and the biggest boy, Tyler with four boys, he announced they would play "shirts and skins." He led the boys in stripping off their shirts, then noticed Carlie staring. She tightened her mouth and blushed bright red when he caught her eye. He was amused, but he also liked the idea of her liking his body. Walking toward her, seeing her back up a step before she could stop herself, Tyler grinned. When he reached her, he slipped a fingertip over her lips, then chucked her chin, all without a single word. She closed her mouth with a snap, stomping to the other side of the hoop. But still, she looked her fill.

Later, after each of the children had taken a few practice shots, Tyler pulled Carlie aside. "They're well-behaved. Only a few of them are a little rambunctious." He laughed. "I heard one of the boys daring another to do a few…indiscreet things. They saw me looking and changed their minds."

"Just remember that when the novelty wears off and they get used to you. They can become a little more than rambunctious."

There were several occasions to point out misconduct, ranging from offensive language to shoving. Once, Tyler had to break up a skirmish between two of the boys. By the time six o'clock rolled around, Tyler was beat and Carlie looked exhausted.

But still, she took the time to make certain each child was bundled up properly. She helped with tying shoes, answered numerous questions and convinced one little boy that he didn't really want to hit another, just because the child had sneezed on him.

Then she gave the sneezer a tissue.

"I'm impressed," Tyler told her, his eyes on her flushed face. "You're really good with kids. You never once lost your temper."

She shrugged off his compliment. "I enjoy them. They're fun, and honest to a fault."

Tyler felt a tug on his hand, and looked down at a little girl named Lucy. She was smiling at him, showing him the stuck zipper on her coat. He helped her get her coat closed, then tweaked her nose. As he started to stand, she threw her skinny arms around his neck and squeezed him tight. "Thank you, Mr. Ramsey. I had fun."

Surprised, he looked toward Carlie, then ruffled the girl's tangled hair. "I did too, Lucy." She giggled, and Tyler grinned at her. "You'll be here Monday?"

"Yes, sir." She skipped away, leaving Tyler to stare after her.

"Whatever could that little girl have done to deserve detention? She's a doll."

Carlie waved goodbye to the last little boy, watching as he climbed into his parent's car, before allowing the heavy gym door to close. She turned to Tyler, chuckling softly. "Lucy has a problem with her language. She could make a sailor blush when she puts her mind to it. Personally, I think she just wants attention. Her father took off about a year ago, and her mother has her hands full trying to take care of five kids, all under the age of fifteen. Lucy sort of falls into the middle of the group.''

Tyler turned away, his left hand rubbing the muscles of his neck. ''I hate hearing stories like that. They make me want to strangle somebody.'' He began idly bouncing the ball, just to give his hands something to do and his mind something to focus on other than the problems of innocent children. But it didn't work. The issue was a sensitive one with him. ''Why is it the kids who have to get hurt?''

''It's always the ones who are most vulnerable. That's simply human nature.'' She shrugged philosophically, then took him by surprise, snatching the basketball out of his hands and dribbling it across the court.

Tyler watched her antics, knowing she was trying to distract him, and appreciating her efforts. Being with the children today reminded him of his own childhood. It had been rough for him and Jason, and when they'd become teenagers it had only gotten worse. Tyler had always pretended with his friends, bragging about the freedom he and Jason had, making it sound as if raising themselves had been a lark. And he had refused to admit to the embarrassment of having a mother who was the town ''lightskirt.''

God, it had been hard. Luckily, he'd had Jason. But it wasn't the same. Children needed an adult to look up to, someone they respected and who cared about them.

These kids had Carlie, but he wanted to help, too, wanted to make a difference.

"All right, Tyler," she said, breaking into his thoughts. "Enough moping over things you can't change. I hereby challenge you to a little one-on-one. The first to make ten baskets wins."

His grin was slow and filled with wicked delight. He put his hands on his hips, watching Carlie as she continued to expertly dribble the ball. "What are we betting?"

"That I can beat the pants off you." Her tone was smug and taunting. And then she understood exactly what she'd said. She flushed scarlet.

"My pants? Well, Ms. McDaniels! It wasn't enough to ogle me without my shirt? You want to strip me of all modesty?"

"That would be impossible." Her face was still hot, but she began dribbling the ball again. "You don't possess any modesty and probably never have."

His grin widened. He approached her slowly, his eyes never leaving her face. "I'm ready when you are, sweetheart. But the stakes have to be worthwhile. Say…dinner? At the winner's choice of place?"

Carlie gave him a confident smile. She did a fancy little feat of bouncing the ball behind her back, then between her knees, before shouting suddenly, "You're on." She raced down the court, scoring the first basket before he realized the game had started.

"Oh, ho! Getting tricky on me, huh? I like a woman who can take me by surprise." Carlie faltered at his words, nearly losing the ball. Tyler lunged, staying right on her, his body looming over hers, his arms outreaching her, his legs able to cover the same amount of ground more quickly. Carlie claimed it was an even match.

She was good, real good. She dunked the ball three times before he had a chance to score. Then he got serious. But all the while, he grinned. He felt better than he had in a very long time.

They were both sweaty by the time the score was evened up, eight all. Tendrils of hair had come loose around Carlie's face, sticking to her forehead and flushed cheeks. She looked done in, but still very determined to win. And she was laughing, obviously enjoying herself.

Then Tyler accidentally hit her. He made to jump for the ball, and his elbow smacked against her temple. Stumbling backward, she landed on her butt, her glasses slipping off her nose and dropping into her lap.

Tyler was horrified. "Oh, God, Carlie. I'm sorry!" He knelt beside her, taking her face in his hands, staring into her dazed eyes. Wide, hazel eyes. "Are you all right?"

She managed a slight, shaky smile. "I'm okay." Then she looked up at him.

His eyes locked with hers, and his fingers moved an almost imperceptible amount. As he studied her, something seemed familiar, some memory tickling at the back of his mind. Those wide eyes....

Then Carlie broke the contact, pulling away from his hands.

"You knew you were about to lose, right? That's why you belted me?" Her voice shook, and she tried another grin, but it was a weak attempt. Tyler wondered how badly she was hurt.

He was too busy trying to analyze the situation to answer right away. Carlie stuck her glasses firmly back on her nose, then called, "Yoo-hoo? Anybody home? Tyler?"

Finally, he shook his head, chasing away the errant confusion. "Sorry. Here, let me help you up."

"I'm fine, Tyler. I don't need any help." He helped, anyway, giving Carlie no choice in the matter.

He turned her, holding her chin in his palm. "Let me look at you. I think you have a lump coming up already."

She jerked away. "I told you, I'm fine. Quit fussing."

Tyler propped his hands on his hips, worried and filled with guilt. "I'll concede the game. Dinner is on me."

Carlie looked down at herself, then shook her head.

"Dressed like this? I don't think so, but thanks, anyway."

Her refusal didn't surprise him, but it did annoy him. "You have to eat. It's been a long day."

"I have stew in the Crock-Pot at home. You're free and clear."

He picked up his shirt, drying the sweat from his chest and arms with it. He didn't particularly want to be free. "Stew sounds good. We bachelors don't get a home-cooked meal all that often."

Carlie raised her eyes to his, a look of disbelief mirroring her thoughts.

As hints went, his was blatantly clear and he held his breath while waiting to see what she would say.

"*You* are wrangling *me* for an invite?"

He shrugged, but the movement felt stiff. "I figure anyone who can play basketball as good as you, must surely be able to cook, too."

"Your logic escapes me, and besides, I don't think I made enough."

It was almost as if she was challenging him. He wanted to spend more time with her, but she was determined to put him off. He didn't like it, not one little bit. They *would* spend the evening together, despite the woman's ridiculous reservations. "I'll stop at the bakery and pick up some sourdough bread to go with it."

Carlie narrowed her eyes at his persistence. "Don't

you have some female somewhere waiting for you to call and check in?''

"Nope. And I'm hopelessly lonely. Be kind, Carlie. Take me home.''

"Like a stray dog? If I feed you once, will I have trouble getting rid of you?''

He managed to look hurt. Shrugging his bare shoulders, he said, "Never mind. I didn't mean to intrude. I just thought since we were both going home alone, we could share a meal. I had fun today. I don't get to goof off all that often anymore, regardless of what you think.''

Carlie froze. He knew she wouldn't be able to handle hurting his feelings. Carlie was, despite her efforts to prove otherwise, a real softie. He watched her out of the corner of his eye and knew the moment she relented.

"I had fun, too, Tyler. And I suppose it would be nice to have someone to chat with over dinner.''

Tyler raised his head, all remnants of self-pity disappearing. "Terrific! I knew you could be reasonable.''

"Why, you big fraud!''

He simply laughed, not the least bit concerned with his deception. "Go get your things. I'll follow you to your house.''

He watched Carlie stomp away. He could see her silently fuming. Damn, but he enjoyed her company. She was prickly, independent, determined to do things her way. She didn't pout, didn't treat him to the silent bit. No, when Carlie had something to say—and she usually did—she said it. She was so unpredictable, so *unexpected,* she chased boredom right out the door.

ner eyes. She tamed, walking away. Tyler sat in the Grand
Am, on a tear, realizing refusing to answer he asked the
woman deliberately. She was so uncertainly knowing
embrace. He cleared a throat right out of his

CHAPTER FIVE

TYLER DROVE behind Carlie, noting the slow, careful
way she maneuvered her car. He was on the verge of
laughing out loud. He shook his head, bemused. He
couldn't recall ever having such verbal skirmishes
with a woman. Women didn't react to him that way.
But damned if he didn't like it. It was fun.

For that matter, Carlie was fun.

And he'd never thought of a woman that way before. She appeared totally immune to his flirting, but
it wasn't because she was shy or withdrawn.

On the contrary. She was one of the most outspoken women he'd ever met. And intelligent. He enjoyed her company.

It was like having a pal, someone he could
exchange mild insults with and still smile. But it was
so utterly different with her being female. It was as
if a whole new facet had been added to the relationship. It went a long way toward relieving his distraction over the mysterious—and missing—masked lady.
And that in itself was a major feat.

Carlie pulled into her driveway and parked beneath
a carport. Tyler pulled up to the curb out front, then

he stared. He wasn't sure what he'd expected, probably a mud-colored house with a barren expanse of lawn and not a single speck of color. She took him by surprise. Again.

Her house was a small Cape Cod cottage nestled at the end of a narrow side street. A farmer's fields were on the right side of the house, a heavily wooded area to the left. Behind and in front of the white-and-yellow wooden structure was a well-tended lawn. Daisies were blooming everywhere, and her mailbox was designed to look like a small, colorful barn.

Tyler looked around, captivated. There was a tire swing hanging from the gnarled branch of an ancient oak off the back corner of the house. A curving porch circling to the right of the front door had a rattan porch swing attached to the overhang.

"A real swinger, aren't you?"

Carlie shrugged as she dug her key from her purse. "I'm not an idle person. I don't like to be still, even when I'm relaxing."

Tyler tried to imagine the classic picture of a woman superimposed with Carlie in a flowery dress, her hair loose, swaying in the breeze and humming softly while her bare feet maintained the gentle motion of the swing.

He wasn't quite that imaginative.

The inside of her house was also a contrast, so different from the woman he was getting to know. There was little furniture, only the basic necessities.

It was an eclectic mix of modern and antique, light oak and glass, chintz material and delicate doilies. There were no photographs, but there were framed prints of the most outrageous things. Each room appeared to have a theme.

The living room was spring, with a large, brass-framed picture of a bee, busily collecting pollen from a daisy. Porcelain flowers decorated each tabletop and filled one curio cabinet.

The dining room, which was minuscule, was decorated with birds. A border of them circled the room, a dainty, delicate figure sat looking over every corner, and in each plant, one peeked from between the leaves.

The kitchen was whales.

He raised his eyebrows at her in question. "How did you choose whales, may I ask?"

Carlie had been busily putting their jackets on the coat tree and checking the stew. She looked at him over her shoulder as she lifted the Crock-Pot lid. "One of the children at school gave me one, once. I said I liked it, and…" She smiled.

"They all decided to give you one?"

"Each class seems to take it into their head that I need a new collection of something. But I don't mind. It makes for consistent Christmas presents. There are bunnies in the bathroom and cats in my bedroom."

"What are you going to do when you run out of rooms?"

She tilted her head. "Mix and match?"

He smiled at her wit. "Can I help you set the table or something?"

"No. You can turn on the television if you like. I'm just going to heat the bread and set the table."

Tyler wandered into the living room again. His attention was drawn to the television set and an array of tapes sitting on top. He looked through them, and stopped when he spotted a "Work Out With the Oldies," video. He carried it with him into the kitchen. "Whose is this?"

Carlie paused in the process of serving the stew. "Mine. Who else would it belong to?"

"You work out to the oldies?"

"I like older music. It's more fun than this new stuff kids listen to."

"So do you hop and jostle around in a pair of tights?"

She smirked at his expression. "You're looking at my workout clothes." She spread her arms in the air. The shirt raised a bit and he caught a glimpse of the pale flesh of her belly.

To his disbelief, and annoyance, he felt a brief spurt of interest. It had only been a flash, an instant of white skin, gone too quickly to really appreciate, if indeed, there had been anything there to appreciate.

She was slightly overweight. At least, he thought she was. With the clothes she favored, it was hard to tell for certain. But she definitely had a large bosom.

He'd established that today when she was exercising, her body bouncing in all the right places. And from that prominent point, her clothes fell almost straight down, giving no hint of curves or dips and hollows.

But her arms had felt slim when he'd shaken her the other day. And when she'd come into the house, she'd kicked off her shoes, showing narrow feet and trim ankles.

It was simple curiosity, he decided, that was making him react to her. Not that he would ever consider doing anything about it. She was a school teacher, which was bad enough as far as dalliance went, but on top of that she was too damn prickly, and was his sister-in-law's best friend, to boot. She was so far off the scale of available females, he knew he didn't have to concern himself. But he did, anyway.

He'd never met a woman so dedicated to a cause, so at ease with children and so giving. She was totally disinterested in his supposed prowess, in his community standing, in his reputation. All she wanted from him was his help in achieving a worthwhile goal.

Disgruntled with his thoughts, and his overactive imagination that kept him guessing at her elusive, and presumably plump, figure, he stalked toward her and asked bluntly, "How much do you weigh?"

Carlie halted in the middle of opening a package of butter. "That's none of your business!"

"You're working out, so you must feel you need to lose some weight, right?"

"Wrong. I work out to keep in shape. Everybody should." She poked him in the middle. "Don't you?"

"Of course. But that's different."

"Why?"

"I go to a gym. I'm a man."

"Well, I can't afford to go to some fancy gym. And no one ever told me being a man was synonymous with being outrageously snoopy and impertinent. I would have thought a man your age would have learned some manners by now."

It was her teacher's voice again, and Tyler saw that he'd made her truly angry, though she was trying to hide it. He watched as she slammed bowls onto the table, then practically threw the spoons next to them.

"What are you drinking?" he asked cautiously, waiting to see if she would end up throwing something at him.

"I'm drinking milk. You can find yourself something in the refrigerator."

He did. Milk.

After sitting down to eat in perfect, strained silence, he ventured, "I'm sorry…?"

"You're not sure?"

"Of course I'm sure. I just didn't know if you would want me to speak to you. I, ah, seemed to have hit a nerve."

Carlie sighed, dropping her face into her hands.

Tyler had the awful suspicion she was going to cry. In a near whisper, he asked, "Carlie?"

Her shoulders shook, and Tyler's heart stopped. "Aw, Carlie don't. Sometimes I just stick my foot in it. You shouldn't pay any attention to me. Really. Carlie?"

She slowly raised her head. A wicked grin spread across her features. One look at Tyler and she broke into peals of laughter. He fell back against his chair, glaring at her.

"Oh, Tyler. You didn't hit a nerve, honestly." She chuckled again, then removed her glasses to wipe her eyes. "Actually," she put in, obviously intent on controlling her hilarity and not entirely succeeding, "you're finally acting exactly as I thought you would."

"Is that right?"

"Yes, it is."

He felt the sting of her insult, deliberate, he was certain. "So, you assumed all along that I was a jerk? Is that it?"

"Not a jerk. Not really. You're an okay guy. But you think you can make up your own rules and everyone, especially females, will abide by them. You deliberately provoke me, and you're purposely outrageous. You don't even try to follow normal codes of manners or behavior. And why should you? Women relentlessly fall at your feet, despite your attitude, so why should you change to accommodate polite society?''

He didn't like having her categorize and analyze his faults as if he fell into an expected mode of ''male behavior.'' ''All this lecturing simply because I commented on your weight?''

''Because you felt it didn't matter if you were rude. After all, I'm not a woman you'd aspire to sleep with. You have no personal, sexual interest in me, so why go out of your way to be charming? There wouldn't be any benefit, now, would there?''

He studied her, his eyes probing. Damned if he wasn't letting her get the best of him, again. So far, that was how it had been. She consistently sliced him up, verbally at least, while he was sitting there admiring her. Laughing with him was one thing, but Carlie was actually laughing *at* him. It was intolerable. ''I'll be honest with you. For some inexplicable reason, I'm intrigued by you.''

Her eyes widened enormously, and she choked on a breath. Her amusement was instantly, and completely, gone.

He waited impassively until she'd regained her breath. ''I've decided it's because you're so damned mysterious.''

She sent him a wary look, then shook her head, refusing to meet his eyes. ''No. No, I'm not. I'm an open book. You simply refuse to accept there's a woman who isn't bowled over by your charm.''

He pretended she hadn't spoken. "What does your body look like? That's what I'm wondering. How plump are you? How big are your breasts, how bountiful is your bottom? I'm used to looking at a woman and seeing what's there, be it attractive or not, not this infuriating guessing game, trying to see beneath layers of ugly clothing."

Very slowly, Carlie laid her spoon by her bowl. She stared at him, then tightened her mouth. "You're terribly spoiled. You think nothing of going for the jugular just so you can win. All right. So I'm overweight." She lifted one shoulder in a stiff shrug, holding his gaze. "It runs in my family. And flaunting my body would be a bigger crime than hiding it. But so what? I don't need a man's approval to feel good about myself. I'm a very nice person, and I do a very good job, and I *care*. About this community, about the children, about people in general. Can you say the same, Tyler? So you're handsome. So what? What real contribution have you ever made to your own small part of the world?"

He spooned up a bite of stew, saluting her with it before putting it in his mouth. He chewed thoughtfully, feeling her simmer beside him, her anger growing with his nonchalance. Finally, knowing he'd pushed her far enough and sensing that she was ready to throw her stew at his head, he said, "You do a good job of going for the jugular, as well. I can't think of a single important thing I've ever done in my life.

But I don't do bad things, either, discounting my comment on your weight, of course. I pay my taxes on time, I don't drink and drive, I donate to charities—although, only when they actually catch me. I'm a gentleman and I'm kind to older people. Surely all that counts for something?''

''Not much.''

''Come on, Carlie. Can't you forgive me? I was only curious, after all, not being deliberately insulting. If I was too nosy, well it's only because I think you could be very attractive. No, don't make rude noises at me again. So you're not a beauty. Big deal. You are intelligent, very intelligent. That's something to be admired. If you made a little effort with your appearance, you might have plenty of equally intelligent men knocking your door down. You would probably have a very busy social schedule.''

''I don't have time for a…busy social schedule.''

''It's not a disease, you know. You're a fun person to be with. You should be involved with someone special.''

Carlie tilted her head back to survey the ceiling. Without looking at him, she asked, ''Why do you care, Tyler? I'm not some bird with a broken wing you need to teach to fly. I don't want to fly. Walking is much more my speed.''

''I have an idea,'' he announced, very pleased with himself.

''Oh, no. Now we're in it deep.''

He laid his palms flat on the table, and raised himself out of his chair to loom toward her. "Date me."

Carlie eyed him as if he'd grown a second head. As she kept him waiting, he reseated himself, tapping his fingers on the table. "Well?"

"I'm waiting for the punch line."

"All right. Here it is. You might like it. You might enjoy my company."

She made a show of stifling her laughter. "You should get paid. You're a professional."

"Professional what? Or should I ask?"

"Comedian, of course."

"I'm being serious here. The least you could do is listen to me."

"No, the least I could do is make you go home and take your insanity with you." She seemed almost angry—and flustered. Her cheeks were a warm, rosy pink, and her hands trembled just the tiniest bit. Then she widened her eyes comically, gasping. "You don't think it's catching, do you?" She shoved her chair back, holding her hands up in a defensive gesture.

Tyler slowly rose from his seat. "All right, you. I think I ought to take you in hand. Talk about *my* manners!" As he advanced on her, circling the table with a menacing stride, Carlie shrieked and jumped to her feet, moving quickly to keep the table between them.

"All right! All right! Tell me what you have to say."

Tyler advanced. "Too late. You've challenged my masculinity. And with my ego as enormous as you claim, that must surely be grounds for assault. Now you'll have to pay."

She was trying not to laugh. He watched the grin grow on her face, and felt satisfaction. Chuckles emerged from between her tightly drawn lips. She clapped a hand over her mouth, still moving cautiously. He followed.

Then Tyler lunged across the table, grabbing for her. She screeched in surprise, but it was already too late. He had her.

Hauling her body across the table, his grip firm on her upper arms, Tyler grinned at her. She was laughing, her glasses were askew, her chest heaving. And he had the insane, almost overwhelming urge to kiss her.

What the hell? he thought, and leaned closer, his eyes on her soft, slightly parted lips. He was filled with an anticipation that even surpassed what he'd felt at the pool house with the masked lady, and that had been shocking in its intensity. What he felt now was so alien to his jaded senses, he actually jerked when she spoke.

Her voice wasn't breathless. It was low and menacing. "Back off."

He did. Slowly regaining his wits, mortified by what he had almost done—to *Carlie,* for Pete's sake—Tyler managed an unconcerned shrug. "I've never really...played with a woman before. I was only going to—''

"Oh, please. Spare me. I know what you were doing."

"Uh, what?" Maybe she could tell him, for he certainly hadn't a clue what had been in his mind. *Carlie?* Good grief.

Carlie fussed with her glasses. "You're playing games. I already told you, I won't have it."

That sounded plausible, though not entirely true. But it helped him to regain his aplomb. "Of course I was playing. And so were you. That's why you should date me. Ah-ah, just hear me out." He waited until she sat down again. "Now, don't storm out on me. I think we could enjoy each other's company, at least, as long as we keep it platonic. I hope you didn't think I meant—"

"Why?" she interrupted, her tone sharp, her look suspicious. "Why would you want to spend more time with me?"

"I like you. *Really* like you. You make me laugh." Then he added, "And you keep me humble."

She snorted, then ignored his chastising look at the rude noise.

"It would be good for us both. You would learn to relax a little, to concentrate on something other than your obligation to the school, and like I said, I enjoy your company."

"Surely there are other women whose company you would enjoy more?"

"Perhaps. But for different reasons." She opened her mouth, and he raised a hand in surrender. "I know. Uncalled for. Acquit me. But I've been really bored lately and…"

He frowned at her bubble of laughter. "I'm perfectly serious, I'll have you know. Here I am, laying my heart out to you, and you're rudely stomping all over it."

"You know what, Tyler?"

He didn't trust her grin. "Probably not."

"It has been fun at odd and varying moments, which if you're being sincere, is surprising to us both."

He grabbed his chest, feigning a heart attack. "What? You admit to enjoying my company? I'm not totally without redemption? I'm not totally cast down? Carlie McDaniels likes my company! What more encouragement could a man ask for?"

"At odd and varying moments," she clarified. "Okay, so where would we go and what would we do on these experimental, platonic dates?"

"Then you'll do it?"

"Absolutely not. Not until you answer my question."

"I don't know." He hadn't really thought things through. "The usual stuff?"

"Such as?"

"Dinner? Dancing?" He grinned, ready to elaborate and add to his list. "Roller skating? Bungee jumping? Body surfing?"

"I could maybe handle a movie. It's dark there and nobody would have to know I was out with a maniac."

He beamed at her. "Excellent choice. Tomorrow?"

"Tomorrow is Saturday. Don't you have a real date?"

"Carlie, Carlie, Carlie. This *will* be a real date. Up to, but excluding, the good-night kiss."

Carlie twisted her mouth in apparent thought, chewed the corner of her bottom lip and studied her short, neat nails.

"You're not contemplating death, you know," he said dryly. "I'll even let you choose the movie." He watched the fleeting expressions on her face, and saw her indecision, her...nervousness? Damned unaccountable female. He couldn't remember the last time he'd had to actually beg for a date. It was a rather disturbing experience.

"I can choose what we'll see?"

His heartbeat picked up speed. "Absolutely."

"A true concession. All right. I'll go."

Tyler felt his muscles ease, and only then realized how stiff he'd been. He felt as if he'd accomplished something major. Carlie was no easy nut to crack. But he was determined to help her loosen up. He could help her with the children, easing some of her obligation, and also show her how to have a good time.

He suddenly realized that things were starting to pick up. Boredom was a thing of the past. First there was that night with the mysterious, timid masked lady, whose identity Brenda refused to reveal, no matter how he cajoled. His curiosity over that little episode was still extreme; he'd never met a woman like her before. Sooner or later, he *would* find out who she was.

Of course, he'd never met a woman like Carlie, either. She was as unique as any woman could be. He smiled, thinking of her again. Prickly, independent, outspoken Carlie. He surely had enough excitement to keep boredom at bay for some time to come.

"I CAN'T BELIEVE you chose this movie."

Carlie smiled in the dim theater, very aware of Tyler sitting beside her. He was dressed in jeans and a dark sweater. She could smell his after-shave, and his own natural, masculine scent. It was comforting, stimulating and very distracting. "I love Mel Gibson."

"Now, why does that surprise me? Oh, yeah. You've made it clear to me on several occasions that macho, sexy men are low on your list."

"No. I made it clear that men who *thought* they were macho, sexy men were low on my list."

"Don't look at me like that! I never claimed to be macho."

"Are you claiming to be sensitive, instead?"

"Certainly. Especially in specific areas. Like low on my stomach, the top of my spine…"

Carlie's breath caught and her skin suffused with heat. He wasn't lying. She remembered all too well just how sensitive he was in those particular areas. Throughout that one special night, he'd shown her how to give as well as take, and she'd thoroughly enjoyed each lesson.

She elbowed him roughly to cover her reaction. "You're impossible."

"Naw." He waited a heartbeat. "Just *very* sensitive."

"Hush, the movie is starting." Carlie knew she sounded rude, but she didn't care. Tyler's flirting was just that, flirting. He did it with every woman he came into contact with, be she nine or ninety. It shouldn't mean anything, and likely wouldn't if she wasn't the mystery woman. But she was, and his words affected her in numerous ways. Her head knew he wasn't serious, but her heart jumped into a wild cadence of excitement every time he teased.

"Lesson number one, Carlie. You don't rudely tell your date to hush."

She shifted her gaze, peering at him in the growing darkness. "Not even when the movie is starting and he's yakking on about his sexuality and very personal preferences?"

"That's right. You should have told me where you're sensitive, too."

"Oh. Well, let's see. My feet?"

"You're not trying to get in the mood here, are you?"

She chuckled, feeling some of her tension ebb at his dry expression. Leaning slightly toward him, she nudged him affectionately with her shoulder. The action surprised them both, and Tyler whispered, "That's better," then boldly put his arm around her.

It felt good. Comforting and exciting at the same time. But she had to remind herself this was only a game to him. And she was only a distraction.

"You shouldn't stiffen up so, either," he added. "I'm not getting fresh. Just relax."

The words had been whispered gently in her ear. She could have added it as another sensitive spot, yes, indeed. He was being so careful with her, lightly teasing and so solicitous. She wanted to lean against him, to feel more of his heat against her side. Instead, she stared straight ahead. "Shh. Don't make me miss the movie."

It would be okay, Carlie thought, once she managed to relax a little. Tyler would never connect her with the pool house. And he wasn't attempting to fondle her; his hand wasn't moving from her shoulder and he wasn't drawing her nearer to his body. He was just…there. Firm. Nice. Male.

They shared a huge bucket of extra-buttery popcorn

and a large cola. Carlie felt Tyler's eyes on her when she unconsciously licked the butter from her fingers, but when she turned to him, he didn't say a word. He looked perplexed, annoyed and exasperated. Carlie frowned at him, but he shook his head and looked away. She couldn't begin to decipher his thoughts, and a few seconds later he excused himself to go buy candy. He returned with a box of chocolates.

"After all that popcorn, you have room for candy?"

Her tone had been whisper-soft, and he answered in kind. "You're doing it again. You don't talk to your date as if he's a glutton. You should say, 'Oh, candy!' and thank him for it."

She contrived a blank expression. "Oh, candy! Thank you."

He laughed out loud, prompting the people behind him to grumble a complaint.

Carlie whispered, "I gather by your display of humor, I didn't do it right?"

"You are amusing, Carlie. You really are. Thank you for coming with me tonight."

Her throat felt tight when she tried to smile. She dropped her gaze to her lap for a moment, then raised it to look at him. "I'm having a good time, too. Thank you for asking me."

He held her eyes a moment longer, tightened his arm around her in an affectionate squeeze, then turned his attention back to the screen. Carlie silently studied his profile. He wasn't the puffed-up, conceited ego-maniac she'd accused him of being. At least, not now, not with her.

Probably because he was with her; he wasn't trying to impress or seduce her. He'd claimed boredom, but she wasn't at all certain that was possible, given his reputation. There was no doubt Tyler Ramsey could have a different date every night of the week, without resorting to asking her out.

But it was nice being with him, knowing he didn't really see her as a woman, but rather as a companion, someone to spend a few hours with. She thought of the party and trembled.

Tyler accepted that she was heavy, plain and greatly lacking in good taste. He'd made no bones about detesting her choice in clothing. But it had taken only a few small modifications—a wig, colored contacts—and he hadn't recognized her at all.

With each passing hour, she found herself growing more attracted to him. It had started out being strictly physical. After all, Tyler Ramsey was the kind of man girls dreamed about and women fantasized over. And Carlie had recently lived a few of those fantasies. But now, she realized how easily she could lose her heart.

Carlie thought about the woman she used to be, so frivolous, so anxious to attract her husband's atten-tion, wanting and needing his approval. She'd failed dismally then, and eventually had learned a valuable lesson. Not that she blamed her husband entirely, for she had failed him in numerous ways. But he hadn't even tried to be patient with her. He'd thrown out accusations without remorse or consideration to her age and inexperience. At first, she'd been crushed that she wasn't a sexual person, that she'd failed in the most basic female concepts.

She was older now, wiser, no longer taken in by men and their obscure promises. Her husband hadn't wasted any time in finding someone who suited his sexual tastes better than she did. It didn't hurt anymore to remember, nor did it fill her with disappointment and self-reproach. She'd vowed never again to be that vulnerable. And she'd never been tempted to waver from that pledge.

Until Tyler. Now she had a night to herself, a special night to remember when she felt the loneliness that would surely come one day.

Gaining Tyler's friendship was fun, but knowing him as a man, for that one special night, was a memory she would repeatedly indulge in recalling. Without even trying, he'd made her feel things she'd never felt before, things she'd thought herself incapable of feeling. He'd proven her husband had been wrong about her. That would have to be enough.

She would have to be very careful that he never became suspicious. Any more friendly, casual dates would have to be forgotten. She couldn't risk it. The possibility of emotional hurt was too great. But the program? Could she distance herself, even while working with him for hours on end?

It wouldn't be easy, but she had no choice.

"TELL ME about Carlie."

Brenda paused in her efforts to finish folding her laundry. "Carlie? What do you want to know about her?"

Tyler shrugged. "I don't know. How long have you known her? Why isn't she married?"

Brenda swallowed, then looked away. "She was married. When she was very young. But it didn't work out. And since then...she just hasn't found the right man. She's intelligent, bright and funny and caring. She's very special."

Tyler was frowning slightly, then waved away Brenda's defense of Carlie. "You don't need to convince me. I've been with her a lot lately, and I like her, too." He was silent a moment, then shook his head. "I didn't know she'd been married. It was rough, huh?"

"I...ah, Carlie is very private, Tyler. I don't feel comfortable talking about her."

"I didn't mean to pry. I just think it's a shame she doesn't have anyone special."

Brenda turned and looked at him. "She told me you two went to the movies."

"Yeah. It was really fun. I enjoyed it. It's nice to be out with someone without having to worry about how the night will end. It was actually better than being with the guys. I didn't have to listen to, and return, all the raunchy jokes about sex and who had enjoyed the latest conquest. It was comfortable. Do you know what I mean?''

Very gently, Brenda smiled at him. ''Don't look so confused, Tyler. I know exactly what you mean. Jason says he felt the same way after he met me. With other women and with his male friends, there was always a certain face he had to wear, a certain way he was expected to act. Around me, he could just be himself.''

''There's a major difference here, Bren. Jason couldn't keep his hands off you.''

Her sudden burst of laughter was quickly cut off. ''That's true enough, thank heavens. I don't suppose you suffered the same thing with Carlie?''

''Carlie? That woman gives new meaning to *bad taste*. Her clothes alone are enough to keep my stomach churning. And there were several times I would have dearly loved to yank those damned glasses off her nose and stomp on them.''

''I've had the same thought myself, Tyler. But Carlie won't ever change. She won't dress to suit other people. And she's comfortable with herself and the style she's chosen.''

''What style? There is no style to her.'' He grinned suddenly and admitted, ''I've wondered what she would look like buck-naked, without her hair being tortured behind her head in that braid.''

Brenda's mouth dropped open, then she sputtered. "Tyler Ramsey! Don't you dare seduce my friend out of idle curiosity. I'd never forgive you!''

Tyler stood, glancing at his watch. He sighed philosophically. "You don't want me to have any fun, Bren.''

"Have *fun* with some other woman. But you leave Carlie alone.''

"Carlie is safe enough.'' Then he added, "You sure you won't tell me who the harem girl is?''

"I can't. I promised her I wouldn't.''

"But why? What is she hiding?''

"She...she knows your reputation. And...and I guess she just doesn't want to get involved.'' Brenda shrugged. "I'm sorry.''

Tyler worked his jaw in frustration. "She doesn't trust me?''

"Well...no.''

He exploded. "What is it with you women? I am not some overcharged male bimbo! Doesn't anyone allot me the benefit of having scruples?''

"You women?'' Brenda grinned at him. "This sounds like a Carlie lecture. Has she been rough on you?''

"One minute, yes. I get the feeling she doesn't think very highly of me. But then she'll laugh and be outrageously funny.'' He paced a few feet away. "She keeps me guessing.''

Brenda walked him to the door. "I know you have scruples, Tyler. And I think you're a very nice man, despite everything.'' She skipped away when he turned, grabbing playfully for her. Laughing, she continued, "But Carlie's different. I don't want to see her hurt.''

"Hurt? Carlie's about as vulnerable as a porcupine. But if you're worrying I'll make her promises I can't keep, don't. I've told her I like her friendship, that's all. I admire her, despite her atrocious clothing. And unless she's hiding a big surprise beneath those ugly clothes, I doubt I'd be even tempted to go beyond platonic with her. She's safe enough.''

Even as he said the words, Tyler thought what an adept liar he was. He was tempted, more than tempted. It was just that the temptation had come in a different package. Carlie's looks didn't appeal to him, but her character was extremely alluring. As often as not, he wanted to simply touch her, on the hand, on her smooth cheek. Holding her would be nice.

"Thank you, Tyler. I'm glad you've befriended Carlie. She needs some fun and excitement with men other than those stuffed shirts on the school board.

Tyler had been in the process of walking out, but he halted abruptly. "I didn't get the impression she was dating anyone in particular.''

"Carlie doesn't consider going anywhere with them a date, because she works with them. She thinks that their interest is purely work-related. But I don't think so. I think they're as curious as you are, but probably don't have the conscience you have." She looked up at him, frowning. "So far, Carlie hasn't allowed them the chance to appease their curiosity."

"What about Carlie? Doesn't she get curious?"

"Carlie?" Brenda fidgeted with her hair, looking away from Tyler. "Naw. She just isn't interested anymore. Like her clothes, she thinks spending a lot of time on a social life is a waste of perfectly good brain waves."

Tyler grinned. "I can hear her saying that." He glanced at his watch again, then asked quickly, "So you knew her in school?"

"Carlie and I have known each other for years. Without her help, I'd never have made it through college."

Tyler was silent a moment, acknowledging Brenda's words. "Carlie's like a mother hen, isn't she? She *likes* helping people."

"Yeah. That's Carlie, all right."

Nodding in satisfaction, Tyler left, late for his appointment. His trip to his sister-in-law's had been spontaneous. Carlie had refused to see him again except at practice, claiming she had too many papers to grade and a big test to prepare. He'd missed her.

Carlie seemed to have an innate rapport with children. When he was younger, he'd thought it was only his mother who didn't like and understand kids. Women, in general, were supposed to be maternal, he'd thought. But as he'd matured, he'd learned exactly how wrong he could be.

His mother hadn't wanted him or Jason because they hampered her life-style, which basically meant they curtailed her sexual freedom. At least she claimed they did. Tyler could never recall his presence slowing her down.

From a very young age, he'd known what women did with men. He'd *seen* what women did with men. His mother hadn't been circumspect. His mother hadn't been much of a mother.

And since then, he'd met too many women who seemed to share her sentiments. Life was for enjoying; as long as you had money and looks and prestige. It was a life-style most women sought, with no place for kids. Children interfered with careers or ruined otherwise perfect figures.

He would probably never have any children of his own. His life wasn't conducive to raising kids. And he would never cheat a child of the warmth and love they deserved. Children should enrich life; they should be cherished and protected, not considered a burden to be tolerated.

An image of Carlie, married and cradling a baby of her own, flitted through his mind. It left behind conflicting emotions; tenderness, because he knew she would be an excellent mother. But also possessiveness, which made no sense at all. He refused to dwell on that sentiment, and put the image firmly from his mind.

It disturbed him, how much she occupied his thoughts. Especially when he had other things to think about. He wouldn't give up on the mystery woman—he wasn't a man to leave a puzzle unsolved. But time and again, he found his thoughts veering to Carlie and her unusual wit, the gentleness and patience she gave her students.

Anyone who took the time to really know Carlie, would realize there was nothing plain about her, despite the horrendous clothing she wore. She was about as complex and complicated as any female could be. He hadn't exaggerated when he said she intrigued him.

Though he knew she'd had a good time with him, she had refused any future dates. She didn't return his calls, either. He would almost swear she was avoiding him, but why?

He would take his time, and sooner or later he would figure her out.

He intended to enjoy every minute.

CHAPTER SIX

CARLIE SAW Tyler's car pull up to the curb in front of Brenda's. His arrival was unexpected, and she went perfectly still. He jerked the car into Park, then jumped out, appearing determined—more than determined, if the look on his face was any indication. He disappeared past the window, then came to the kitchen door.

He knocked sharply, once, then stepped inside without waiting for an answer. Brenda met him there, her hands on her hips, blocking his vision of the kitchen table where Carlie sat.

"Tyler! What are you doing here?"

"I insist you tell me who she is."

"Who?"

He gave her a look of impatience. "Enough, Brenda. You know who I mean. The harem girl. Who is she?"

Brenda rolled her eyes. "For the last time, Tyler. No!"

Carlie wanted to disappear. It was a miserable Sunday morning, aptly suiting her mood. She'd come to Brenda's for solace, her emotions in turmoil. Nothing was as it had been only days before. She didn't know what to think, what to do. She'd learned so much lately. Too much.

One thing was certain: she couldn't just look at her experience with Tyler as a sexual lesson. Her one "date" with him had proven that. Tyler had touched more than her body. He'd thrown away the misconceptions she'd had about herself, stolen her fears and her disappointments.

And now that she saw him nearly every day, she feared he might very well steal her heart.

She couldn't let that happen. She needed time to think, to reason out her reactions. But here was Tyler, wanting to know who she really was. It was too ironic to bear.

"Your friends are something else, Bren. They're driving me crazy." He ran his hands roughly through his hair, the gesture filled with frustration.

"Friends?"

"Don't sound so innocent. First the harem girl refuses to tell me who she is. Then Carlie refuses to return my calls. I ask her out, and all she can say is no. I swear, that woman is totally—"

Brenda interrupted him then, clearing her throat loudly and gesturing with her eyes to draw his attention to the kitchen table. He looked, and Carlie saw his beautiful eyes narrow slightly.

His annoyance seemed to disappear; he became almost cheerful. "What the hell's the matter with you? You look awful."

After shooting him a disgusted frown, she turned away. "I have a cold," Carlie said. She sincerely hoped he wouldn't question her further, because her swollen, sleepy eyes had little to do with illness.

"And that made your hair all frizzy?"

"No, that didn't make my hair all frizzy." She mimicked him perfectly. "I jogged over here in the rain, and the rain makes my hair go frizzy."

Tyler scrutinized her. "You just said you had a cold! Why the hell were you out in the rain?"

"I jog every Sunday. Why should today be any different? A little rain never killed anyone." She knew she was being more waspish than usual, but she hadn't planned on having to face him this morning. Her heart ached, and her head followed suit.

"No. Rain doesn't kill, it just makes some people's hair go frizzy." Tyler grinned. "At least a few strands found the excuse to escape that infernal braid. It's probably a hair rebellion."

He laughed at his own jest, and Carlie stiffened at the sound. She pushed her glasses up, then lifted her chin. "Maybe I should go now, Bren. Tyler obviously has something he wants to discuss with you. And I'd hate to get stuck in the downpour, anyway."

Brenda smacked Tyler, then hurried to Carlie. "Don't go, yet. We haven't finished…talking."

"Yeah, Carlie." Tyler pulled out a chair and straddled it, facing Carlie with a huge grin. "I probably won't get any information out of Brenda, anyway. She's looking very stubborn, don't you think?" Then he turned to Brenda. "But you and I will talk later."

"It won't do you any good. I already told you I'm sworn to secrecy."

Exasperated, he looked at Carlie pointedly. "Do you really want to discuss my personal life in front of company?"

Brenda scoffed. "Carlie isn't company."

"Gee, thanks, Bren," Carlie said.

"You know what I mean, Carlie. Besides, I'm sure you couldn't care less about Tyler's love life. Right?"

Carlie tightened her mouth, feeling caught in a nightmare. Brenda was trying to tease; she still wanted Carlie to tell Tyler the truth. Only Brenda didn't know what the truth was, and Carlie had no doubt she'd be shocked if she did. For that matter, Tyler would be shocked, too. And probably disappointed. Carlie couldn't bear that. "You're right. I don't care to sit through any details. So—" she stood "—I'm off."

Tyler caught her wrist. "You can't walk home, now. It's raining."

"Believe me, it won't bother me a bit."

"Now, Carlie, don't be obstinate."

"Tyler, I'm dangerously close to laying you low." She had to get away from him. Now.

"Violence? My, my, your cold is making you surly."

She tugged, but he didn't release her. "Tyler, what did you intend to do today, before you came here and decided to harass me?"

"I was going to harass Brenda, but you'll do better."

She could feel the warmth of his hand on her arm, feel the probing intensity of his eyes. "Let go. I want to leave."

Tyler looked down at his hand, still wrapped around Carlie's wrist. She saw what he saw. His fingers entirely encircled her. She had slim, fine-boned wrists. He said, "You've been avoiding me."

Her breath caught somewhere in her diaphragm, causing her chest to ache. It took a great deal of effort to banter with him. "I've been busy. And why are you calling me on a weekend, anyway? Surely your social calendar is fully penciled in."

He flashed her a grin. "No, and there were numerous disappointed ladies, I can tell you."

She knew him well enough now to know he was only baiting her. He wasn't nearly the egomaniac he pretended to be. A reluctant smile curved her lips. "Tyler, quit fooling around. Let go."

"Not until you promise to help entertain me. Let's do something, go someplace. I'm bored and despondent. I need company."

"Despondent?" He was charm personified, and

much too appealing. It was strange, but not only had she played the part of two different women, she *felt* like two different women. Tyler was managing to lighten her mood, even though he was the cause of her foul disposition in the first place.

"That's right. And with good reason." He grinned at Brenda. "I got shunned by someone at Bren's party the other night, and now she won't tell me who the woman is."

With a theatrical gasp meant to cover her uneasiness with the topic, Carlie stared. "No! It can't be true."

"Sadly, it is. I fell in love, and the wench dumped me."

The words had obviously been said as a jest, but still Carlie jerked. Brenda said quickly, "He…he met a friend of mine during the party. They seemed to hit it off, but…she doesn't want to see him again. Ever." She ended with a shrug.

"Just tell me who she is, Bren. I can handle the rest."

Wanting to play her part properly, Carlie asked with laudable suspicion, "You don't know who she is?"

"Absurd, isn't it? But she refused to remove her mask, just so I wouldn't know who she was."

Carlie struggled to relax her tense muscles. "Smart girl."

"Oh, she wasn't a girl." He gave her a taunting

smile, obviously irritated with her snide comment. "She was very much a woman. A damned sexy woman." He turned to Brenda, a mocking plea in his eyes. "Please! Tell me who she is. I promise you, she'll thank you later."

Brenda grinned at his woeful expression. "I don't know. What do you think, Carlie?"

Carlie would certainly strangle Brenda later. She cleared her throat. "I think if a woman had enough sense to avoid getting involved with Tyler, you should respect her wishes."

Tyler lost his smile, then said, his words deliberately precise, "There you go again, casting aspersions on my character. What makes you think you know so much about me, Carlie?" She tried to tug free, but he tightened his hold. "I've never coerced a woman into a relationship—other than you, of course, but that's a different matter, isn't it? Usually, the women are trying to coerce me. And they're up-front about it. They say what *they* want, what *they* need out of a relationship, and undying devotion isn't on top of their list. Now, that would make me the used, not the user, wouldn't you say?"

"No, I wouldn't. I have no interest in commenting on your exploits one way or the other."

"But you do often enough."

"Then I apologize." She stared down at his hand, still grasping her wrist. Her heart was thundering so rapidly, she could barely breathe. She'd never seen

Tyler so intense, so direct about his private life. Maybe she had been misjudging him. It was something she needed to think about in the quiet of her own home. "Now, if you'll turn me loose, I'll get out of your hair."

His mood seemed to switch mercury quick. "But I want you in my hair today. Haven't you been paying attention? Even though you're wearing the most disgusting outfit I've even seen on man, woman or beast, I still want your company." He hesitated, then asked reluctantly, "Where did you find that, anyway? Surely there isn't a store that actually sold you that thing?"

Carlie looked down at her khaki green nylon jogging suit. It was lined and very warm. She was wearing a gray sweatshirt underneath.

"I wasn't trying to be fashionable, Tyler. I was jogging. In the rain, not on a runway. What does it matter how I look?" She gave one final yank and freed her arm, then headed for the kitchen door. "I'll call you later, Bren."

Carlie hurried out the door, then jogged away in a loose-limbed stride, feeling the rain immediately soak her hair and drip down her face. She was nearly a block away, when Tyler caught up with her.

He pulled his car up to the curb and rolled down his window. "Hello, Carlie."

Without looking his way, she said plainly, "Go away."

He drove slowly, keeping pace with her. She ignored him. "You know, Brenda said I hurt your feelings."

That effectively stopped her. "Not on your best day, with your best shot."

"Then why are you so ill-tempered today?"

"Me! What about you?"

"I asked first."

Carlie briefly considered her options, then decided on one truth she could share. "I'm concerned about one of the children at school. His father's in the hospital, and it doesn't look good. When I called yesterday, their phone had been shut off."

They had both stopped. Tyler lowered his head. "That's rough."

"Yes, it is. I wish I knew some way to help."

"Maybe I can help."

"How?"

"I don't know. Let me think about it, all right?"

Carlie started off again. "Fine. And while you're doing that, leave me alone."

He shook his head sadly. "Can't. I told you. I'm despondent." Then in a clear pleading tone, he added, "I need you, Carlie."

Water dripped down her nose. She blinked at him, feeling her heart jump several beats and her throat go dry. He was a cad, a beautiful cad, but still, she couldn't give herself away. So she laughed. Hard.

"You're a cold, cruel woman."

She laughed again for good measure.

"Come on, Carlie. Get in before you get too wet. I don't want you to ruin my seat covers."

"I'm already soaked to the bone, Tyler. And you have leather seats. I would surely ruin them."

"I'll forgive you. I promise."

She could feel herself weakening against his insistence. "You really want company so badly?"

"No. I really want *your* company. You're good for my ego."

"Then I must be slipping."

Tyler got out and went to the passenger door. He opened it with a flourish, bowing for her to enter.

Carlie gave in gracefully. She realized that she didn't have it in her to deny him. She wanted his company too much. Already, she felt more buoyant, more alive. He didn't treat her like any other man she knew. He was honest with her. She knew where he was coming from and what he was thinking. She could trust him.

Tyler hurried back around the car and slid in behind the wheel. He sighed, then turned to grin at Carlie. "I'll take you home to change before we go to a movie."

"When did I agree to see a movie?"

"You will, won't you?"

Carlie waited a moment, then asked with a degree of curiosity and disbelief, "You're really bothered that this woman walked out on you?"

He didn't answer right away, and she prompted, "Tyler?"

"I liked her. So, yeah, it bothers me. We...well, things just really clicked. It was like I knew her already, you know?"

"But you see a lot of women."

He didn't dispute that, but he didn't confirm it, either. Again, she wondered if she'd misjudged him.

"What about you, Carlie? Have you ever met anyone that really felt *right* from the very beginning?"

"Brenda and I were instant friends, even though we're so different."

"That's not exactly what I meant, and you know it."

No, she knew what he meant, but she couldn't very well confide in him about her lack of a love life, about a lack of love, period. Until that night in the pool house, she hadn't believed she would ever enjoy the sexual side of a relationship. "I was married once. But things didn't work out."

She jumped when Tyler reached across the seat and took her hand. "Tell me what happened."

"No. Let it suffice to say, I was young and foolish and made some dumb mistakes. End of story."

"You must have been hurt."

A nervous laugh escaped her, and she covered her mouth with her hand. He'd said similar words at the pool house. She was playing a dangerous game, and it was wearing on her.

Tyler frowned at her. "Was that funny? I think I missed the punch line."

She shook her head. "No, I'm sorry. It's just…yes, I felt bad about it at the time. But as you can see, I got over it. Don't worry about it, okay?"

His hand tightened on hers, and he appeared disgruntled. "You know, you should probably be really careful about hooking up with anyone again. I mean, guys can really take advantage. You deserve to be treated special."

Carlie looked at him questioningly, seeing that he was agitated, but not understanding why. He smiled.

"You want to go home first to change and get dried off?" he asked.

"Yes. But you should know right now, Tyler, you won't like my change of clothes any better than you like this outfit. I refuse to dress up on Sundays. It's my day off, a day for comfort." And besides, the sloppier she looked, the less likely Tyler was to recognize her. Not that he had the slightest suspicion now.

"Fair enough. But can I at least request you avoid shades of green? It makes my stomach churn."

Carlie flashed a crooked grin. "I'll see what I can do."

"Ah, just what I like. A submissive woman."

That comment earned him a playful smack.

After they reached Carlie's house, she disappeared into her bedroom to change and Tyler nosed around her living room. Carlie emerged minutes later, her hair only slightly damp and combed into place, her wet jogging suit replaced with a dry one. It was blue, and hopefully less objectionable, at least in color; the fit was still very loose and concealing.

A short while later, they were back in the car, on their way to Tyler's house. The storm intensified, covering the streets with debris and filling the car with a steady drone of raindrops hitting the roof, interspersed with rumbling thunder. Carlie was relaxed in her seat, unconcerned with the weather.

"The storm doesn't bother you?"

She lazily swiveled her head toward Tyler, not raising it from the back of the seat. She was exhausted from too little sleep, and mind-weary from fretting about things she had no control over. "I love storms."

He grinned. "I should have known better than to think they would frighten you."

She smiled, her eyes still on his profile. "When I was a little girl, I used to sit on the porch and listen. The rain would blow under the overhang, wetting my legs and sometimes my face. But the smells...so clean and fresh. I've always thought of storms as being peaceful, despite their noise."

Tyler glanced at her, his eyes drifting over her face. He grinned teasingly. "I've always thought storms were sexy."

Carlie's heart jerked, memories of the storm the

night they'd spent at the pool house flooding into her memory. She cleared her throat, but still her words emerged as a dry croak. "Is that right?"

He laughed. "Hmm. They have one hell of an effect on me."

"Good grief." Carlie had to joke to cover the heat that surged through her. A vivid mental picture had surfaced with his words, and she had to rely on wit to hide her feelings. "You won't embarrass me by attacking some poor, unsuspecting female at the movies, will you?"

His grin was wicked. "You're not concerned for your own safety?"

She snorted.

"You do that really well, you know? I don't think I've ever heard another female snort with quite your flair. It's very descriptive."

"Thank you."

Tyler laughed at her dry tone, then shot her a narrow-eyed look. "Have you ever made love during a storm?"

Forcing herself to breathe normally, Carlie peeked at him, then quickly looked away. She felt hot from the inside out, her skin tingling, her stomach coiling tight. *She had to lie.* She shook her head, then realizing he was watching the road, she whispered, "No."

That should have ended it, but she couldn't stop herself from asking, still in a whisper, "Have you?"

Tyler glanced at her again, his look unreadable. His words were quiet and carefully measured. "I thought you didn't want any details on my exploits."

She felt disgruntled by his evasion after she'd summoned up the nerve to ask. "No details. Just a statement. Yes or no?"

He stared straight ahead. "Yeah." He sighed. "Yeah, I have."

Carlie turned away. His husky tone nearly melted her, and she said without thinking, "It would probably be nice."

Tyler's eyes skipped quickly to Carlie and then back to the road again. "Carlie?"

"Hmm?"

Her head was laid back against the seat, her eyes closed. She could never have another sexual interlude with Tyler, but just being with him was nice, too. Maybe she should let that be enough, she thought. Maybe she should try to relax and enjoy her time with him, even though it was risky.

She didn't see his incredulous expression, or the way he was watching her.

"Carlie, did you mean you thought it would be 'nice' to make love to *me* during a storm?"

Her eyes shot wide open, her relaxed position shot to hell. She felt tense from her toes to her eyebrows, her heart going into spasms. She peered at Tyler, totally speechless.

They stopped at a traffic light and he turned to face her, bracing one arm on the back of the seat. "Well?"

Her laugh sounded a bit forced. "I didn't mean you specifically. I meant…the storm in general. Someone who really enjoyed sex would like it in this kind of weather." She was babbling, but she couldn't seem to stop.

His gaze was disturbingly intent. "You don't enjoy lovemaking?"

"I never said that!" She was flustered and had to struggle to keep from looking away. "I just meant there are a lot of people who don't. But someone like you, someone who appears, by all accounts, to like it very much, probably would enjoy it during a storm. I…I think I would, just because I love storms, I mean."

Carlie ground to a painful halt, her rambling finally at an end. Tyler stared at her, and Carlie didn't want to know what he was thinking.

He cleared his throat, but the words came out sounding husky. "You should definitely try it sometime."

Conversation, after that bit of advice, was nil. When they arrived at the video-rental store, Carlie gaped. "What are we doing?"

"Renting a movie."

Uh-oh. "Renting a movie, to watch…where?"

Tyler shot her a grin. "My place. You said you

didn't want to dress up, so I thought you'd be more comfortable at home.''

Her home, maybe. Not this. She didn't want to go to his...

''Wait here, and I'll run in and get it. No reason for both of us to get soaked.''

Carlie sat in his car, stupefied. How could she refuse without looking ridiculous? How could she explain the difference between being in a crowded theater and being *alone* with Tyler?

She was still pondering that problem when he returned, the tape tucked inside his jacket, his dark hair glistening from the rain. ''All set.'' He took his seat and started the car. ''You're gonna love this movie.''

She had her doubts.

There was an underground garage at Tyler's building, so they didn't get wet going in. Carlie walked slowly, hesitant to enter his private domain. But, like his office, Tyler's home was fairly generic. It was large, with a fantastic view, and very tastefully decorated. But everything looked...cold and impersonal. He explained it was a furnished apartment, and a cleaning crew came in weekly.

Carlie thought that was a sad way to live.

Tyler must have picked up on her sentiments, because he said, ''Not exactly 'home sweet home,' is it?''

''If you don't like it, why did you move here?''

He shrugged, looking around the apartment.

"When I was a kid, we lived in a dirty little hellhole with ratty furniture and peeling paint. I decided that when I picked a place of my own, I'd make sure it was nice." He shook his head. "At the time, I suppose I thought this place was nice." He winked at Carlie. "But I like your house much better."

She grinned. "Thank you. I like my house, too. I picked it because it's small. Grandfather had a huge old farmhouse. It was always cold and empty. I hated it."

"You said your parents died when you were young. Your grandfather raised you?"

Carlie nodded, but looked away. "My brother was already old enough to be on his own, and I didn't see him much. It was just me and Granddad."

"Were you lonely?"

"I suppose." Then she changed the subject. Talk of her childhood always made her melancholy. "So, are we going to start this movie or not?"

Tyler took her hand, gave it a soft squeeze, then left the room. After fetching colas and pretzels from a sterile kitchen, he turned off most of the lights. "A scary movie has to be watched in the dark...for effect."

Carlie relaxed, settling herself into the soft leather sofa. "I know why you wanted to come here to watch the movie." She waved a finger at him. "You didn't want witnesses when you get scared and start screaming."

"Perceptive girl." After putting in the tape, Tyler took his seat next to Carlie. He sat very close, his damp hair pushed back from his face, his long legs stretched out.

Unexpectedly, Carlie leaned toward him and nudged him with her shoulder. "You're all right, Tyler."

He stared at her, grinning crookedly and looking very pleased by her offhand compliment.

He gently touched her cheek. "I'm glad you think so."

It was such an easy and natural thing to do. She leaned into his hand, and his fingers found a stray wisp of hair escaped over her temple. He toyed with it, running it through his fingers, then giving her a gentle tug.

He could make her stomach flip with just a word or a look, but he also made her feel accepted, made her a part of things in a way she'd never been. Being raised by her grandfather had left her sheltered but alone. Brenda had been her first real friend.

Now she had Tyler, too.

"I like you, Tyler. I'm...really glad we're friends."

"I am, too. Though I'll admit, I've never been just friends with a woman before." He tucked her hair behind her ear. "And by the way, this is another date. Try to remember the rules."

She immediately put on her best vacant expression,

removed her glasses and batted her eyelashes. "Tyler," she whined, looking pathetically vulnerable, "I'm scared of the dark. Hold me."

He grinned and reached for her. She promptly shoved him back into his seat. "You've got the basics down right, but you're supposed to be clinging to me right about now."

"You big coward." She shook her head at him. "You better control yourself during this movie, Tyler. I mean it. Date or no date, I don't want you crawling all over me just because you chose a movie you couldn't handle."

He smiled slyly, apparently enjoying himself. "Did I tell you, I've seen this movie before? I'd be willing to wager that about halfway through, *you'll* be crawling all over *me*."

"I'll take that bet." She grabbed his hand and pumped it. "What will you give me when you lose?"

"I won't lose. You will. Then you'll invite me over for another home-cooked meal. Agreed?"

"Fine. But when *I* win? What do I get?"

"A kiss?"

"Ha! Why play if the stakes aren't worth much?"

"You're saying my kisses aren't to be devoutly sought?"

"Not by Carlie McDaniels."

"Carlie, Carlie. You've already forgotten that this is a date. You should have been more determined to win, with a kiss as the prize."

Carlie twisted her lips into a wry smile. "How about you help me grade tests next Friday night when you lose? You're college-educated. You could probably handle third-grade math."

"I would, of course, endeavor to do my best—if I lost, which I won't. Now, hush, the movie is about to start."

The picture began with a bloodcurdling scream, then continued with screams for quite some time. Ten minutes into the movie, Carlie was glaring at Tyler. "This is awful!"

"I know. Don't you love it?"

"Oh, I don't believe this! They almost die at the hands of a monstrous alien, and now, while hiding in a dark, dank hole, they're getting aroused?"

Tyler put his arm around her, reacting with world-weary logic. "These things happen."

"Good grief!" Her eyes were glued to the picture. "From blood and guts to pornography! It's obscene."

Halfway through the movie, Carlie was watching through her fingers, her hands covering her face. She was leaning toward Tyler, or he was pulling her close, she wasn't sure which.

But she liked it. Tyler kept smoothing his hand over her shoulder, not paying the least attention to the movie. When she gasped and moved close to him again, his arm tightened, instinctively offering her comfort.

He was unbelievably hard and warm. And he

smelled good, like the storm outside, fresh and alive and very male. She wanted to cuddle closer, to turn her nose into his chest and breathe deeply of his unique scent.

Instead, she forced herself to pull away slightly.

Tyler refused to let her move too far. He turned her chin toward him. "You about ready to give up and crawl into my lap?"

"Very nearly," she whispered back, seeing the glimmer of his dark eyes in the dim light. She could feel the firm, unyielding muscles of his upper arm pressing into her breast, and there was a strange tension in the air. Carlie wondered if Tyler felt it, too. Probably not.

She was beginning to accept how easily he could make her react to him. She'd never had the problem with any other man, and in fact, had been repulsed when they'd tried to become romantic. But not so with Tyler. He could easily infuriate her one minute, make her laugh the next, then fill her with sensual heat with only his smile.

But he didn't want her. He wanted a masked harem girl.

Suddenly, there was a particularly grotesque scene, accompanied by a blast of startling noise. Carlie launched herself against Tyler in reflex, and he pressed her face into his throat. Just as she turned her gaze back to the screen, she felt Tyler's lips skim her temple.

She went perfectly still, unable to believe what had just happened, wondering if she'd imagined the fleeting touch. But then she felt his breath, warm and gentle on her cheek, and the feel of his lips on her skin again, tentative and soft. He sighed quietly into her ear, sending ripples of sensation over her skin.

Oblivious to the movie, Carlie shuddered with the shock of the erotic kiss. He lightly circled the rim of her ear with the tip of his tongue, then delicately slipped his tongue inside, teasing her with a leisurely attentiveness to detail.

Softly, with consternation, she asked, "Tyler?"

"Hmm?" He was laving her ear, tracing the swirls, his breath warm and moist.

"What...exactly...are you doing?"

"Exactly?" He asked the question against her temple, his voice husky and low. "Putting my tongue in your ear."

Carlie pulled back, incredulous at the easy way he made that confession. "You're putting your tongue in *my* ear?"

Tyler stared at her, his dark eyes appearing almost black in the dim shadows. "Well...yes."

"Whatever for?"

"You, ah, didn't like it?"

Carlie searched his face, unable to tell if he was being serious or clowning around again. She thought it must surely be another of his jokes, like the lessons in dating. "I don't know. I suppose you took me by surprise. I thought this was to be strictly platonic."

He shrugged, totally unconcerned. "I love women's ears. Yours are very nice."

Carlie opened her mouth, but then closed it again. He was playing with her, and she didn't like it. "I'm not at all certain you should be doing this, Tyler."

He ignored her vague protest. "I want to know if you liked it, Carlie."

"Why?"

"Most women have sensitive ears. I just—"

"No. I mean, why me? Why should you care if I liked it?"

"Curiosity?"

She frowned at him a moment, struggling to hide her disappointment. She shouldn't have asked, and now she wished she hadn't. Turning back to the movie, she pushed on her glasses. "I think it would be best if we forgot the idle curiosity."

"Aren't you just a little curious, too, Carlie?"

His insistence annoyed her. "I'm curious about a lot of things, Tyler. But sometimes curiosity is better left unappeased." She refused to look at him again, overwhelmed with uncertainty.

"I didn't mean to upset you."

"You didn't."

"You provoked me, you know."

She slanted him a quick look of exasperation, pretending a great interest in the movie. "I did no such thing."

"Sure you did. You crawled, just as I said you would, into my lap. I'm only a man, Carlie."

She gave him her full attention. He was behaving exactly like the cad she'd accused him of being, flirting with her simply because she was female and available. What other reason could there be? "Were you this pushy with your lady friend from the party?"

Tyler rubbed a hand over his face, then stared at Carlie in chagrin. "You know, as incredible as it seems, I'd all but forgotten about that little incident. I don't think I'll thank you for reminding me." He looked away from her, then said, "I knew you'd help me forget the mystery woman's desertion, but I didn't think you'd deliberately bring it up again."

"This morning, you acted as if you had to know who she was. How could you forget about her so easily, anyway?" As soon as she'd asked the question, Carlie wondered if she was losing it. She was purposely treading on very dangerous ground.

"You don't want to hear about my conquests, remember?"

"Ah, so it was a conquest. Not that I'd ever doubted otherwise, given your reputation. But it is unfortunate the lady was masked, don't you think? Otherwise, it might have been her here now, and I'm sure she'd be more appreciative of your charms than I am."

Tyler caught Carlie's hand, demanding her attention. "It isn't like that, Carlie. I—"

His innocent look of confusion infuriated her. "Isn't like what? I like you, Tyler, I really do. But I don't appreciate being treated like a fool. Does it make you feel macho to come on to every woman you meet, even those you don't really want?"

Tyler looked startled by her anger. He visibly collected himself. "I like you as a friend, too. More than I've ever liked a woman. I feel completely at ease with you. And I'm not 'playing' with you, Carlie. You're a woman. That's an irrevocable fact. I can't help being—"

"Don't you dare tell me again that you're *curious!*"

His hand came up to cradle her cheek. Smiling slightly, he said simply, "Then you'll have to stop being so unique, so intelligent and witty and fun to be with."

"So." Carlie tightened her mouth, and moved out of his reach. "What about your masked lady? Have you given up on finding her?"

She could see the frustration that replaced his smile. "I don't know." He gave her another smile and shrugged. "You know, I'd never met a woman who could so easily confuse me, and now I've met two. Not really sporting, is it?"

"Tyler…"

"Shh. Stop fending me off and just relax, okay? I

promise not to attack you again. I won't lose my head and have my wicked way with you."

He was back to normal, or what she accepted as normal. When he talked complete nonsense, she was comfortable with his attention. Carlie finally smiled, then playfully slugged Tyler in the arm before giving her attention back to the movie. "You're impossible."

Carlie wanted to linger once the movie ended, but Tyler didn't invite her to stay, and she didn't know how to ask. It didn't feel as though he was tired of her company, but rather that he was tired of his apartment.

He said, "I'm not here all that often. I only come home to sleep." Then he laughed. "I've probably only used that television a handful of times. But it was fun today, with you."

She berated him all the way home for showing her such an outrageous movie. And then he reminded her she owed him dinner.

"All right, though I don't think you played fair. You'd already seen the movie and knew what to expect."

Tyler grinned. It was still storming, and the driving was slow. The inside of the car was warm and humid and Carlie's hair had once again rebelled. She tried to get the damp tendrils back into place, but gave up after Tyler shook his head at her. He reached across the seat and took her hand with easy familiarity. "I suppose I did have the advantage. So how about I help you grade your papers, anyway? I wouldn't mind.''

Carlie smiled. It would probably be best to refuse, but he gave her fingers a gentle squeeze, and she found herself agreeing. "Very sporting of you, Tyler. Thank you.''

"You're welcome. And I'll bring dinner. Pizza or something. Okay?''

"Why are you so conciliatory all of a sudden? You're making me very suspicious.''

They pulled up in front of Carlie's house. Tyler put the car into Park and turned off the engine, then shifted in his seat to face her. The air, sealed by the heavy rain outside, smelled of damp flesh and wet hair and Tyler, masculine and seductive.

"I meant what I said today, Carlie. I can't recall ever enjoying another person's company as much as I enjoy yours. I like helping the kids and I like the exercise. But I think I like arguing with you most of all. You get riled so easily.''

"Arguing with you is my pleasure. And as to the rest, the children and I should thank you. You're making a difference, and we appreciate it.'' Tyler looked embarrassed by her praise. She knew she shouldn't, even debated with herself for several moments, but she couldn't resist inviting him in. "I don't have anything pressing to do. We could play cards or something.''

"I thought that if I sat here in the rain, looking forlorn long enough, you would finally ask."

Carlie indicated the rain lashing the windows. "Are you ready then? We'll have to make a run for it."

Tyler grinned at her. "I'll race you."

They each dashed from the car as the rain pounded them with stinging force. They huddled together, Tyler protectively putting his arm around Carlie, trying to cover her as best he could. Laughing, they nearly tripped each other in their race for the house.

Stumbling onto the front stoop and under the tiny roof, they collapsed against the door. Gasping and winded, with rain dripping from their bodies, they shivered from the chill October air and tried to stifle their laughter.

Carlie pulled off her glasses and swiped at her eyes. She looked at Tyler, then burst out laughing again, falling against his shoulder. "Oh, Tyler, you're soaked!" She reached up and pushed a wet strand of dark hair from his forehead.

Tyler didn't move. She was huddled under his arm, her hair plastered to her skull, her glasses in her hand. He raised a finger and brushed gently against her eyelashes, spiked from the rain. Carlie smiled up at him.

Then his eyes dropped to her lips, and she parted them, without speaking, without even breathing. The tension was back, nearly choking her now. She ached so badly…

"Carlie?"

His voice was husky. Carlie tried to lean away, but he held her firm. His eyes drifted over her face and she blinked at the tenderness there.

And then he kissed her.

CHAPTER SEVEN

CARLIE GASPED and squirmed against him. The sound of Tyler's breathing was even louder than the rain pelting the roof of the overhang. Carlie felt his tongue touch the seam of her lips, and without conscious decision, she parted them. He groaned low in his throat, held her face between his hands and slanted his mouth over hers, stroking deep inside, imitating the lovemaking she was only recently familiar with. It made her body tingle with remembered heat.

He released her mouth, his lips traveling over her cheek and temple and the bridge of her nose. ''Carlie...'' He murmured her name wonderingly, over and over again. His hands slid down her shoulders, and one palm ventured forward to cover her breast, rubbing over her nipple with tantalizing expertise.

It was that expertise that brought her to her senses.

Shoving him away, Carlie covered herself with her hands. Tyler stood staring at her, apparently dazed. ''Carlie...?''

''You...you...'' She couldn't believe what she had almost let happen. Her thoughts were in turmoil, her emotions sensitized, and it was all his fault. "How dare you!"

He frowned, his eyes black with a mixture of passion and frustration. He shook his head the tiniest bit, then growled, "I don't know. I...hell." He turned his back, his hands flexing, but when Carlie began struggling with her keys to unlock the door, he jerked around to face her.

She flinched from the hand he reached toward her. She felt so confused and angry at Tyler for complicating things further, for apparently wanting his mystery woman, but willing to toy with her, as well. She concentrated on the anger, unreasonable as it seemed. "Don't you touch me! You lied!"

"About what?" His shout matched the volume of her words.

"You said you wouldn't attack me!"

"I didn't attack you, dammit! I kissed you. There's a big difference."

"You...you pawed me."

He loomed over her. "I touched your breast. That's all. Your nipples were hard and I saw that and—"

She gasped loudly at his audacity, feeling her face pulse with heat. "It's cold out here, you ass! My... my..."

"Nipples," he supplied, smirking at her.

His attitude infuriated her. "It's because of the cold, certainly not because of you."

"I know that. I'm not stupid to women's bodies. But the sight made me lose my head a little." He suddenly looked solemn, and a little confused himself. "You have very nice breasts, Carlie."

Her heart raced in her chest. "My…my…"

"Breasts!" He stared at her irritably. "They're called breasts, dammit."

"Well, they're none of your business! Keep your opinions to yourself."

"You're repressed," he accused, sounding disgusted with her. "It was no big deal. Forget about it."

No big deal. The words crushed her. And to call her repressed…that was the same label her husband had applied, though she now knew it wasn't true. She had the same feelings as any other woman, but right now, she wished she didn't. Maybe it wouldn't hurt so bad if the accusation was true. She swallowed, staring at Tyler and his dark expression of irritation. "I'd sooner forget you, Tyler Ramsey." And she meant it. "Go home and leave me alone."

Carlie turned, finally unlocking her door. She tried to enter, but Tyler stopped her. "You invited me in."

"I changed my mind."

"We need to talk, Carlie. This isn't going to go away."

"Of course it is. Just as soon as you do."

"No, it's not." He took her arm and forced his way into her house.

Carlie refused to close the door. She was trembling inside and felt ready to snap. She was furious, with herself, with Tyler, with the circumstances. "Get out."

"No. I want to talk to you."

She snorted. "You have a funny way of talking."

"Look, Carlie..." He tried to sound reasonable, but his eyes dropped to her breasts again, almost unintentionally, it seemed. "Let's get dried off. Then we can sort this out."

"There's nothing to sort out. You crossed the line and I don't want you to ever do that again."

"Well, I'm damn well going to do it again, and real soon if you don't get your butt in the other room and find something dry to wear that isn't showing off your..."

She fled the room, and purposely slammed her bedroom door. Hard.

Odious man! Carlie yanked off her sodden clothing, repeatedly shoving her glasses up on the bridge of her nose. And all the while she rained silent curses on Tyler's head. Talk about fickle! First, he claims to be depressed because he's without a date; then, he wants to see the mystery woman again and can't; and then, he makes a move on her, Carlie. She stopped in the process of pulling a thick terry-cloth, floor-length shift over her head.

He'd actually done that—made a pass at her. And he couldn't have been completely toying with her. He'd been affected also, she could see that. Slowly, she sat on the edge of her bed.

Tyler Ramsey wanted Carlie McDaniels? Good grief.

But, her thinking continued, he also wanted her alter ego, the mystery woman, and had already slept with her. *She* knew they were one and the same, but Tyler didn't. Was he only biding his time with her until he could discover the identity of the masked harem girl?

It was equal parts ridiculous and unreasonable, but she was feeling jealous of herself.

She finished dressing, then left the bedroom. Tyler was pacing the living room, his shirt discarded, a towel in his hands as he tried to dry himself off. He'd removed his shoes and socks and had left them by the front door. His jeans were dark, soaked from rain and molded to his thighs and buttocks. Carlie cleared her throat.

Turning, Tyler stared at her. She was nervous, she couldn't help that. Everything had suddenly shifted again, so many changes converging on her all at once. She was at a loss as to how to deal with it all.

His eyes swept over her, from her still-wet hair to her naked feet. He didn't say a word, but held her eyes, his hands hanging from his sides.

"I apologize if I overreacted," she said. "You took me by surprise. I never once suspected you might…"

A reluctant smile curved his mouth. "You acted as if I'd defiled you in some way. Was it really so bad, honey?"

"No." She shook her head, her heavy braid swinging behind her. "But I really don't think getting phys-ical is a good idea. I like being friends with you too much to complicate things. And it wouldn't have the same effect on you—our being…involved—I mean, as it would on me."

He approached her slowly, then stopped in front of her. She lowered her eyes, unable to meet his probing gaze. He crouched slightly to look her in the face. "Carlie. Don't sell yourself short. You can't know how I might react to you."

But she could, because she knew how he'd reacted to the mysterious and provocative harem girl. She was simply Carlie. Plain and boring. "You're used to beautiful women. Tons of them."

"Tons, huh? Well, that's not true." He wrapped the towel around his neck, holding the ends. "I haven't had an ounce of experience with any real re-lationships. In fact, the only relationship I've ever had that was worth a damn was with my brother. And now Brenda. But that's not what we're talking about, is it? So give me a break here, okay?"

She stared up at him helplessly, and then he cupped her cheek, his thumb stroking her temple. "I like the way we are together, Carlie. We could have a good relationship."

She needed some space. With Tyler standing so close, she could see the water drops still clinging to the dark swirls of hair on his chest. His body was moist from the rain, his muscles slick and smooth.

Her nipples tightened again and she stepped away. Space. She definitely needed space.

"Why don't you tell me what you really want, Tyler." She walked into the kitchen as casually as possible and pulled two mugs from the cabinet.

She was filling the glass coffeepot with water, when she felt Tyler behind her. His hands lifted to her upper arms and he pulled her back against his chest. He murmured against her temple, "I'm not sure. I know I like spending time with you. And I know I'm going to want to kiss you again."

Carlie closed her eyes. "What about other women?"

"What other women?"

"Your masked lady, for one. Are you only wanting to spend time with me until you can convince Bren to give you her name? And if your harem girl wants to see you again, what then?"

She could feel the added tension in the way Tyler's hands gripped her. "You're jumping the gun, Carlie. Hell, I didn't ask you to marry me. I'm not asking for a lifetime commitment."

She pulled away, embarrassment vying with the anger rising within her. He made her sound desperate! "That isn't what I meant, Tyler. I certainly don't aspire to tie you down. I don't aspire to do anything with you. It's just that I know how you are about commitments, and I'm trying to point out that you would only be using me until something better came along. Right now, I like you as a friend. I'm grateful for the time you donate to helping the children. But if you…that is…if we…''

Tyler rolled his eyes in exasperation. "If I made love to you. That *is* what you're trying to say, isn't it?''

"Yes. If we…did that. I'm honest enough to admit my heart might get involved, and then my pride would suffer when you decided to toss me aside. I don't think I could forgive you, and our friendship, which I count more important than a bit of hanky-panky, would be ruined.''

She couldn't look at him after that little speech. Instead, she went about setting out cookies and preparing some coffee. She felt like a fraud.

Tyler narrowed his eyes in disbelief. "You're amazing, you know that? I'm surprised you didn't carry your predictions through to the end of Time. And you forgot to cover a few scenarios. I mean, what if that jerk you told me you used to love suddenly reappeared? Or what if one of your teacher buddies caught your eye? You could ditch me!'' He stormed around the kitchen, his hands on his hips, his dark eyebrows lowered in a fierce frown. "I wasn't talking about some time in the distant future, dammit. I was talking about now.''

Carlie choked on the sip of coffee she'd just taken. Tyler grumbled and proceeded to pound on her back.

"All right, all right! Don't beat me to death.'' She sucked in several desperate breaths, then glowered at him incredulously. "You're wanting to…to…''

He rolled his eyes again, and sighed loud enough to rattle the windowpanes. "Make love. It's called making love, Carlie. People have been doing it since the beginning of Time. They'll continue doing it until the end of Time. It's a necessary and enjoyable part of life, you know."

She gave him her patented snort. "I'm not as cavalier as you, Tyler. *I* certainly haven't been doing it." She realized her slip immediately. Tyler was looking at her curiously, and she stammered an explanation. "It isn't necessary. Enjoyable, maybe. But not necessary."

"God save us from liberated women." He advanced on her, and Carlie held her coffee cup between them like an insubstantial shield. Tyler took it from her. "Do you care about me, Carlie?"

"I care about a lot of men. That doesn't mean I want to sleep with them."

He stiffened, and his eyes grew hard. "Who? Who do you care about?"

"Jason, for one."

"My brother?"

"Yes. And several teachers who I've been friends with since I started teaching here. I care about some of the parents I've gotten to know, and a few of my neighbors…"

"Carlie." Tyler laid his finger against her lips. "There's caring, and then there's *caring*."

She nodded. Tyler removed his hand from her

mouth, then stroked her cheek. "Tell me you care about me."

"This sounds suspiciously like a seduction routine you've practiced to perfection."

Tyler stepped back, shoving his hands into his pockets. "Obviously, I haven't practiced it enough."

Carlie smiled, her first real smile since he'd kissed her. He looked every bit as confused as she felt. "Tyler, be reasonable. I'm not going to jump into bed with you, just because you suddenly find me strange and interesting."

"I never said—"

"I'm different from other women you know, and the main difference is that I'm *not* trying to wend my way into your bed. You're just stymied, not really aroused. Go home and take a warm bath and you'll feel better in the morning."

He shook his head, being very precise. "I won't."

Carlie chuckled. "Don't pout, Tyler. Surely some woman somewhere has told you no before."

"Not that I would admit to. And just because you're not interested right now, doesn't mean I'll stop being interested. When you get used to the idea and accept it as a fact, you'll see that I was right."

She looked at him suspiciously. "About what?"

Quickly, before she could move away, Tyler bent down and kissed her, hard and fast. "We'll be good together. I'm sure of it. Very good."

That was an already proven fact, but Tyler couldn't

know it. She mustered a shaky smile. "Bragging, Mr. Ramsey?"

"No." He stared intently into her eyes. "Making a promise."

Carlie felt the heat building in her stomach. But then Tyler pulled out a seat at the table and sprawled in it. "In the meantime..." He raised his arms and clasped his hands behind his head. "No pressure. You're the best friend I ever recall having. I suppose I can be content with that. For a time."

Carlie felt relief, and quelling disappointment. "Good. Then we can stop all this nonsense and play some cards." She pulled a deck from a drawer and sat across from Tyler.

"What would you like to play?" She looked at Tyler.

"Strip poker?"

Carlie started to rise, her mouth drawn in annoyance, but Tyler stopped her. He was laughing. "Okay, okay. Bad jest. Sorry."

She nodded grudgingly. "So. What should we play?"

With a twinkle in his eyes, he asked innocently, "Old maid?"

She threw the cards at him, then sat there glaring.

"Well, I suppose that decides it." He grinned wryly, a card sitting on top of his head, the rest scattered in his lap and on the floor. "Fifty-two pickup it is."

TYLER TRIED to keep his mind on the basketball game they were playing, but he couldn't keep his eyes off Carlie. She was trying to treat him the same as always, but he wasn't going to let her get away with it. Everything was different now, the way he felt when he was around her, the effect her smile had on him. She was doing her best to ignore his attention, but there was only ten more minutes before practice was over. Then he'd be going home with her again. That fact had his stomach in knots.

When was the last time he'd so anticipated spending time with a woman?

But Carlie wasn't just any woman. She wasn't impressed by monetary things. In fact, she almost seemed disdainful of them. And she wanted nothing from him, other than companionship and help with a group of children who deserved someone better than him.

He'd thought about that, too, about ways he could help. He'd never given much of himself—money didn't count, because that wasn't him. But for Carlie, for the kids…for himself, he was going to try to make a difference. And he had a plan he hoped would work.

Practice ended, and Tyler found the little boy whose family's phone had been disconnected. He walked him out to his mother's car. After discreetly questioning the woman, Tyler discovered that she used to be a secretary. He casually mentioned that he always had papers that had to be transcribed, and would be glad to have her assistance. When he mentioned what he was willing to pay, and that she could do the work at home, she readily accepted. He arranged to start sending her documents next week.

And in the meantime, he explained a scholarship of sorts he was setting up that would enable her to enroll her children in the extracurricular activities that they'd been forced to drop out of due to lack of funds.

By the time Tyler finished convincing her to take advantage of his offer, he was feeling pretty good. It was a damned nice thing to know you'd been some small help. But when he came back into the gym, he realized instantly that Carlie was disgruntled with him for having excluded her.

Well, that was just too bad. He intended to surprise her when things were settled, and not a moment sooner.

She was ready to leave, her keys in her hand. He realized he hadn't even changed out of his sweaty shirt yet.

"I'll just be a minute," he said, and started toward the change-room door. She didn't answer, just stood there, tapping her foot. He chuckled. "I know what you're thinking. Curiosity is written all over your face."

She gave him a haughty look, and he prepared himself, knowing he was going to get an earful. "Actually," she said, a slight blush on her cheeks, "I was thinking how...sexy you look right now."

That stopped him. "Is that so?" He advanced

slowly, seeing her struggle to stand her ground. "Enough to warrant a kiss?"

She leaned toward him, her expression smug. "Nope."

Tyler reached for her, but she ducked away. "You're a terrible tease, McDaniels!" Then he grinned. "I think I like it."

She was waiting for him to tell her why he'd been outside so long. He knew, and deliberately kept silent. Her mouth pursed, then she asked, "Are you still coming over?"

"Only if you'll give me a kiss. You can't tell a man he's sexy, then just walk away."

She shrugged. "Sure I can."

He grabbed her arm, grinning. "*No.* You can't. Besides, you want to kiss me. You know you do. What are you afraid of?"

Her lips parted, then she drew in a shaky breath, her gaze going to his mouth. "I'm not afraid of anything."

Tyler leaned back, bending his knees so he was looking directly into her eyes. Carlie squirmed, and he knew she was feeling much the same thing he was, even if she denied it. Finally, satisfied by what he saw, Tyler held out his arms. "Okay, if you're not afraid, then give me one kiss. My hands won't move, I promise."

It was a challenge, and he was willing to bet she wouldn't be able to resist. When she placed her hands on his shoulders, he felt his breath catch. When her gaze dropped to his mouth, his muscles clenched.

Going up on tiptoe, she lightly, quickly, brushed her lips over his, then settled back for his reaction.

His mouth twitched with humor. He left his arms outstretched. "Well? Are you going to kiss me or not, honey? Oh, you mean that little wisp of air that blew over my mouth was your kiss? How disappointing. I thought you could do better than that."

She blinked at him. "You didn't...like it?"

"I have no idea. It was over with before I could decide. Hell, Brenda kisses me better than that. In *front* of Jason."

Her eyebrows lowered and she shoved her glasses higher on the bridge of her nose. Tyler could practically see her mentally hitching up her pants, and he had to fight a smile.

She tightened her hands on his shoulders, and came up again, this time pressing her mouth more firmly to his. Tyler lightly licked her lips, moving his mouth against hers. She went still for a single heartbeat, then accepted his challenge, and returned the gesture. But once her tongue touched him, he drew her inside, and the kiss became ravenous.

He heard her soft moan and instantly grew hard. The game was over. He pressed against her, forcing her to step backward until they reached the wall, then he trapped her there with his body. His hips settled against her groin, rubbing insistently. His mouth now took over, eating at hers, his tongue plunging inside, feeling her own tongue move in a way that made him tremble.

He had to stop. He groaned and raised his mouth. "Damn." His head dropped onto her shoulder, his face turned inward so he could inhale her scent.

He could feel her shaking. His body was laid against the length of her own from shoulders to knees. Her legs were open, accommodating his hips.

His chuckle was wry and filled with wonder. "I asked for that, I suppose." He lifted away from her shoulder, but kept his body close to her. His voice dropped to a whisper. "I want you, Carlie."

She shook her head.

He pressed his hips closer, holding her gaze. "You can feel how much I want you, sweetheart."

She snorted, then pushed him away. "This isn't the eighth grade, Tyler. So you're aroused. So what? It's the same reaction you'd have to any woman you were kissing."

He propped his hands on his hips, feeling his lips twitch with amusement again, despite the ache in his body. "Not quite."

Carlie waved away his rebuttal. "Are you also going to tell me you're in pain? That's next, isn't it?"

"I am in pain." He started toward her. "Your screeching denials are giving me a headache."

"I wasn't screeching! I was only pointing out... Tyler, don't you touch me again!"

He took her by the shoulders, and pulled her body roughly against his. With his nose touching her own, he gently demanded, "Admit you want me, too, Carlie. Now."

She hesitated only a second. "*I do.* It's just that…"

He released her. "I'm willing to give you all the time you need, honey, but…"

She snorted, louder than usual.

Tyler grinned. "Okay, so I've been pushing. I'm having a hard time keeping my hands off you. But you know you can trust me, Carlie. I would never try to force you to do anything you didn't want to do."

He waited, all shreds of humor gone, and finally Carlie nodded. "I know that."

"Good. Then don't keep denying everything I feel. Believe it or not, I want you. You, Carlie, not some other woman, not because you're handy, not because I can't get somebody else." He stroked her cheek. "You're special, sweetheart. And what I feel for you is special."

Her eyes searched his, and she asked, "And what is it you feel, Tyler?"

He should have known she'd ask. "I'm not sure, yet—and don't snort at me!" He grinned again. "I'm trying to be honest here, Carlie. Be patient with me."

Carlie swiped up her gym bag from the bleachers and headed for the door. Tyler trotted after her. "Am I still invited for dinner?"

She didn't slow her pace. "If that's all you want. Because dinner is all you'll get."

"I promise not to do anything…that you don't want me to do."

GET 2

HOW TO GET YOUR
2 FREE BOOKS AND FREE GIFT!

1. Peel off the MIRA® sticker on the front cover. Place it in the space provided at right. This automatically entitles you to receive two free books and an exciting surprise gift.

2. Send back this card and you'll get 2 "The Best of the Best™" books. These books have a combined cover price of $11.98 or more in the U.S. and $13.98 or more in Canada, but they are yours to keep absolutely FREE!

3. There's <u>no</u> catch. You're under <u>no</u> obligation to buy anything. We charge nothing – ZERO – for your first shipment. And you don't have to make any minimum number of purchases – not even one!

4. We call this line "The Best of the Best" because each month you'll receive the best books by some of today's most popular authors. These authors show up time and time again on all the major bestseller lists and their books sell out as soon as they hit the stores. You'll like the convenience of getting them delivered to your home at our special discount prices . . . and you'll love your *Heart to Heart* subscriber newsletter featuring author news, horoscopes, recipes, book reviews and much more!

5. We hope that after receiving your free books you'll want to remain a subscriber. But the choice is yours – to continue or cancel, anytime at all! So why not take us up on our invitation, with no risk of any kind. You'll be glad you did!

6. And remember...we'll send you a surprise gift ABSOLUTELY FREE just for giving THE BEST OF THE BEST a try.

BOOKS FREE!

THE BEST OF THE BEST™ — Here's How it Works:

Accepting your 2 free books and gift places you under no obligation to buy anything. You may keep the books and gift and return the shipping statement marked "cancel." If you do not cancel, about a month later we will send you 4 additional books and bill you just $4.74 each in the U.S., or $5.24 each in Canada, plus 25¢ shipping & handling per book and applicable taxes if any.* That's the complete price and — compared to cover prices starting from $5.99 each in the U.S. and $6.99 each in Canada — it's quite a bargain! You may cancel at any time, but if you choose to continue, every month we'll send you 4 more books, which you may either purchase at the discount price or return to us and cancel your subscription.

*Terms and prices subject to change without notice. Sales tax applicable in N.Y. Canadian residents will be charged applicable provincial taxes and GST. Credit or Debit balances in a customer's account(s) may be offset by any other outstanding balance owed by or to the customer.

If offer card is missing write to: The Best of the Best., 3010 Walden Ave., P.O. Box 1867, Buffalo, NY 14240-1867

BUSINESS REPLY MAIL
FIRST-CLASS MAIL   PERMIT NO. 717-003   BUFFALO, NY

POSTAGE WILL BE PAID BY ADDRESSEE

**THE BEST OF THE BEST
3010 WALDEN AVE
PO BOX 1867
BUFFALO NY 14240-9952**

NO POSTAGE
NECESSARY
IF MAILED
IN THE
UNITED STATES

He felt smug when her step faltered. But he also felt determined not to rush her. Carlie was worth waiting for, and she evidently needed a lot of reassurance. He could give her time. He could behave himself. It wouldn't be easy, but... He'd never known women could be so different. He'd never known a woman could be like Carlie.

And he no longer cared if he found out who the mystery woman was. Carlie, with her bristly independence and concealing wardrobe, was mystery enough to keep his attention for a long, long time. Maybe even forever.

"HELLO?"

"Tyler?"

There was a pause, then, "Who's this?"

"We...ah, *met* at the party..."

Another pause. Carlie waited breathlessly, her hand gripping the receiver so tightly her fingers ached. She had deliberately disguised her voice, but it was shaking so badly, it had probably been an unnecessary measure.

"I didn't expect to hear from you again. Brenda refused to tell me how to reach you."

"I know. I...it has to be that way."

"I'll admit I'm curious to know why."

Traitor, Carlie thought. She was huddled in the middle of her bed, her nightgown twisted around her updrawn knees. Her hair was loose, hanging down to shield her face, which, even though Tyler couldn't see, was burning. "I'm sorry."

"You have no reason to be afraid of me."

"I know. But…"

"You ran out on me."

"Yes." Carlie squeezed her eyes shut. This wasn't going the way she'd planned. She'd convinced herself to call him, hopefully to find out how determined he was to meet the mystery woman or if he even still cared. He claimed to want her…"her" meaning Carlie. But could that be true if he was still intent on meeting another woman? Even if the other woman was herself? But he didn't know that…so…. It was just too confusing. Her brain felt muddled, and she was willing to try anything that might give her some real insight as to how Tyler truly felt about her.

But Tyler wasn't giving her a chance to question him. He was too busy pressing her.

"Tell me who you are." He sounded more annoyed than ever.

"No! I just…wanted to talk to you. To ask…"

"Ask me what?"

Surprised, Carlie accused softly, "You're angry."

"No, I'm frustrated. I don't like games. You're a grown woman. I understand what happened between us was unexpected. You couldn't have been any more surprised than I was. But it's too late to change things now." Then, very persuasively, "Tell me who you are."

Carlie shook her head, as tears gathered in her eyes. If only she could. ''No.''

''Dammit!''

She squeezed her eyes shut. ''Please. Don't be angry.'' There was a tremor in her voice, and Tyler reacted to it.

''I'm sorry.'' He sounded almost weary. ''We can talk. That's why you called, isn't it?''

Carlie was afraid to speak again. This was a stupid idea. She should hang up now before he figured out who she was.

He said again, ''Do you want to talk about it?''

''Maybe you should just forget…''

''Not without knowing.''

Those words, said so sincerely, washed over her. Her heart ached. If he wouldn't forget, then she would have to stay away from him entirely. She drew a deep breath, calming herself. ''Why?''

It was Tyler's turn to be thoughtfully silent. ''It was different. You were different. More intense. It didn't seem like just sex.''

''No.'' It had been more, at least for her.

''You felt it, too?'' he asked.

''I did.''

''I want to meet you. I want to know who you are. Stop playing games.''

''It's…it's not a game,'' she said. ''You would be angry…''

''I'm angry now! This isn't the eighth grade, dammit!''

Carlie jumped at his raised voice. He'd unconsciously repeated her defense. It seemed like a betrayal. "Aren't you seeing anyone else?"

She hadn't meant to ask that. This wasn't a test he had to pass. She'd only wanted to understand why he was so determined to find her. But it was too late to call back the words.

She could feel his frustration, it was so keen. His reply, when it came, was carefully modulated, the words exact. "I'm not intimate with anyone right now, if that's what you mean."

"I see."

"How could you, when I don't? I hate this!" He growled in frustration. "I don't want anything from you! But I hate knowing you might pass me on the street, and I wouldn't even know it. I hate that you have intimate knowledge of me, but I don't even know your name."

Carlie trembled. She hadn't thought of it that way, how it would be for him. She was very sorry. "Tyler, please…"

"You'll see me somewhere and remember. While I'm saying hello, how do you do, you'll be thinking of how it feels to climax with me deep inside you."

His words were harsh now, deliberately taunting, baiting her. He was being ugly, and even while she understood his frustration, she hated it. "*Stop. Please.*"

"*Tell me who you are, dammit.*"

"I can't." The words were rushed, husky with

need. Carlie had to get them out before she did or said something she'd later regret. "It's impossible. I'm so sorry." Then she added in a tiny whisper, "You were wonderful, Tyler."

"Don't hang up...!"

Very gently, Carlie laid the receiver in the cradle, then curled onto her side. It had been a mistake to call him. She had to stop torturing herself and Tyler. Her heart ached with her decision.

He was right. She was behaving like a teenager with a sorry crush on the captain of the football team. She was leaving him to wonder about a woman who didn't exist. On Friday, when he came over again, she'd tell him. She wouldn't take the coward's way out by sending him a letter or giving her explanation and then running. It would be face-to-face, and she would accept his anger, for he would surely be enraged.

Carlie found sleep impossible that night. She pondered a thousand different ways Tyler might react. But it all came down to one final, irrevocable conclusion.

She had lost him, when she'd never really had him in the first place. And until now, she hadn't fully realized how badly she wanted him.

CHAPTER EIGHT

TYLER SET the pizza on the table, then turned to Carlie. She'd been quiet, too damned quiet, all day. He caught her as she walked by to set the table.

He pulled her into his arms. She was more rigid than usual. "I missed you, Carlie. How about a hug?"

Her arms remained at her sides, and she looked beyond him. He was stymied. "What is it? Are you mad at me about something?"

"No, I'm not mad."

"Then what is it?" He bent to look into her eyes. "You can at least give me a hug, can't you?"

She did as he asked, but it was a measly effort at best. Tyler let his hands drift down her back, and realized suddenly that it was the first time he'd ever done so. Her back was narrow, her flesh firm, and her waist tapered in. His hands started to explore there, but she pulled away. He touched her chin, seeking her eyes again. "What is it?"

"We need to talk." She peered up at him, her eyebrows lowered in a nervous frown, and shook her head. "But later, after we eat."

"Ah, intrigue. You don't have to work at keeping my interest, you know. I'm already caught."

Carlie slapped a huge piece of pizza onto his plate, splattering tomato sauce over the table.

Tyler raised his eyebrows. "You are entertaining, Carlie. When we don't have practice, I have nothing to look forward to at the end of the day. I think of you, though."

Carlie stopped in the middle of pouring the wine. She turned to Tyler, her expression serious. "Why?"

"What do you mean, 'why?' I like you."

"But *why*, Tyler? What is it about me that you like?"

He considered her question with grave seriousness. She was being very sober. His answer obviously mattered a great deal to her. The first thing that came to his mind was her honesty. "I can trust you. You don't play games, and I don't think you would ever lie to me. You're straightforward and genuine, blunt to a fault. I've never known a woman like you before."

Carlie looked stricken, which wasn't the reaction he had expected. She crossed her arms over her chest and turned away. He walked up behind her and wrapped her in his arms, holding her close despite her stiffness. He still felt frustrated and angry over his mysterious phone call, and now, with Carlie seeming so intent on separating herself from him, he actually felt needy. It wasn't a feeling he enjoyed.

"Carlie, talk to me. I don't like this. I'm used to you giving me hell and making me laugh and then making me so hot I can't breathe. I'm not used to this silence, sweetheart.''

She turned abruptly, throwing her arms tight around him and he groaned in relief. His arms were around her middle, and it registered, rather abruptly, that she was actually slim. She was wearing her usual basketball clothes that consisted of baggy sweats, and since the day was cooler, she was layered under several pieces. But his hands were stroking up and down her ribs, and it amazed him how tiny her waist was. He pulled back, shocked.

Carlie was watching him. "Don't even say it."

He was amused by her fierce expression. "What?"

"Whatever you were thinking. I know you were checking out my weight again. I'm not stupid."

"No, you're not stupid. But you are a big faker." His mouth tilted in a quizzical smile. "There's not an ounce of extra fat on you, is there?"

Carlie propped one hand on her hip in an arrogant stance. She glanced down meaningfully at her chest, the implied message very clear.

Tyler choked back his laugh. "That's not fat, sweetheart. That's a bonus from Mother Nature." Then his eyes slid over her, and his amusement slowly disappeared. "I want to see you."

"You're looking right at me."

"You know what I mean."

Warm color bloomed in her cheeks. "Oh? You want me to strip naked and dance on the table perhaps?"

"Damn! You're not as unreasonable as I thought." He pulled out a chair and made a big production of seating himself. "Go ahead. I think I'm ready. Wait! Do you have smelling salts available? I'm not sure my heart can take this."

Carlie stared back at him blandly. Then she pulled out her own chair and sat down. She shoved a glass of wine toward him. "Eat. You need something to occupy that mouth of yours."

"True. But I could think of other...mmm!"

Carlie had jammed the piece of pizza into his mouth without concern for his clean face. He ended up laughing, and wiping pizza sauce from his nose and cheeks.

They ate in near silence but for the music Carlie had playing in the background. Tyler watched her, simply enjoying her nearness. After a moment, the quiet began to bother him. "I meant what I said earlier. About your being different. Until I met you, I thought all women were the same."

"That's an asinine comment unworthy of recognition."

"I know it sounds cynical, but it's true. Most of the women I've known were users. They would lie or mislead, even jump into my bed, just to get what they wanted."

Carlie looked slightly dazed. "What did they want?"

"Marriage, usually. You may not believe this, but I'm considered a prime catch. I'm single, and Jason and I run a successful law practice. I'm financially secure, and I drive a flashy car. That's all the criteria most women require. It wouldn't matter *who* I really was.''

''I can't believe that.''

''That's because you're just a little naive, honey.'' He studied her affectionately. ''Other than Brenda, no woman has taken the time to really get to know me. Except you.''

She searched his face, her eyes bright with curiosity. ''What about your mother? Or other relatives?''

''I don't have other relatives. And all my mother ever wanted was for me and Jason to get out of her hair. Most times we did. It didn't matter where we went, as long as we weren't around to interfere in her affairs.'' He didn't quite meet her gaze, feeling her empathy, and not entirely comfortable with it. Discussing his past was not something he was familiar with.

''Jason was the one who convinced me I could get a degree. And at the time, that was no easy feat. I was so busy indulging in my bad-boy popularity, I'll admit I was something of a punk.''

Carlie touched the bridge of his nose. ''Brenda told me you broke your nose in a fight.''

He sent her a small, brief smile. ''Yeah. I did a lot of fighting back then. Mom loved it when I kicked ass. It was the only time she ever gave me any recognition.'' Tyler was amazed the words were coming so easily. But then, it was always easy to talk to Carlie. "You see, it really didn't matter who I was. It was what I did that was important."

"It always matters, Tyler. If not to someone else, then to yourself."

He was filled with satisfaction. "There, you see? You know that, but no other woman I've ever met has thought so. When Mom took off, and that was some time ago, she couldn't have cared less who I was or what I might become."

Carlie looked down at the remains of her pizza, then tightened her fingers around his hand. "You can't categorize all women based on one, Tyler. That isn't fair."

Tyler laughed wryly. "Don't go getting psychological on me. My mother and her many faults didn't form any lasting impression on me. It's the dozens of women since who've done that. All but you." He lifted her fingers and kissed them. "You, I'm convinced, are incapable of guile."

Carlie jumped to her feet, picked up the plates and carried them to the sink. "I'm just your basic female, Tyler, subject to the same flaws as anyone else. I can make mistakes, I—"

Tyler stood, going to Carlie and taking her face between his hands. She stared up at him, her body taut with apprehension. "You would never hurt me, Carlie. I know you wouldn't."

"You sound so positive."

He smiled as his thumbs stroked her cheeks. "That's because I know you care about me. You grouse and grumble and complain, but you do care, don't you?''

Her gaze was direct and fiercely earnest. "Yes, I do.''

He hesitated, his smile disappearing. "A little?''

"A lot, Tyler. A lot.''

He ached. She made him feel important to her. And most of all, he believed her. She truly cared for him.

His kiss wasn't meant to seduce, but rather to show tenderness and understanding. "Thank you, Carlie. For caring.''

He was still cradling her face, but their bodies weren't touching. Carlie bit her lower lip, then hugged herself to him. Tyler had the awful suspicion she could look into his soul and see his vulnerability. It shook him, and he sought casual conversation to break the mood.

"It was the same for Jason, until he met Brenda. You should have seen him in action. He had women throwing themselves at him, and he seldom ducked to get out of the way. After we opened the law practice, it only got worse. It seemed every client who came in knew someone or was related to someone, or *was* someone, who they thought Jason should get to know intimately. It grew old real quick. He started sending the younger female clients to me.''

"And now look how incorrigible you are.''

He chuckled. "That's right, honey. Put the blame where it's deserved. I'm just a product of circumstance.''

"You're a product of indulgence." Carlie leaned back to smile up at him. "I remember when Brenda went to work for Jason. She said he was gorgeous, charming and entirely insufferable. He tried giving her a bracelet once, you know."

"I remember. She threw it at him. Damned thing was heavy, too. Left a bruise on his shoulder."

"It was at the Christmas party you two had, that she kissed him under the mistletoe. She seemed to float for two days."

"Yeah. I got the load of the cases because Jason was too busy wooing Brenda to bother with anything as trivial as work. She really ran him ragged." And, Tyler thought, he now had a much better understanding of what his brother had gone through. Carlie could tie him up in knots with just a look.

But there was one major difference. Jason loved Brenda, whereas Tyler had no idea exactly what he felt for Carlie.

"She made him chase her until she caught him. But they both enjoyed it, and look how everything turned out." Carlie said the words quietly, with a strange, wistful smile.

"Brenda isn't the type of woman I would have figured Jason to fall for. Don't get me wrong. There's not a better person than Brenda. She's good for Jason, and I love her. But Jason always had a preference for tall, busty sophisticated brunettes. Not short, perky, domesticated redheads."

Carlie darted him a quick look. "I guess you never can tell."

"No." Tyler tilted his head, studying her, and then he agreed. "You never can tell."

Tugging her closer, he watched as her thick lashes lowered behind the lenses of her glasses. She gave a feeble protest when he reached up and removed them from her nose, laying them carefully on the table. "Tyler…"

"You're very pretty, Carlie." He toyed with her braid, dragging his curled fingers over the length of it. He reached the end, felt the cloth-covered rubber band holding the braid secure, and pulled it free. Carlie's eyes widened, but he didn't give her time to stop him.

His fingers sifted through the strands, separating them, then pulling her hair over her shoulders. It rippled with waves, a dozen different colors highlighted by the overhead light. It was beautiful—she was beautiful—and Tyler never felt so needful of anyone in his life.

Bunching her hair into his fists on either side of her head, he pulled her face up to his. "I want you, Carlie."

The kiss was devastating in its intensity, powerfully erotic, and sensually sweet. Her body leaned into him. Tyler walked her backward to the counter, then pressed himself hard against her. He swallowed her gasp and gave his groan in return.

And still he kissed her. He was in no hurry to speed

things along. No one had ever tasted so good, so right and so perfect.

His hands moved down her body languidly, exploring, excited by the feel of what he'd never expected, never imagined. She was all full, soft curves, lush. Fine-boned, her arms were slim, her wrists and elbows tiny. Her waist was slight, her soft belly only a marginal curve, very feminine, utterly seductive. His palm lingered there. He heard her shuddered breathing as he stroked her, feeling her muscles quiver.

He palmed her bottom, finding it exquisitely soft and equally firm. He pulled her against his aroused body, rubbing and stroking. Carlie clung to him, and he loved it. He couldn't get enough of her or her response.

"I want to see you, honey."

"No." Her face dipped down and she pressed her lips into his throat. "Please…"

He kissed her again, his tongue thrusting, his breath coming in harsh pants.

"Take me to your bedroom, Carlie." He held her face until she opened her eyes and looked at him. "I'm going to make love to you."

It was inevitable. "Yes."

He threw back his head and closed his eyes for an instant. Then he pulled her from the counter and turned her toward the hallway. "Your bedroom."

She slowed as she neared her bedroom door. "I haven't showered."

"It doesn't matter." Nothing mattered except making her his, completely.

"But we...the basketball..."

Tyler shoved her gently inside, closing the door behind him. The room was in shadows, dim and close and intimate. It smelled of Carlie, her elusive, feminine scent. He reached for her in the dark. "Believe me, it doesn't matter."

He held her close, one hand caressing her full, lush breasts, finding a stiffened nipple and tugging on it lightly, hearing her groan and then palming her, crushing her soft flesh delicately in his large hand.

"Where's the light?" The question was tinged with his haste, his need.

"No." Carlie threw herself against him. "Not tonight, Tyler. Give me tonight."

He didn't understand her, but he relished her obvious urgency. He forgot the light—there was enough moonlight to illuminate the room with vague, slanted beams of opalescence. The shadows were thick and heavy, but he could see Carlie, could read her expression by the gleam in her beautiful hazel eyes, the wet sheen of her tongue as she flicked it over her lips. Her hands touched his chest tentatively, her fingers kneading the muscles, as inquisitive about his body as he was about hers. They explored each other leisurely, their excitement growing, the air thick with sexual tension. Tyler kept trying to calm himself, to call on his control, but it was nonexistent. He throbbed with need, and he was with Carlie. It was unbelievable.

Carlie kicked out of her sneakers and pulled off her socks as Tyler simultaneously whisked off her sweatshirt. They nearly toppled each other to the floor, but Tyler caught her by the waist and they landed on her bed. The covers billowed around them, soft and fragrant as Tyler's weight pressed Carlie deep into the mattress.

"You feel so good, Carlie." He rubbed against her, but she protested, tugging at his sweatshirt. Going up on his knees, Tyler jerked off the shirt.

An instant later, they were together again, each frantic to touch the other. Carlie raked her nails gently through the dark, curling hair on his chest.

Tyler reared back, unable to control himself with her innocent, curious touch. He stared down at her partial nudity—a stray beam of moonlight slashed across her breasts, showing them to be milky white and smooth, full and firm. His hands covered her, and she arched into him.

"God, Carlie. I can't believe how you hid yourself. Never again, sweetheart, do you hear me? You're mine now. I won't let you hide from me again."

He lowered his head, unable to wait a moment longer, and caught a nipple, nibbling with his lips, lightly flicking with his tongue.

"Tyler, please…"

"Yes, honey. Soon, soon." His sharp teeth closed on her, carefully tugging, and when she groaned, throwing her head back and turning her face away as she gripped the blankets in fierce pleasure, he tugged again, pulling sweetly, taunting her. Her hands settled in his hair, urging him closer toward her. He drew her in, suckling gently, then hard, until her hips were writhing against him.

He hadn't planned his seduction, didn't have pre-meditated intentions of devastating her with his finesse. It just didn't occur to him to end the pleasure any time soon. He'd waited so long, a lifetime, it seemed, for Carlie to be like this with him, and his senses were rioting, his body moving of its own volition.

He was mindless to everything but taking and giving pleasure. And at the moment, hearing Carlie's gasps and soft feminine moans gave him more pleasure than he thought he could endure.

Tyler slid to the side of her, his hand coasting languidly over her midriff and beneath the waistband of her pants to caress her soft belly. Carlie turned to face him. "Tyler, I think I'm going to die."

"No. You won't die, sweetheart." He sat up. "Let me get these other clothes off you."

She was trembling all over, her body taut and aching, and as Tyler slid the pants down her long legs, his fingers touched her, skimming over her soft flesh, teasing the insides of her thighs. He pulled the pants free of her ankles, then sat there at her side, simply looking at her. Restless, her long legs moved in subtle, impatient turns. She looked at him, seeing his gaze so intent on her body, then turned away, her eyes closing, only to look at him again.

"I can see all of you, Carlie, despite the dark." His hand slid down her thigh, stopping at her knees, slowly easing her legs farther apart. She gasped, and he smiled in the moonlight. "I love looking at you, a woman with a woman's body. You have nothing to hide, nothing to be ashamed of."

"I'm…I'm…" Carlie gasped again, not able to get the words out.

His finger sifted through her curls, finding her flesh hot and swollen, wet with need. He wanted to shout with excitement. "You're perfect. Just the way nature intended a woman to be." As he talked, he stroked her, slowly, one finger dipping just inside her, withdrawing when her hips rose sharply.

"Feel how wet you are for me, Carlie." He pressed his finger inside her again, this time deeper, and she groaned, her legs spreading wider without his instruction. Her every move inflamed him, she was so special…yet somehow, it all seemed familiar.

His body rocked with his pounding heartbeat and he bent to press his face into her belly. He could smell her, the spicy scent of her desire filling him, shaking him profoundly.

Sliding off the bed, he went to his knees between her legs. Before she could voice a protest, before he could even think about what he was doing, he'd caught her thighs and tugged her to the very edge of the mattress. Her legs hung over the side, Tyler between them. She raised herself on an elbow, peering down at him in confusion, and he quickly lifted her knees over his shoulders, then pressed his face into her heat.

Her gasp was immediate, her protest loud. He ignored her, locking his arms around her hips, holding her still. "You taste so good, Carlie. So damn good." She fell back with a low cry, lifting herself to his seeking tongue.

Her trembling increased, her body arching from the mattress. He caught her sensitized flesh carefully between his teeth, holding her captive for his hot tongue, intent on her climax now, devastating her, enjoying her, driving her closer with each and every movement he made. She called his name, softly, over and over. He slid his hands against her, abruptly pushing two fingers deep inside her.

Wild, shattering sensations swept through her body, and Tyler could feel her contractions against his mouth and tongue, pressing closer, relishing every second of her pleasure. It seemed to go on and on, and he pushed her for more.

When Carlie finally went limp, Tyler raised himself, scooting up to lie upon her. "You're beautiful." Her hair was tangled about her head and a fine sheen of moisture glistened on her skin. He kissed her slack mouth, then stood, quickly removing his pants.

Carlie opened her eyes, but she didn't smile. She seemed dazed, her gaze intent on his body. Tyler leaned forward, naked, to brush his fingers through the curls between her thighs. She sucked in a startled breath, her hips pressing into the mattress.

His touch eased, barely skimming her, and she trembled. "Too sensitive?" He watched her nod, seeing the confusion in her bright eyes. He palmed her, his hand still and warm.

Sitting on the bed beside her, he looked over her body. Her legs were still sprawled, her knees bent so her calves hung over the bed. Her arms were limp, lying palm up beside her head. She was watching him closely.

He looked at her breasts, still heaving slightly, and leaned down to gently take a nipple between his teeth. She groaned, her body clenching once again. "Tyler, *please*."

"Just a minute, sweetheart. I have to protect you."

It took him only a moment, but she was frantic with need, and Tyler closed his eyes in anticipation. He felt her thighs open wider, accommodating him, and with only the subtlest of movement, he was ready to enter her.

Poised on his forearms, he watched every nuance of her expression as he slowly, inexorably, sank into her, giving her his length, stretching her with his hardness.

She moved anxiously against him, and forced him past his control. Thrusting smoothly and deeply, he wound his hands in Carlie's hair, anchoring her head so he could kiss her, swallowing her gasping breaths and soft, broken moans.

When he felt her tightening again, this time around his arousal, squeezing him, giving him unbelievable pleasure, he found his own explosive orgasm. Closing his arms around her, he held her tight until the spasms had faded.

It was several minutes before Tyler found the strength to move away from her warm body. He rolled to his side, but immediately pulled her close. He felt oddly disturbed, and frankly disloyal. He'd never known anything like what he'd just experienced with Carlie—except for that one night in the pool house. He hadn't wanted those memories to interfere. They no longer mattered; he no longer cared.

But thoughts of that night, images and heated memories, had danced through his mind even as his senses filled with Carlie. *His Carlie.* He squeezed her closer, trying to chase away the images, but they didn't budge. Carlie leaned up to look at him.

"Tyler? What's wrong?"

She sounded anxious, and he rushed to reassure her. "What could possibly be wrong? Other than the fact I think you may have killed me with pleasure. I'm certain I no longer have legs. At least, if I do, they're totally useless right now." He cupped her cheek. "You're incredible, do you know that?"

She cuddled back down to his chest, her hands stroking through the dark curls there. "No. It was you. You were wonderful, Tyler."

He froze. The masked lady had said virtually the same thing on the phone. It unnerved him. Especially since the two women were so different. The woman at the party had been reserved, nearly frightened and so timid about each move he made, but Carlie had participated wholeheartedly. She was everything a man could want or hope to have in a mate.

He felt as though he'd somehow tainted the otherwise exquisite experience by envisioning another woman. No matter that the thought had come out of the blue. *How* could another woman, any woman, have intruded when he was with his Carlie? And she *was* his now. Savage possessiveness gripped him; he would never let her go.

Thinking that, he lowered his head to press a kiss to her temple. "You can't ever close me out again, Carlie. I won't let you."

Her reaction was immediate, and again, unexpected. She went perfectly still, almost stunned. He ran his hand over her shoulder. "You're mine, Carlie. I need you."

She looked at him from beneath her lashes. "Tyler, there's something you need to know."

He didn't like the sound of that. She was already trying to escape him, but he wouldn't let her. He kissed her again, then rose from the bed. "*Now*, we need that shower."

Her eyes widened. "I can't...!"

"Of course you can. Come on, I'll wash your back. And anything else that needs my attention."

He could sense her thinking, plotting. She twisted

her hands in the sheets. "I'm too tired. You've exhausted me. Please, just come back to bed."

It hit him like a lightning bolt. She didn't want him to see her, really see her, without her clothing hiding her figure, making her look frumpy. He frowned thoughtfully, uncertain how to proceed. If she had a scar or some other reason to be embarrassed...but he'd touched every inch of her; certainly he would have noticed if anything was wrong. Still, her anxiety was very real, almost tangible, and he couldn't push her. Not after all she'd already given him, not after sharing herself so completely.

He touched her cheek. "I'll be right back."

He walked out of the room unconcerned with his own nudity, returning only moments later with a damp cloth. He left the lights off and seated himself beside her, content with the way she followed his progress. "Your eyes are so wide, you must think I'm intending some kind of mayhem."

Carlie shifted fretfully. "What are you intending?"

"Only to wash you. Now lie still and behave."

With a rapid peddling motion of her long legs, she scooted backward until she was pressed against the headboard. "Tyler, no! Good grief, I'm perfectly capable of tending myself."

He caught her foot, stroking the damp cloth up her calf and behind her knee. "But I want to do it. Now relax and stop fighting me."

She remained stiff, but she didn't struggle against him. "You're outrageous, Tyler."

"Don't sound so sulky. Before long, you'll learn to enjoy my outrageousness, I promise."

Tyler was thorough, using the cool cloth to stroke slowly over her body, removing all traces of their lovemaking. Carlie finally gave up her inhibitions, relaxing and enjoying his ministrations. Tyler chuckled when she moaned softly, then he bent to kiss a soft pink nipple.

"Sleep, Carlie. We need sleep." She frowned at him, and he stroked her one last time. "I'll be right back."

Tyler showered in a hurry, not wanting to take the chance Carlie would recover and send him home. He wanted to hold her in his arms all night.

He wanted to wake in the morning and look at her in the full light of day. And make love to her again.

She was an enigma, but he was slowly coming to understand her, completely and without doubts. She was trustworthy, the only trustworthy woman he'd ever known.

With his hair still damp, a towel wrapped loosely around his hips, he reentered the bedroom. He could see Carlie's huge golden eyes shining at him in the darkness. He hesitated, waiting only a heartbeat, and she leaned forward, throwing back the blankets, silently inviting him into her bed.

He dropped the towel over a chair and slid in beside her. She immediately curled against him, settling her hand on his chest. In the smallest voice he'd ever heard from Carlie, she whispered, "Thank you, Tyler."

"Thank you? That's an unusual sentiment from a woman who just gave herself to a man."

"I didn't. Give myself to you, that is. You gave yourself to me. And you did it perfectly. It was wonderful, you were wonderful, and I thank you."

His chuckle nearly jarred her from her position against his shoulder. "You're very welcome...and by far the most appreciative woman I've ever made love to."

Her hand moved slowly over his chest, kneading the swell of muscle, teasing her fingers through the fine, dark hair. "We'll talk in the morning, okay?"

She sounded wary, unsure of herself. Tyler kissed the top of her head, then yawned hugely. "We'll talk, but only after I've gotten a chance to enjoy waking up with you."

Carlie was silent, her face turned into his skin, and he felt the sweet, very brief touch of her lips. He wasn't certain what to make of this new mood of hers, but then, it didn't matter. She was his, and nothing was going to change that. He wouldn't let it.

IT WAS THE SUNLIGHT streaming in that first stirred Tyler. His eyes opened slowly. Remembrance came in a rush of contentment, and he looked down to see Carlie still close to him, but now turned so that her bottom was nestled securely against his groin. His palm rested on her breast. Her skin was warm and silky and smooth.

She was peaceful in her sleep, her body lax, one hand curled beneath her cheek giving the illusion of childlike innocence. But she was no child.

Very quietly, Tyler raised himself onto one elbow, gazing down at her, a strange, stirring mix of emotions swamping him. He wanted to wake her and make love to her; he wanted to lie down and hold her forever.

He forced himself to be considerate and do neither. She was exhausted, and she needed her sleep. She didn't move so much as an eyelash when he carefully slid out of the bed.

The first order of business was a shave. His morning beard was harsh, and he didn't want to scratch her tender skin. And he didn't want to have to avoid kissing her in all the most delectable places because of beard stubble. He smiled at the thought.

Carlie wasn't the straitlaced, narrow-minded prude he'd expected. All her talk of reputations and gossip had been misleading. She was magnificent. Wild and open and honest with her feelings. She'd told him he was wonderful.

The mysterious masked woman had told him the same thing.

That wayward thought had him scowling at himself in the mirror. It was traitorous. Carlie deserved much better. He was a cad to still concern himself with another woman's identity. If he never discovered the truth, it wouldn't matter.

Deliberately, he shoved those disturbing thoughts from his mind. The mystery woman may have been a fantasy come to life, but Carlie was a living fantasy. Her effect on him was unbelievable, and he couldn't seem to get enough of her.

Naked, he stood in the bathroom and looked around. Surely Carlie had a razor somewhere. He checked in the vanity drawers, then the medicine cabinet. He didn't find a a razor, but a small contact case caught his attention.

Smiling, he envisioned Carlie wearing contacts, relegating the ugly glasses to the desk drawer forever. She had beautiful eyes, the hazel clear and unique and pure.

It was idle curiosity that prompted him to open the case. For a moment, he stared stupidly at the colored lenses. They were a very bright, familiar blue. Then his face reddened.

He'd seen that color before. The night of the party.

Reality beat a swift path into his brain.

His guileless, forthright, *honest* Carlie had played him for a fool. He remembered the recent phone call, and his face burned, the heat of humiliation spreading rapidly down his neck. He was filled with fierce blinding anger, and the most devastating disappointment he'd ever known.

He'd thought of Carlie as near-perfect; dedicated to the children and to loftier causes for the common good. He'd thought her stubborn, headstrong and thoroughly independent. But not a liar.

She was still sleeping when he entered the bedroom. He was intent on his course, not about to be swayed by the alluring picture she made. Deliberately, he sat on the side of the bed, promptly waking her.

Her long lashes fluttered and her eyes opened slowly. She looked up into his unsmiling face, and reached for him.

"Tyler." Her hand landed on his naked thigh, and she stroked him. He dropped forward on one elbow so they were nose to nose. "Good morning, sweetheart. I trust you slept well?"

Her hand came up to his cheek, and she nodded. She felt his stubbly chin, then smiled slowly. "You're so very dark."

His look was grim. Pushing away the covers, he surveyed her body. "You're certainly not." His eyes fell to the tight curls between her thighs. "Light brown. Close to the color of your beautiful head. Maybe not as golden. Certainly not black."

She gasped.

"Who are we today, Carlie? Maybe you'd like me to run home and fetch my pirate costume? I could pretend you were a virgin maiden, and 'pillage' you to my heart's content."

He saw her pale throat move as she swallowed, but otherwise she remained still, not even blinking. The hurt in her golden eyes enraged him all the more. He couldn't stop himself from taunting her. "No? You don't like that idea? Then how about I rent a sheikh costume? That role you would surely approve of. After all, you wear the veils so well. Maybe I could convince you to dance for me. I'd like that, I'm sure."

She pulled away without touching him. Her look was distant and wary. "You don't understand, Tyler."

"Now, there's where you're wrong." He reached out to wrap a lock of long hair around his finger, tugging her face closer to his own. "I understand perfectly. You wanted to experiment, and were too much the coward to come out from behind your spinster disguise. But now there's no reason to pretend. Hell, I enjoyed myself last night. What red-blooded male wouldn't have?"

"Tyler…"

"Don't look so concerned, sweetheart. I'm still willing to play. I only wish you'd told me the way of it sooner. Just think of all the time we've wasted. We could have been enjoying ourselves quite a bit." He gazed mockingly down the length of her exposed body. He ignored the way her pulse beat frantically in her slim throat, just as he ignored the horrified expression on her face, the tears starting to glisten in her eyes. He wouldn't be a fool again. Once was more than enough. It was more than he could bear.

He hurt so badly. He had never felt so betrayed in his life, not even when he'd finally realized how little he meant to his mother. He'd expected deception and manipulation from her. But he'd trusted Carlie. *Fool.*

Not for the world would he let her know that. He forced a wicked grin, hiding his hurt. Then he bent to press a hard, possessive kiss to her parted lips. He hadn't completely lost, he thought. He was still with her, and they were both in bed.

He could prove to her it didn't matter, that she meant little to him.

And then maybe he could prove it to himself.

CHAPTER NINE

"No, damn you!" Carlie gave Tyler a shove that nearly knocked him from the bed. She scrambled away from him, quickly rising.

He lounged back, surveying her with a look of arrogant annoyance, his arms behind his head. "Calm down, Carlie."

"Get out! Get out now." She was trembling from head to foot, still completely naked, her hands squeezed together so tight her knuckles ached. Did he actually think he could make love to her while he was angry?

His eyes coasted over her slowly, with deliberate insult. But his words were a contrast, and terribly hurtful. "You're magnificent."

Carlie was speechless for just a moment. Then she narrowed her eyes. "I want you to leave now, Tyler." Her words quavered, but she couldn't help it. Everything had fallen apart. Tyler was acting like a stranger, treating her with the same callous insolence her husband had always employed whenever he'd been angry with her. She couldn't bear it.

Realizing that she was standing there, completely

naked, waiting to see what else he would do or say made her throat go dry. She wasn't helpless and she was no longer young and naive. She angled her chin toward him, then forced a semblance of calm into her voice. "I won't let you do this, Tyler."

"Let me do what? You're the one who lied and made a fool of me, Carlie." His gaze pierced her, hot and hard and filled with contempt. She briefly closed her eyes against the pain of it.

"I'm sorry. I never intended it to be this way. I should never had done any of it. You're right to be angry. I knew you would be. That's why I decided to put off telling you until this morning."

"You want me to believe you would have actually confessed? I'm not stupid, Carlie. Look at you. You're shocked that I know. You wouldn't have said a word if I hadn't stumbled across your contacts and found out on my own."

She couldn't deny she was shocked, but it was because of Tyler's reaction, his disdain. She expected anger, but not disgust.

She watched Tyler rise from the bed, unmindful of his nudity as he stalked toward her. She couldn't bear his touch, not now, not with the way he felt about her. She pressed back against the wall.

Tyler glared at her retreat, then roughly ran his hands through his hair. Carlie realized, rather stupidly, that he was even gorgeous in the morning, beard stubble and all. His voice, when he spoke, was practically a sneer. "What's with the timid act, Carlie? I thought that little charade ended at the pool house.''

Of course, it hadn't been an act, but she wasn't going to remind him of that. She understood his anger completely; she simply couldn't deal with it at the moment. She scooped up his pants and threw them at him. ''Get dressed and go, Tyler.''

She pulled a robe from her closet and quickly slipped it on. Tyler watched her, his eyes taking in every minute movement of her body. She hated his scrutiny.

His sweatshirt hit him in the chest when she threw it. He caught the garment, but made no move to put it on. He clutched the clothing in his big hands and started toward her again.

Carlie steeled herself, pushing away her guilt and nervousness, calling on her anger. No man would ever intimidate her again. She held up her hand, and Tyler halted. ''I'm sorry for what happened, Tyler. Sorrier than you can know. I take full blame and I understand your anger. But it's over now. I won't bother you again. I promise.''

His eyes looked dangerously bright. ''Is that right?''

''Yes.'' She swallowed heavily. ''I understand how you feel…''

Tyler threw back his head and laughed harshly. ''Lady, you haven't got a clue. How could you understand my feelings when you don't have any of your own? Hell, you're not even real. You're make-believe—and there's too damn many of you for me to keep track of.''

"I don't know what you're talking about." She hated feeling defensive, and she hated lying. Deep down, she knew exactly what he was talking about.

"Who are you now, Carlie? I haven't met this woman before. The harem girl I know intimately, I met that timid little kitten at the pool house. She blew my socks off, wanting my body and very little conversation. A good woman if ever there was one. And then I met the school teacher. Prickly woman, with the worst taste in clothing I have ever seen. Of course, she made up for it with her show of honesty and compassion and concern. A born actress. And now you. A woman who offers abject apologies left and right. A woman who lied and manipulated without a single qualm, and now, apparently, is sorry for it. It's a good act, I admit, but somehow I can't quite believe you're all that repentant. You played your little game too damn convincingly.''

Carlie's mind went blank. All her barely contained emotions settled into one dull ache that she suppressed deep inside herself. The more emotion she gave him, the more he would mock her. And she couldn't bear it. "You're right. But each of those women had something in common, Tyler. Something you obviously missed. They were each a fool and an idiot. And you can believe me this time—liar that I am—they're gone. You won't see them again. Well, perhaps you'll see the school teacher, but that's entirely up to you. If you wish to quit the program at school, I'll understand. I even encourage you to do so. I'll find someone else. It would be for the best if we didn't expose the children to any animosity.''

She turned and began pulling clothes from her closet, all but dismissing Tyler. She wasn't going to continue to apologize. He obviously didn't want to hear it, and just as certainly, he didn't believe her regret. She'd learned long ago, if one apology wasn't sufficient, a hundred wouldn't do, either.

Tyler caught her arm, turning her to face him. ''You're trying to make me out to be the villain here, Carlie.'' His eyes were clouded with confusion. ''I'm the one who was used, the one who was made to look like a fool.''

Carlie jerked her arm free. His touch was still disturbing, regardless of all that had happened. ''I've thought you many things, Tyler, but never a fool. And as I recall, you didn't object overly to being used. *You* initiated the…intimacies. And as far as the other…well, you should remember I tried to keep our relationship platonic. You're the one who pushed, not me.''

''You called me one night,'' he accused softly, ignoring her words. ''Why would you do that except to taunt me?''

Carlie managed a casual shrug, but it was difficult. Her humiliation was gone, buried with her regret. But he was so large and imposing, she couldn't help being very aware of him, of his maleness in contrast to her femininity. He was naked, he was angry and there was no avoiding a confrontation.

She refused to cower, to lower her eyes from his perceptive stare. ''I already admitted to being a fool. Just think of that call as another example of my foolishness.'' She wasn't about to tell him she'd been searching for some truth behind his attentiveness, some sign that he wasn't just playing with her. She'd already given enough of herself away.

''But why, Carlie? Why the damned charade in the first place?'' He was back to shouting, his face dark with renewed anger.

And he still hadn't put a stitch of clothing on.

Carlie stepped quickly away from him, and headed for the bathroom. She had to get away, had to find a moment's privacy to collect herself and call up her reserve. She had the choking need to break down and cry like a baby. She would never feel a loss as greatly as she felt it now. She had lost Tyler.

Who was she kidding? She'd never had Tyler in the first place. She'd reminded herself of that often enough. But somehow, because they had shared sex— she would no longer consider it lovemaking—she had allowed herself to indulge in a whimsical dream. She was such a fraud.

She turned back to Tyler, and caught him watching her intently, a look closely resembling concern shining in his eyes. She disregarded that possibility. He hated her now. She could feel it. ''The charade was unintentional, if you'll remember correctly. I had left the party. *You* followed *me*. But I suppose some part of me was pathetic enough to appreciate the attention you gave me. It surprised me. It…'' She swallowed. ''I was flattered. But I learn from my mistakes, Tyler. Believe me.'' She laughed, then, a bubbling, nervous sound. She lowered her head with the force of it.

She felt Tyler move toward her and reach out a hand. ''Carlie?''

The single word was sharp, edged with a vague emotion Carlie couldn't begin to fathom. She stepped away from him, still chuckling. ''Oh, it's too funny. Tyler Ramsey, the stud of the community, feeling used by Carlie McDaniels! It's too absurd to be real. But don't worry, Tyler. I won't tell a single soul. After all, who would ever believe me?''

He flexed his jaw, his stance deceptively mild. ''You think it's funny?''

Her smile twisted into a sneer and her eyes narrowed. ''I think it's hilarious. One of those too-strange-to-be-true scenarios better shoved to the back of the closet, never to be thought of again.''

Tyler caught her chin, and her grin vanished instantly. ''You won't be able to forget, Carlie. At least be honest with yourself now.'' His thumb teased over her bottom lip, and there was genuine regret in the words he muttered. ''You won't ever be able to forget.'' Then he straightened, all signs of disappointment magically disappearing. ''I'd actually thought you were different. And in a way you are. You were able to fool me completely. No other woman has done that. You're to be congratulated.''

Carlie nearly cried out at those words. Instead, she bit her lip, whirled and slammed into the bathroom, locking the door behind her. The pain nearly suffocated her, making her knees weak and stealing her resolve. She sank, defeated, to the edge of the tub, her fist in her mouth to stifle her low sobs.

She stayed there, hearing Tyler dress quietly, hearing the sounds of him preparing to leave. And then the closing of the door, so soft, so final, so very, very real.

And she broke, crying with all the energy of someone who knows she's lost something invaluable. Something she's never had but always desperately wanted.

''TYLER! My goodness, you're a sight!''

''Why the hell didn't you tell me, Brenda!'' He stuck his face close to hers. ''I'm your brother-in-law! I'm family! I can't believe you would stab me in the back like this!''

Brenda covered her chest with one hand, her eyes wide. ''Whatever are you shouting about? What's happened?''

Jason entered the room, took one look at his brother and put himself in front of his wife. ''Calm down, Tyler.''

''Calm down! Do you know…?''

''Yes.'' Jason's voice was very quiet in comparison

to Tyler's. "I know. But I can't let you yell at my wife. Now settle down."

Tyler was thunderstruck. "You knew, too?"

"Don't look so shocked. No one told me, but I figured it out quickly enough. I have to admit, I was surprised you didn't."

Brenda gasped then, shoving her husband aside. She faced Tyler with the most alarmed expression he'd ever seen on her face. "This is about Carlie? You've found out?"

"Yes, dammit! Your little game is over. Did you two sit down to tea and laugh over watching me make a fool of myself? Did she give you all the juicy details?"

Jason opened his mouth, but Brenda didn't give him time to interject. "Oh, Tyler, it wasn't like that!" Then she bit her lip. "You're angry. You…you didn't hurt her, did you?"

Tyler threw up his hands in a gesture of despair. "I don't believe you asked me that! Since when have I been such a bastard that I'd hurt a woman? I may have felt like strangling you both, but I would never—"

"I don't mean physically. I know you would never lay a hand on a woman." Then she reached up to touch his cheek. "But she's so fragile, Tyler. She's been hurt so much. Please, tell me you didn't do or say anything to hurt her feelings."

She was looking so anxious, Tyler frowned at her. Reluctantly, he admitted, "I was damned angry."

Brenda searched his face, then turned to Jason, her eyes huge. "I'm going to go check on her."

Jason nodded, then bent to kiss her cheek. "Be careful driving. Don't hurry. I doubt she's going anywhere." He handed Brenda the car keys from a hook by the phone, catching her just before she started out. "Everything will work out."

Brenda glanced quickly at Tyler, who only looked back in exasperation. She sighed. "Don't be so sure of that, Jason. I'm not."

Tyler watched her rush out, then turned to his brother. "Aren't you the least bit irate on my behalf? Do you even know the whole story? I was *lied* to."

Jason sat, crossing his arms on the kitchen table. "No, you weren't. Unfortunately, Carlie's been honest with you from the start. She's been herself, and that's as honest as it gets. Now, I sincerely hope you're going to sit down here and tell me you didn't just manage to ruin the best thing that's ever happened to you."

Tyler sat, but it wasn't a concession as much as he suddenly needed the stability of a chair. He could hardly credit his brother's defection. "A woman who lies to me and plays juvenile games is the best thing that's ever happened to me? What the hell would be the worst?"

Jason gave him a long look, then sighed. "The worst, the way I see it, is if you just did so much damage, Carlie crawls back into her shell and never gives you a second chance. And that's a very real possibility." Jason looked his brother over, taking in Tyler's still-disheveled hair and unshaven face. "Why don't you tell me what happened?"

Tyler realized how foolish his part sounded in the charade, but he needed to talk. He could barely absorb the reality of what he'd discovered. "I just realized that Carlie and my mystery woman are one and the same." He laughed in self-derision. "Do you know, I was actually feeling guilty because I thought I cared so much for Carlie, and yet I was still curious to know who the other woman was. What a joke."

"What did you do?"

Tyler winced at the suspicion in his brother's words. "I kicked up a fuss, of course. I mean, Carlie knew it was her I had—" Tyler halted. He hadn't told anyone he'd made love to his harem girl—and he was pretty certain Carlie hadn't said anything either. Regardless of what had happened now, that night was special, and he wouldn't ruin it. He stared at his brother, then looked away. "Hell, Bren probably told Carlie I'd been asking about her. It's all so humiliating."

"Yeah. Imagine how Carlie feels."

Tyler's jaw dropped open, but he shut it with a snap. "What about me?"

Jason snorted in disgust. It was a good simulation of Carlie's snort, but without her flair.

"You're a big boy. You've been around. So you were a bit embarrassed? You two could have talked about it, about why Carlie felt so unsure of herself as a woman that she'd have to hide behind a disguise in the first place. Who knows, you may have even been able to laugh about it.''

''Fat chance!''

There was silence, and Jason got up to pour Tyler a cup of coffee. After setting the cup on the table, he clasped Tyler's shoulder, giving him a brotherly squeeze.

Tyler shook his head. Jason always did that. He could give Tyler hell about something, but he always let him know he cared, either by a pat on the back, a squeeze to the shoulder or an occasional bear hug. They were closer than most brothers, and Tyler never doubted his loyalty.

He waited another second or two until Jason had reseated himself, then he took the bait. ''So why is Carlie so insecure?''

Jason idly traced the edge of his coffee cup with his fingertip. ''Don't you think that's a question you ought to ask Carlie?''

Swamped with emotions he couldn't sort out, Tyler chose to go on the defensive. ''I shouldn't have to ask. If she has a good reason for doing what she did, she ought to come to me and tell me.''

''And if she doesn't do that?''

Tyler stubbornly shook his head. ''I don't know.''

''I think you better make up your mind fast.''

That was impossible to do. God, things could get so tangled. He'd only just decided he loved Carlie.... Tyler felt his chest squeeze tight. *Love?* That word had the ability to scare him spitless, but that was probably what it was. Because now that things had soured, he was hurting worse than he'd ever hurt in his life. Surely only love could do that to a man. And what if Carlie did have good reason for doing what she'd done? He hadn't even asked her. He'd let his injured pride guide him, when in his heart, he knew Carlie was incapable of simply using anyone. If she felt she had to resort to deception, she must have had a very good reason.

And he'd probably just ruined whatever trust she'd previously had in him.

Tyler dropped his head onto the table, and it landed with a solid thud.

Jason went on, apparently unmoved by his brother's dejection. "This is going to be really hard for Carlie to take. It's not enough that you know, but now both Bren and I do, as well. I would imagine she's feeling utterly alone right now. She doesn't have anyone, you know. No family, no—"

Tyler raised his head, and pounded it back down on the table. Twice.

"Tyler, quit trying to shake your brains loose and tell me what you're going to do."

He sat back up, his eyes bloodshot and burning, his head aching abominably, feeling totally defeated. "I think I might have blown it, Jason. Some of the things I said…"

"So you're going to try to work it out?"

Tyler covered his face with his hands. "I don't know. Hell, she'll probably never speak to me again."

"Give her a few days. She'll calm down."

"Yeah, maybe." But he didn't believe it. He thought of the look on Carlie's face as he'd hurled accusations…the way she'd backed away from him. Her nearly hysterical laugh.

Tyler closed his eyes, and pinched the bridge of his nose. He was afraid he'd thrown away something precious. All because of his injured pride. "She's incredible, you know. Absolutely incredible."

Jason raised an eyebrow. "Are we talking about in bed?"

Tyler looked up, a frown solidly in place. "No! I mean…" He narrowed his eyes at his brother, then shook his head. "I was talking about other things."

Jason watched him, a slight smile on his face. Tyler didn't even notice. "She's terrific with the kids. So patient and gentle, but boy, do they ever listen to her. They go out of their way to please her. And the parents! They hang on to her every word, as if she speaks the gospel. And she's so intelligent. Loads of common sense—except when it comes to her own worth. She hides behind those damned ugly clothes. I hate that."

Tipping his head back, Tyler stared at the ceiling, feeling hopeless and lost. "We had fun, Jason. Real, genuine fun. I would have sooner spent time with Carlie than anyone I know."

"You love her."

Still staring at the ceiling, Tyler said, "Yeah. I think I do. But love is a damn strange thing. I can't decide if I like it or not."

"I know I hated it when I fell for Brenda. I went through major denial. But then I'd see some clown talking to her, and I'd want to kill him. And I couldn't keep my hands off her. She'd yawn and I'd want her. She'd smile and I'd get hard as a rock."

Tyler scoffed, even though he was suffering the same thing. "I remember. You were warped."

Jason merely grinned. "I still am. It's terrific."

Tyler made a quick decision, and immediately felt better. "I have to go see her."

Jason gave him a cautious look. "Do you think that's wise? Carlie needs time to—"

"I don't mean right this minute. We both need time to think and I'm not sure I can think straight at all when I'm around her." Then he grinned. "Hell, I can hardly think when I'm not around her. At least, not about anything other than her."

Jason clasped Tyler's shoulder, walking with him to the door. "It's love, all right." Then he grew serious. "But you have to be sure, Tyler. You have to be certain of what you want. Get your own thoughts straight before you make matters worse. The way you look now, you'd only go there and end up fighting with her again."

Tyler smiled ruefully. "Don't worry. It's not fighting I have in mind."

Jason slapped him on the back. "Remember that."

WHAT A WASTE of time crying was.

It never solved anything and it was embarrassing. Brenda was sympathetic, but Carlie didn't want sympathy. She wanted solitude, she wanted time to think, and luckily, Brenda was a good enough friend to realize it.

It had been almost two days since she'd last seen Tyler, since the morning he'd walked out her door with the obvious intent of never coming back. Luckily, there hadn't been any basketball practices scheduled, so she didn't have to worry about seeing him at school.

At least, not yet. She had no idea how Tyler intended to handle that. *She* certainly wouldn't quit. That would smack of cowardice, and she had too much pride to be the first to give up. But the thought of seeing him, of trying to be sociable under the circumstances, was nearly too much. She had to get her act together, and she had to do it now.

A warm shower helped to revive her somewhat, and she tried to concentrate her thoughts on the children, on figuring out some way to help the more financially unfortunate families. She also needed some exercise to rid her of her tension.

She had a plan. It was foolproof, which was necessary, since she'd proven herself several times a fool. Part of the secret of recovering from shame and heartache was to make everyone else believe it didn't matter one whit, and pretty soon, after convincing them, you automatically convinced yourself.

Carlie dressed in several layers of sweats, tied her sneakers neatly, and went out the door. The November air was very brisk, and the sky was overcast and gray. The wind was playful, blowing hard one minute, sending stray wisps of hair slashing across her eyes, and then dying, leaving the air strangely still and silent.

Carlie breathed deeply of the scents of approaching winter. It would snow soon, and before long the holidays would be here. That fact meant nothing to Carlie. She hadn't celebrated a holiday since she'd finally escaped her husband over two years ago. Holidays brought memories, and memories only served to destroy her carefully erected peace of mind.

She ran hard for the first few blocks, and then, winded, her lungs aching, she switched to a slow-paced jog. She usually ran for about three miles. It was what she had always done for peace and contentment. Hopefully, it would work again.

But the hurdles seemed insurmountable today. Every step she took brought back thoughts of Tyler. And each thought ended with the angry flash of his dark eyes. What he must be thinking of her now....

It was as if she'd conjured him with her worries. She rounded the corner, laboring for breath, her cheeks stinging from the cold, and there he was. He was watching her, sitting on her front step, his hands shoved deep into the pockets of his leather jacket.

Her heart lurched, her throat went dry and her skin

felt tight—much too tight. But she smiled, a serene, undisturbed smile. "Hello, Tyler."

He blinked. Obviously that wasn't what he'd expected to hear. Especially not in such a cordial tone. Carlie was very pleased with herself.

He stood slowly, his eyes drifting over her jogging suit in obvious distaste. "You were out jogging."

"Very astute of you. What gave me away? The suit itself or the fact that I just returned, still huffing?" She was trembling inside and her stomach was tied in knots, but she hid it well, knowing she'd rather die than have him know how badly he'd hurt her.

Tyler tilted his head, studying her warily. "I thought we should talk."

Carlie bent over, placing her hands on her thighs. It looked as though she was trying to catch her breath, but in truth she needed a moment to regain her emotional balance. She hadn't expected to see him again this soon. She wasn't ready. The fact that Tyler was here, so near and looking so handsome made the chore of feigning nonchalance that much more difficult. She drew one last deep breath and straightened.

"I'm sorry, I really can't right now. It's a bad time for me. Papers to grade, lessons to plan. And I have a few phone calls to make." She smiled politely.

"Carlie…"

"Yes?"

He rubbed the bridge of his nose. "Things didn't go exactly as I planned the other day. It took me by surprise—"

"That's putting a pretty face on it, Tyler. It shocked the hell out of you. And enraged you. And I understand completely. I probably would have felt the same. But I've already apologized. There's nothing more I can do. I can't change what's already been done. Believe me, I wish I could."

"What would you change, honey?"

Oh, that tone, so sweet and gentle. Carlie forced herself to stand just a little straighter. "All of it, of course. From the day Brenda invited me to that stupid party, to yesterday. I'd erase it all." She smiled at him serenely, hoping to put him at ease with her declaration. But it cost her. Her stomach felt so tight now, she feared she might throw up.

Tyler had probably come over with some vague notion that she might pursue him. She'd die first.

He touched her cheek briefly. "Then I'll be eternally grateful you don't possess magic powers. Because I wouldn't trade the time I've spent with you for anything." He waited a moment, then added softly, "I don't really believe you would, either, Carlie."

CHAPTER TEN

OH, GOD, oh, God. He couldn't know that. Carlie summoned a smile, but her serenity had about run out. "You're wrong."

"I've been wrong about a lot of things."

Her eyes widened behind the lenses of her glasses, and she pressed a hand dramatically to her heart. "No! Not you, Tyler! Say it isn't so, or all my grand delusions will blow away in the wind."

"Dammit, Carlie…"

She chuckled. The sound was just a bit rusty, but convincing, all the same. "Go home, Tyler. It's cold out here, too cold to stand around trading recriminations." She went up the steps, fishing her key out of her pocket.

Carlie went inside and then turned to tell Tyler goodbye. He didn't give her the chance. Pushing his way through, he was over the threshold before Carlie could voice a complaint.

He didn't smile. He closed the door and leaned against it, watching her.

Warily, she faced him. "What are you doing?"

Tyler hesitated, then shrugged. "I can help you grade your papers. I still owe you, don't I?"

"I don't remember. But I'd rather you didn't. I don't have time to be distracted."

He came away from the door. "Do I distract you, Carlie?"

She blinked at him, then laughed. "Turn your hormones off, Tyler. I was referring to your inane chatter."

"You can't be that indifferent to me, Carlie. I was there that night, too, you know. I recall perfectly everything that happened between us."

Carlie moved away from the heat of his gaze. It was almost tangible, covering her in waves, penetrating her flesh. She sauntered as casually as possible to the kitchen, Tyler following.

She pulled out a chair and lowered herself into it, while all the time her mind was working furiously. This time, it wasn't as easy to affect a carefree air. Her feelings were even more deeply involved now than when she'd first got divorced. She wasn't a kid who had been disillusioned. And her feelings for Tyler surpassed infatuation.

When Tyler automatically sat opposite her, she regarded him seriously. "Maybe we should talk."

He seemed relieved. "Yes. I want to explain—"

"Let me go first, Tyler." Her heart was racing, her breath was shallow, but she knew she had to have her say and get it over with as cleanly as possible. Even though it cost her, she leaned forward and placed her hand over his. He couldn't know how hurt she was. Pride was all she had left.

Tyler turned his palm upward, clasping her fingers. "Tyler," she started uncertainly, "what happened between us was nice. I'll grant you that." His eyes narrowed, and she released his hand. "Don't interrupt, please. I want you to understand. It was nice, and I believe I already thanked you. But it won't happen again. Ever."

"I don't believe you."

"Then once again, I'm sorry. But it's true. If you're determined for us to remain friends, that's fine with me. I like you. You're a good person and you're a lot of fun. But I won't sleep with you again. Sex isn't on my agenda. It was an aberration that we got together at all. Call it temporary insanity, and the key word there is 'temporary.'"

"People can't just turn off their emotions, Carlie. You were with me every step of the way that night, and it was a damned sight more than 'nice.' Hell, it was more than sex, more than anything I've ever known before. It won't go away."

"There's where you're wrong, Tyler. I can make it go away. I can turn off my feelings with a snap of my fingers. I can do anything I put my mind to. And right now, I'm sending you home." She stood, but Tyler didn't budge. Carlie couldn't believe he'd thought she would abide a casual affair. Without mutual caring between them, it was impossible. But obviously, Tyler didn't realize that. It was just as obvious he didn't know her at all.

He eyed her speculatively. "Is that what you're trying to do now? Turn off your feelings, close off your heart. That's no way to live, honey."

Carlie definitely didn't want Tyler Ramsey rummaging around in her head, trying to decipher what made her click. She gave him a sardonic smile, reminiscent of the Carlie he met so long ago. "Wait, I think I can unearth some violin music around here somewhere to go with all this melodrama." She shook her head. "It's the only way to live, Tyler. At least, for me."

Tyler looked down at his clasped hands resting on the tabletop. "I don't think you can do it, Carlie. I think we shared something very special. It may not have been what either of us is used to, but it was still wonderful, almost explosive. And erotic." He slowly raised his gaze, locking it with hers. "Someday, I'd like to see you in that harem costume again. I swear, I get aroused just thinking about it."

Carlie's head snapped back as if he'd slapped her. She tried to compose herself, but vivid, humiliating images were suddenly whirling through her mind. Her voice was a croak as she tried to regain control. "I want you to leave now, Tyler. I mean it."

He came slowly to his feet, his eyes on her pale face. "Before I screwed things up, I think you would have laughed if I suggested that. I'll get you to laugh again, Carlie. I'm not going to let you run away from me like this."

Carlie snorted, recovering slightly with his calm, arrogant statement. "I don't run from anyone. Not anymore. But I'll be up-front with you. If you persist in making sexual innuendos, I won't associate with you. I mean it."

Tyler tried that word out on his tongue. "Associate? Hmm. Sounds suspiciously like a business relationship."

"Or a casual friendship. The choice is yours." It took all Carlie's resolve to maintain eye contact. His eyes appeared almost black with emotion. He looked very tired.

Tyler gave her a gentle, sincere smile. "If the choice was mine, we'd be back in bed right now, everything else forgotten."

Carlie went rigid. "You were wrong, Tyler. I detest your outrageousness. Now please leave."

He scrutinized her. "Talk to me about your divorce."

He was changing subjects as she'd wanted, but she didn't like this new direction at all. She stared at him, annoyed. "Why?"

"I want to understand. And despite all your dictums, I care about you. I'm beginning to realize I always will."

Her heart took a giant leap, but she repressed the feeling his statement incited. She looked at him with indifference, hoping she was masking her reaction. She couldn't be that big a fool. Not again.

"Will you tell me about him, Carlie?" Then Tyler shook his head, his look almost apologetic. "Let me put that another way. I'm not leaving until you do."

Hiding her exasperation was no mean feat. But she did, because to try to deny him would only cause him to dig deeper, she knew. Tyler could be very stubborn on occasion. She shrugged and went to the refrigerator to pull out a soda, without offering him one. It was a deliberate act of rudeness, but to her chagrin, Tyler merely fetched his own, then sat, watching her expectantly.

Carlie crossed her legs and propped one elbow on the table. "I met him in college. He was one of the 'popular ones,' if you know what I mean. I was a nobody. I worked my way through college, and there was very little time for a social life. It took most of my time just keeping my grades up and working enough hours to make ends meet. I was flattered that he paid attention to me. We spent my last year there dating off and on.

"In spite of the time I'd been seeing him, I guess I didn't really know him. Things between us were pretty casual, and he dated other women, too, not just me. But when I graduated, he asked me to marry him, and I agreed. You see, my grandfather had already told me not to come home. And my brother...he never kept in touch. I was pretty much...alone." She smiled, feeling somewhat foolish for pointing out so many details in her defense. It didn't matter what Tyler thought. At least it shouldn't. "I wanted a family. I wanted someone to want me. I thought he did. Pretty dumb reason to get married, isn't it?"

"It's a hell of a lot more reasonable than some I've heard. So go on. When did things start to go wrong?"

"About ten minutes after I said, 'I do.' We'd gotten married at a justice of the peace. It was a package deal, one of those that included a night at a honeymoon cabin. We went there directly."

Tyler was starting to get an idea where the story was going, Carlie surmised, when he began to scowl at her. "You were a virgin?"

She gazed down at her soda can, running her finger around the rim. It was tough to get the words out, remembering how naive she'd been. "Yes. So I didn't understand that it wasn't supposed to hurt so much. His lovemaking was…crude. And rough." Her eyes found his. "It wasn't at all like what you showed me. I hated it. But he said it was normal. I was totally ignorant of men and I wanted to be reasonable, so I accepted his explanations. Only it didn't get any better."

Tyler lunged from his chair, nearly overturning it. He paced across the room, keeping his back to Carlie.

She spoke mildly, as if it didn't matter one way or the other. "If you'd rather not hear this now, I'll understand." The truth was, she couldn't believe she was actually telling him. She hadn't shared intimate details of her past with anyone, not even Brenda. But in a way, it felt good to talk about it, to say things out loud. She drew a deep breath, then looked at Tyler again.

He was watching her closely. After a few seconds, he resumed his seat. "Go on."

His expression was rigid and his eyes blazed despite his obvious effort at control. Carlie couldn't help herself. She felt a genuine smile pull at her lips. "So outraged on my behalf?"

"I'd dearly love to get my hands on him."

He said it so levelly, with so much gravity, Carlie believed him. She was shocked. Without thinking, she patted his arm. "Relax. It wasn't all that bad."

Tyler growled at her. "Don't lie to me, Carlie, ever."

"You mean 'ever again,' don't you?"

"I don't consider your little masquerade at the pool house lying."

Her eyes widened, he seemed so sincere. "You don't?"

"No. You would have told me the whole of it soon enough, if I hadn't jumped the gun and been such a jerk. Now quit dodging the topic and finish your story."

"All right. The first time I really complained, he said it was my fault. He blamed me completely, excusing himself by saying I didn't respond the way I should. He said I should act more like a woman, and dress up a little more. I tried. I always tried to do what he told me to do. It…just didn't work. I couldn't be…ready as quickly as he wanted, and he would get angry, and…it was a fiasco.''

"It wasn't your fault."

He was so vehement, so sure, Carlie felt comforted, despite herself. She nodded. "I know that. Now. But I believed him when he said I was frigid. And I couldn't see making him abstain just because something was wrong with me. I…tolerated him, which only made matters worse. After a while, we grew so distant, I decided it wasn't worth having a home or family or husband if I had to put up with the sex.''

She didn't say another word until Tyler prompted her. "So you asked for a divorce?" He sounded impatient, and she swallowed the hurt that always swamped her whenever she thought of those times.

She shook her head. "I felt so guilty. But then I came home early one day, and I caught him in bed with another woman. *She* didn't appear to be having any difficulty enjoying him. He wasn't overly concerned that I found them, either. In fact, he seemed almost proud. I think he needed to prove to me that it wasn't him. That it was me, and only me, that caused the problem.''

"And you believed him."

It was a statement, and Tyler sounded somehow disappointed with her deduction. She sighed. "What was I supposed to think? I certainly didn't have anything to compare with. But I was more than ready for the divorce. The only problem was, he didn't want it. He was very possessive of me, and he fought the divorce for a long time. He hounded me for so long, I had to move to get away from him. Looking back, I think it would have been impossible for him to accept any part of the blame. It would have been a mark against his masculinity. I can almost understand him, now. But then…I just wanted out.''

''And when you finally got out, you decided you never wanted in again, is that it?''

Carlie tried to draw forth some of the energy she'd been feeling earlier. She needed it now to get her through the next few minutes. It was emotionally debilitating discussing her past, but even more so discussing it with Tyler. She didn't want him to look at her with pity, to feel sorry for the naive, foolish, young woman she'd been.

She angled her head proudly, refusing to turn away from his probing gaze. Surprisingly, she didn't see pity in his eyes. Just determination. ''I'm strong, Tyler. I don't need a man. I'm perfectly capable of taking care of myself. I dress to please myself, and I work at a job I enjoy. What I can't get on my own, I don't really need.''

''I understand what you're saying, Carlie. But everyone needs other people. You can't just close yourself off.''

She stood again. ''I can. I did. I finally got that divorce, finally got my freedom, and I don't intend to ever put myself in that position again. It was difficult and stupid, relying on someone else for my happiness.

But I'm intelligent enough to remember the lesson, even if I occasionally have a memory lapse.''

Tyler stood also, looking very intent. He took a small step toward her. "What we have is more than a memory lapse, sweetheart. And I'm going to prove it to you."

Carlie stiffened. "You're going to go home." Her words were firm and unrelenting.

"Yes. But I'll be back." She relaxed slightly at his easy compliance. Then he continued. "You have to accept that I'm not like him, Carlie."

A rush of soft laughter escaped her. "Don't you think I know that? You're nothing like him. But I'm still myself. And I can't change."

A smile twitched on his lips. "You change so often, I can't keep up with you. I'm only beginning to discover who Carlie McDaniels is."

"Don't be ridiculous. I've told you who I am."

He shook his head. "You don't know yourself, honey, so how could you tell me?" Then he cupped her cheeks in his palms, holding her gently captive. Against her lips, he breathed, "We'll find her together, Carlie. I promise."

His kiss was light and filled with tenderness, a mere brushing of his lips. Then he turned to go. Carlie didn't say a word. What was there to say? He'd find out soon enough she was exactly who she seemed to be. And then he'd leave her alone. She was strong enough to wait him out.

At least, she hoped she was.

TYLER WOULD BE showing up any minute. She'd spent her morning girding herself for the impact of seeing him again. He hadn't canceled on the school project, so she would have to continue working with him. But she was ready.

He sauntered onto the gym floor with his usual air of confidence, and several of the children ran to greet him. Lucy had taken a particular liking to him, and when she threw her arms around him, he tugged on one of her braids.

Tyler took a few minutes to address the other kids, talking with each one, asking about school, joking and teasing and being teased in return.

Carlie felt herself softening. Whoever would have thought Tyler would show so much understanding with children? And it was innate, she was sure, not something that could be summoned forth at will. Children knew if an adult really liked them. And Tyler truly cared about the children.

It hit Carlie then. Tyler, too, had an alter ego, just as she did. In fact, more than one.

There was Tyler the businessman, the astute lawyer who handled cases with flair and savvy. And there was also Tyler, the ladies' man, with a reputation well known by the female population. In fact, Carlie now realized that reputation had been encouraged more by the ladies than by Tyler himself. The things he valued in a woman, as far as she could tell, were intelligence and laughter, not her measurements and unfailing willingness.

And he was also a very perceptive man, considerate and indulgent, with a gentleness toward all things weaker or smaller. That was why he dealt so well with children.

Tyler looked up and caught her scrutinizing him. He strolled over, dribbling the ball. With a slight smile, he stopped directly in front of her. "I know what I'm thinking. Are your thoughts the same?"

Carlie shrugged, stealing the ball away from him. "I was thinking you should get married and have children of your own. You're very good with them." She glanced at him, saw his shock and smiled with satisfaction. "That's all."

"That's all! Hey, wait a minute."

He was too late. She blew the whistle and the children lined up. For the next two hours, Carlie made certain she kept her distance from Tyler, always making sure she had at least one of the kids close to her. It was an ingenious plan—and it was obviously frustrating Tyler. He scowled at her throughout the last fifteen minutes of the practice.

Tyler walked two of the children out to their parents' cars, talking with the moms and dads a few minutes before coming back to the gym. She wasn't going to bother asking him what the discussions were about this time. He'd never confided in her last time. When he noticed she was still in the gym, he headed toward her, falling into step beside her as she started for the locker room.

"I want to talk to you, Carlie."

"Can't right now. I'm running late as it is." That was an easy truth to give, though Tyler didn't accept it.

"Late for what, dammit?"

She didn't look at him. "Don't curse at me, Tyler."

"Then stop avoiding me!"

"In other words, if I don't, you're going to continue to blast me with your foul language?"

He grabbed her arm, halting her. "Talk to me. Please."

It unnerved her, seeing him so abjectly sincere. "I'm sorry. Really. But I'm starting some night courses and I'm running late. I should have left ten minutes ago."

He searched her face. "What time will you get home?"

"Late."

"Too late to see me?"

"There's no reason for me to see you. I told you that."

"And I didn't accept it. I guess we're at an impasse."

"*We* aren't anywhere. I'm late and you should be getting home. Goodbye."

"No. I'm not leaving until you tell me what you meant by that crack about children."

"It wasn't a crack." She glanced at her watch, a deliberate show of impatience. "You'd make an excellent father. You should find yourself a woman like

Bren, and settle down. It would relieve the boredom you're forever complaining about.''

''I haven't complained about being bored since I met you. And I don't want a woman like Bren. I want a woman like you.''

It took great willpower not to react to that statement. Her stomach had lurched and her pulse had skipped a beat. But he was only being Tyler, flirting and teasing. She couldn't take him seriously. ''You want a woman who doesn't want you back? I don't know, Tyler. That might be kind of hard. Didn't you tell me that all the women want you?''

''No. I don't recall saying that. But I know you do, Carlie. Shall I prove it?''

Carlie flushed, silently cursing him for challenging her, especially when she knew she couldn't win. ''I can't deny I enjoyed sex with you, Tyler. That isn't what I meant, and you know it. Why don't you take up a hobby? Collect stamps or something so you can entertain yourself without annoying me.''

''I wasn't trying to annoy you! I'm trying to talk to you. I want you to forgive me, I want—''

''You're forgiven.''

''That was a little precipitous, wasn't it?'' He eyed her suspiciously. ''What are you forgiving me for?''

''I have no idea. You're the one who wanted forgiveness.'' She raised her eyebrows politely. ''You tell me.''

He took a deep breath. ''I'm sorry for yelling at

you, for jumping to conclusions and saying hateful, uncalled-for things.''

"They were called for. And you were justified." She looked down at her clasped hands and made the necessary effort to relax. "Will you forgive me, also? For deceiving you and using you and causing you embarrassment?''

"Carlie." He pulled her against his chest, despite her stiff, unyielding posture. "There's nothing to forgive, honey. I understand why you didn't tell me."

Carlie slowly stepped away, then started toward the gym door. "It's in the past, Tyler," she called over her shoulder. "Forget about it. We're both obviously very sorry and determined not to make the same mistakes again. That's good enough for me. Now, I have to go. I'll see you Wednesday."

"Carlie…"

She didn't stop, didn't turn to him, didn't slow her pace at all. But she could feel his eyes boring into her and just before the heavy back door swung shut behind her, she heard a bang that sounded suspiciously like a fist hitting a locker.

"YOU'RE GOING to have to help out here, Bren!" Tyler said as he paced the kitchen, his hands shoved deep into his pockets. Carlie was being entirely unreasonable. She wouldn't see him beyond practices and wouldn't take the time to talk to him when it wasn't absolutely necessary. He'd about run out of ideas. And he was getting desperate.

Brenda and Jason stared at him as he paced. Brenda shook her head. "Carlie would never forgive me if I got in the middle of this."

"Just try talking to her for me. She'll listen to you."

"Not a chance. Carlie won't listen to anything I have to say. Not with things so fouled up."

Tyler glowered at her. "Things are not fouled up! Carlie and I being together is not a mistake."

"Hah! Carlie's more determined than ever to stay away from men. She won't even go out with that old school-board guy, and he's certainly no threat."

Tyler halted, then looked at Brenda. "What are you talking about?"

"There's some old stuffed shirt on the school board—"

"He's only thirty-six, Bren," Jason interrupted.

"Well, he seems old, he's so uppity." She gave her attention back to Tyler. "Anyway, she's gone out with him a couple of times. Mostly to talk over school stuff, or so he says. Personally, I think he's trying to ingratiate himself. Now he wants her to help him head up a new fund-raiser at the school. Carlie said she needs to get together with him this weekend to discuss the particulars."

"Where?"

Jason stood. "Now, Tyler…"

He ignored his brother. The thought of Carlie with another man made him see red. He repeated, "Where?"

Jason cleared his throat to hide his smile. "At her house, I believe."

"The time?"

Jason glanced at Brenda, who was doing her best to look innocent. "I think she said around noon, but I can't be sure," she said.

Tyler turned on his heel and headed out, not bothering to say goodbye. He didn't see the smug grin on his sister-in-law's face.

Jason pursed his lips. "I thought you weren't going to interfere."

"Of course I wouldn't!" Brenda gasped. "I gave Carlie my word."

"Then what was this little scene you just enacted?"

"A slip of the tongue?"

"Clever. Just what I love in a wife!"

ON HIS DRIVE HOME, Tyler formulated his plan. It was Friday evening—he'd gone to his brother's house, frustrated after another unsatisfying attempt to gain Carlie's attention during the practice. She was getting very good at ignoring him. And after practice, she had to hurry off for her classes. He had no doubt they'd been planned just to thwart him. It annoyed the hell out of him.

But he could be just as devious as Carlie. Since he had no intention of giving up on Carlie, he had to overcome her obstacles.

And he had a secret weapon—his own project he'd

been working on for some time. He'd planned to surprise Carlie with it. Now it would prove invaluable. But first he needed to get her alone for a bit. He hadn't missed her response the day he'd held her only briefly. But he had been stymied by the fact that she seemed to find it so easy to walk away. She hadn't even looked back as he'd willed her to do. Stubborn wench.

At least she was never boring. He remembered the way she had held him so tight when he'd entered her, how she told him she cared. Not a little, but a lot. He had to believe that. She still cared, and she would get over her anger. He'd help her. Hell, he'd insist upon it.

TYLER PLANNED his arrival perfectly, even to the point of driving around the block twice, waiting for the strange car to show up in front of Carlie's house. He parked and got out, whistling, a sheath of papers in his hand.

He knocked on the door, then waited, doing his best to hide his smile. Carlie answered, dressed in her usual distasteful clothes. This time, it was a long skirt, hanging below her knees. Her slim calves and ankles were hidden by boots, the skirt topped by a large sweater which had no waist or any other defining lines. It was ugly as sin.

"You look beautiful today, Carlie." He spoke loudly enough for her company to hear. She glared at him, but he knew he had her. She was forced to be polite when a member of the school board was in earshot.

"Hello, Tyler. What brings you here today?"

He quickly shouldered his way inside before she could tell him she was busy. "I have some things to discuss with you about your project."

"The team?"

"That's right. I had some ideas to go over with you."

A man entered, dressed in a business suit and looking every bit as stuffy as Brenda had claimed he was. He didn't so much as glance at Tyler. "Is something wrong, Carlie?"

She looked harassed. "Ah, no." Then she grudgingly made the introductions. "Tyler, this is Brad Shaw. Brad, meet Tyler Ramsey, the man I told you about. He's proving to be a big help with the after-school basketball program."

The men shook hands. Tyler smiled with devious innocence. "I'm sorry, Carlie. I didn't realize you had a date tonight."

She didn't disappoint him with her reaction. He grinned as she turned beet red. Tyler had the feeling it was mostly due to anger. "Brad is a member of the school board. We were going to discuss a new fund-raiser."

"Is that right? Maybe I could help. I'm always willing to help support the schools."

It was obvious he'd gotten Brad's interest. He may have wanted to be alone with Carlie, but apparently he also wanted financial aid. He opted for the money. "Won't you join us, Mr. Ramsey?"

He grinned. "Tyler, please. I'd be delighted." Then he turned to Carlie. "But I do need to discuss a few things with you, also."

"Of course. We have the afternoon free." Brad was being very charming. "Isn't that right, Carlie?"

With a strained, slightly malicious smile, Carlie nodded. "Certainly. Tyler knows how interested I am in doing what I can for the school."

Tyler watched her, satisfied. He made certain she was aware of his intent in visiting. He wasn't planning to be devious—yet. That would come later. Maybe after he'd lulled her with false confidence.

"Would anyone like anything to drink?" Carlie headed for the kitchen. Tyler watched her, knowing she was only using the excuse to fume in private. He gave her thirty seconds, then left Brad looking around an empty living room so he could "give Carlie some help."

She had her back to him, setting glasses on the counter and filling them with iced tea. Silently, he moved up behind her, then bent and kissed her exposed neck.

Carlie jerked, nearly knocking over one of the glasses. Tyler caught it, set it back on the counter, then met her outraged gaze. "I've missed you so much, sweetheart."

"Don't you *ever* do that—"

Tyler quickly covered her mouth with his own. Her

startled gasp was held suspended somewhere between them.

Her lips were soft and moist, and she tasted delicious. Using all his experience, he seduced her mouth, nibbling at her soft lips, licking gently, reclaiming her, urging her closer.

"Carlie." He forgot his purpose. It seemed so long since he'd kissed her. Without really intending to, his hand came up to cup her breast.

Instinct alone saved him. Ducking and catching her open palm just inches from his cheek, Tyler chided her. "Sweetheart, if you hit me, how will you explain it to your date?"

Through set teeth, she growled, "He's not my date, you ass!"

"Shh. Do you want him to know what we're doing?"

"I'm not doing anything! You're the one…!"

He watched with interest as her chest heaved angrily. Then he smiled. "You don't have to *do* anything. I read the morning paper and I want you. My secretary, who must be going on eighty, brings me coffee and I want you. I see you standing at the counter pouring tea and I positively throb."

Carlie closed her eyes in exasperation. "What are you doing here, Tyler?"

"I had to see you."

She turned away, picking up the tray. "Now you've seen me. Will you please go home?"

"And leave you here alone with Casanova? No way."

Carlie started out of the kitchen. Tyler took the tray from her. "He's only an associate," she said.

Tyler sent her a doubtful look. "With higher aspirations."

She snorted.

The sound was beautiful to his ears, so much like his old Carlie. He grinned at her, and to his besotted happiness, she actually grinned back. Then she shook her head and whispered for him to behave. He made no promises.

It quickly became a business meeting, just as Carlie had said. And surprisingly, Tyler enjoyed himself. He offered a lot of helpful input concerning the fundraiser, legal advice Carlie or Brad wouldn't have thought of, and some suggestions of his own which proved very sound.

Brad was clearly impressed with Tyler, and before they called it quits, he was behaving as if they were old friends. "Could I call on you at your office sometime to discuss any problems that might arise?"

Tyler felt smug, but he hid it behind a facade of graciousness. "Of course. Just tell me secretary I said it was fine. She's a real stickler about keeping out people without appointments."

Brad shook his hand. "I appreciate that. Well, I better be off. I'm sorry I can't stay and help with your project, but I'm running a little late."

"Think nothing of it." Tyler simply wanted him gone. "Carlie and I can muddle through."

"If you're sure, then?"

Carlie stood abruptly and went to the door, obviously tired of playing cat and mouse. "Thank you for coming by, Brad. Let me know if there's anything else I can do to help."

She stood at the door, waiting until Brad had gotten into his car and driven away before closing it and facing Tyler.

He saw immediately that she was incensed. He forestalled her tirade by tossing out his own stack of papers. "I want to start a scholarship fund at your school."

Her mouth, already open to blast him, snapped shut.

"You could use it as you see fit. To pay for sports equipment, to help with school fees or lunches, or even to start special classes. Whatever. I've been giving this some thought for a while now." He gave her a slightly sheepish look. "After our practices, I offered to help out a few of the parents who were having difficulties. It's a tough thing, trying to give assistance without making it look like charity. I sent papers to be typed up at one house, and then gave some plumbing business from our offices to another. But it wasn't enough. I didn't want to offend anyone, so I came up with the idea of a scholarship.

"Jason has agreed to pitch in, too, and I think some of the other businesses in the area will follow suit. It would be great publicity for their services. 'Caring for the community' and all that.'' He drew to a halt. ''What do you think?''

Her expression blank, Carlie walked to the table where Tyler had tossed the documents. She picked up the top sheet and scanned it. She looked staggered by the amount of his donation.

Raising her eyes to his, she whispered, ''You're serious?''

''Of course. I have a contract ready. I hope you don't mind, but I left the distribution of my donation in your capable hands. As others come in, you could put them before a board of advisers if you want. But you already know the kids and their families so well, what they need and so forth, I thought you'd be perfect for the job.''

Carlie was speechless. She stared at him.

''I think the contributing businesses would also agree to hire a few of the parents on a part-time basis. I know I always need papers transcribed and letters sent out. What do you—'' He stopped mid-sentence. ''Carlie? Is everything all right?''

She sat on the edge of the couch, his papers clutched in her hand, looking dumbfounded. ''You're amazing, Tyler.''

He actually felt himself blush. Gruffly, he said, ''I'm just trying to help out. I have the money.'' He shrugged, dismissing her praise. ''I wanted to surprise you.''

Carlie laid her hand over his. ''Thank you, Tyler.

This means so much. I can already think of three families who will really benefit from this.''

He grinned in satisfaction, retaining his hold on her hand. ''There you go! Use it as you see fit. I'll see what I can do about getting some of the other businesses in on it. But in the meantime, if you need more money, let me know.''

That did it. She looked near tears, overwhelmed with his generosity and goodness of spirit. And he felt not a single moment's guilt.

After all, he reasoned, he had donated the money. If the timing of his surprise seemed just a bit suspicious, it didn't matter. He needed all the help he could get.

Seeing her so obviously softened toward him, Tyler eased her into his arms. ''You're not going to cry, are you? I can't abide watery women.''

Pulling away as far as his arms would allow, Carlie gazed at him with a small smile. ''I promise not to cry.'' But no sooner had she made that promise than she broke it, choking on a low sob.

Tyler shook his head. ''So you really think I'm amazing?''

''I do.''

The words were whispered with such sincerity, Tyler caught his breath. And then he smiled. ''Excellent.'' His thoughts slowed to concentrate on one fact: he was with Carlie, and she still cared. But as he leaned toward her, she protested.

''Ah, Tyler, I didn't mean...''

"Shh. Kiss me again, Carlie."

"You kissed me! I didn't…"

"Don't argue semantics. I can think of better things to do." His tone was deep and suggestive as his arms slowly tightened around her.

With slightly narrowed eyes and a dangerously soft voice, she inquired, "Are you suggesting we have sex?"

"I, ah, well, I suppose the thought had entered my mind." About a million times in the past hour, he silently added. But Carlie was suddenly looking so furious, he kept that little tidbit to himself.

"Because you donated money to needy children," she clarified, "you think I should sleep with you? That's despicable! How could you propose such a thing?"

Anger and frustration rushed through him, and he jumped to his feet. "All right, dammit! You don't like that proposition? Well, here's another one." He sucked in a deep breath. "Marry me."

CHAPTER ELEVEN

CARLIE STARED at Tyler blankly. "Don't you think humor is a little misplaced at this point?"

"I…" He shut his mouth. Truth be told, he'd surprised himself as much as he had Carlie with that sudden command. *Marry me.* Damn, but it did seem the right thing to say at the right time.

He grinned. "I'm not joking. I want to marry you."

She eyed him warily. "Why?"

He gave her a mock frown of disapproval over her rude questioning. "You don't seem to know any more about accepting proposals than you did about dates. Let me instruct you. This is the part where you fall into my arms, tearfully showing your gratitude and devotion, and shout a resounding, 'Yes!' You got all that?"

"Provided, of course, the answer would be yes?"

Tyler felt a moment's misgiving. "Don't toy with me, Carlie. I've never proposed to anyone in my life. I could have a major attack of insecurity here, if you're not careful." He hoped his teasing tone belied the truth behind his words. He felt almost sick with dread.

Carlie chewed her bottom lip and her eyes were dark with shadows. "Tyler, I don't want to get married. It's not just you. I don't want to marry anyone. Ever. I followed that route once, and as you know, it didn't go all that well."

Tyler sat beside her and took her hands in his. He needed to touch her, to make her understand. "It wouldn't be that way with me, Carlie. I'm not like him."

She went on, all brisk and businesslike. "Of course you're not. I told you, you're amazing. Kind and compassionate, and too attractive to be turned loose on polite society. But I value my independence. I don't intend to give it up."

It took him a minute to recover from her compliments. He was still beaming when the rest of what she'd said sank in. "I'm not asking you to give up anything."

She gave him a sardonic look. "Be honest, Tyler. Don't you think you'd start hounding me right away over how I dress? Or how I wear my hair?"

"Well," he hedged. She had a point. But a poor one. "You can't go on hiding the rest of your life, Carlie. You're a beautiful woman. That's something to be proud of. It's a part of you. And once we're married, there won't be any reason to look so shabby. I wouldn't let other men ogle you."

She tossed up her hands in exasperation. "There, you see? Not only are you changing me, but you'll be playing barbarian protector as well. I don't need a protector, Tyler.''

"Not dressed like that you won't.''

Carlie sighed, ignoring his provocation. "Please try to understand.''

"I understand. You said you cared for me, but it wasn't exactly the truth.'' He stood, towering over her. He felt dejected, rejected and unbearably weary. He tweaked her chin, giving her a crooked smile. "You know something, honey? You're just a bit selfish.''

Carlie raised an eyebrow at the criticism, but he continued.

"I've bent over backward, made all the concessions I can make, humiliated myself several times now trying to win you over. But you have a hard heart. I don't hold that against you. Considering your past, I suppose it's even expected. But damned if I know what else to do.

"It hurts, Carlie. It hurts to care so much about someone, and then have them turn you away again and again. I've been closer to you than I have to any other soul on earth, Jason included. And I was determined not to give up on you.''

Carlie was staring down at her lap, and Tyler couldn't see her face. He decided it was just as well. He was spilling his guts, laying his heart on the table, and if she looked at him with pity, he might very well lose it. His tone was indifferent now, his expression impassive. "I can't do it anymore. You must be stronger than I am, because I can't take the rejections again. If you want to go on living in a cocoon, there's no way I can stop you. But I won't hang around indefinitely waiting for you to emerge, either.''

She remained silent, and Tyler sighed in disgust. She wasn't making it any easier for him. ''I won't be at the practice on Monday. I'll get Jason to fill in until you can find someone more permanent. Explain to the kids for me, if you will. And if you need any more money, let me know. You can leave a message with my secretary.'' He walked to the door and waited, but she didn't move. He nearly choked on his rage and frustration. Damn her, she had pulled him in, made him love her and now she didn't care.

He walked out, closing the door softly behind him.

CARLIE WAITED on Monday, her stomach roiling, her head aching, her eyes burning. And true to his word, Tyler didn't come. She felt awful, even though she hadn't wanted to marry him, *couldn't* marry him. The idea was absurd.

So why had her heart threatened to burst when he'd proposed? And when he'd left, after such a touching speech, she'd felt like she was coming apart.

Oh God, she hurt.

Jason entered, dressed in an old college sweatshirt and gym shorts that showed his hairy legs. He spared her a glance, then picked up a ball and began bouncing it. Carlie approached him.

''Hello, Jason.''

He inclined his head. "Carlie."

"I appreciate your filling in like this. On such short notice, I mean."

He looked at her. "Tyler needed me. I love him. He's my brother."

"I…I know." She hesitated, swallowing hard. Jason's mood was apparently not conducive to small talk. But she needed to know. "How is Tyler?"

Very casually, still bouncing the ball, Jason said, "Miserable. Thanks for asking."

Carlie flinched at his tone. "Jason, I never meant to—"

"Of course, you didn't. In your book, all men are jerks, right? Tyler certainly can't be any different."

She shook her head, then started to turn away. Jason held the ball. "Carlie? I'm sorry. It's not my place to…"

She didn't look at him. "It's okay, Jason. I understand."

"No. I don't think you do. But it's my opinion you never will, so I'm glad you broke things off with Tyler now, before he got even more involved. I'm the only person he's ever had care for him. His life hasn't exactly encouraged him to trust women. So when he does marry, I damned well want it to be to a woman who's capable of loving him. He deserves that much."

She was crushed by the hard words, but acknowledged the truth in them. Tyler did deserve the best. If only…

Oh, God. She really had done it this time. No matter how deep she buried the past, it always seemed to come back and torment her.

Or was she only tormenting herself?

AFTER TWO WEEKS had passed, Carlie knew it was time to face facts. She loved Tyler and always would. She missed him terribly, and with each day that went by, the feeling grew worse. When she was with him, she felt alive. Without him, she felt dull and drained.

She needed him, and even though she'd sworn never to need anyone again, she felt comforted by the admission. She no longer had to deny herself or her emotions. It wasn't a bad thing to need Tyler. He wouldn't take advantage of her feelings, wouldn't try to dominate her or weaken her to suit his own needs. She believed that. She trusted him.

But she had hurt him badly, and he might not forgive her.

Carlie knew she was too much the coward to call Tyler outright. She needed a reason for calling, and when more donations to the scholarship fund came in from various businesses, she decided that excuse would work well enough. She'd start out by thanking him, and work into telling him she loved him madly.

It was a bold plan, she thought, and would have worked, except that Tyler didn't answer the phone. She got a message saying he was out of the office for some time and all calls could be forwarded to Jason.

When she tried him at home, his answering machine picked up. Concerned, she called Brenda.

What she discovered wasn't encouraging.

Tyler planned to take an extended vacation to Chicago, where he was considering joining a new firm. Jason, of course, was livid and blaming Carlie. Brenda was apologetic, but very upset by it all.

Carlie had a hard time breathing. She knew exactly what was happening. She'd done the same after her divorce. She'd tried to leave the pain behind.

She could have told Tyler it didn't work. Because right now, the pain was unbearable. Everything had gone wrong, and it was all her own fault. She was a miserable coward, and it was time she stopped hiding, just as Tyler had suggested.

She had to do something, and she had to do it now.

IT WAS JASON who answered the door. Just the fact that Carlie was knocking at the front entrance, rather than entering through the kitchen, as usual, was indicative of her uneasiness. She had no idea if she'd be welcome, given the present situation. But Jason was polite. Painfully so.

"Hello, Carlie. Come in."

"Thanks. Ah, Tyler isn't here, is he?"

Jason eyed her. "No. He's been avoiding us as much as you have."

Carlie flushed, but she refused to back down. "I'm sorry about that." She came in and Jason shut the door behind her. With her hands in her pockets, she looked around the room. "Is Bren around?"

"I'll get her for you. Make yourself at home."

It felt exceedingly odd for Jason to say such a thing. It had never been necessary before.

Brenda flew into the room, her eyes alight with expectation. "Carlie! I'm so glad to see you!"

Carlie ducked out of reach. "No hugging, Bren. I'm dangerously close to coming unglued here, and any excess of kind consideration will definitely put me over the edge."

Brenda blinked. "What are you talking about?"

Carlie had been calm enough until that moment. The simple truth was, she still suffered a few qualms over her own appeal. She was unbelievably apprehensive about confronting Tyler, no matter how she tried to deny it. Her lips started to quiver. She felt like a fool, but she couldn't stop it. She clasped her hands, opened her mouth to calmly and intelligently explain, then broke into tears. "I love him!"

Brenda smiled. "Oh, Carlie."

Despite Carlie's objections, Brenda pulled her into a fierce hug. "I think that's wonderful."

"I don't know, Bren." She sniffed, then swiped the tears from her cheeks. "I hurt him. I've never hurt anyone in my life. I can't stand it."

"Have you told him?"

Carlie shook her head. "I can't just go up to him and say, 'Well, guess what? I do love you, after all.' I've been so terrible."

"No, you haven't. And Tyler will understand."

Carlie raised her chin. Enough was enough. She'd had her little show of vulnerability. "I sincerely hope you're right. Because I do love him. In fact, I'm crazy about him. But he's never actually said he loved me. He asked me to marry him, and he makes no bones about wanting me...that way. But he's never actually mentioned the word *love*."

Jason stepped into the room. "Gossiping about my brother again?"

Brenda turned and nearly snapped his head off. "We weren't gossiping! I was going to convince Carlie that Tyler loves her."

Jason rolled his eyes. "Of course he does. Why do you think he's been so impossible lately?"

"Don't tell me," Brenda demanded. "Tell Carlie."

Jason walked over to Carlie. "Tyler loves you. Now, what are you going to do about it?"

Carlie bit her bottom lip. Tyler had tried to tell her the depth of his feelings right before he left her house the last time. But she hadn't responded. At all. It made her ache to imagine how he must have felt. How could she tell him how scared she had been, that she'd been petrified at the idea of accepting too much happiness because it left her vulnerable?

Just as vulnerable as he must have felt when she'd failed to accept his proposal.

Suddenly, she realized what she had to do. "I have to make it up to him. I need to show him how much I care."

"Just tell him," Jason suggested.

But Carlie shook her head. "I have a plan. But I'll need your help."

"Oh, no." Jason put a hand to his head, looking ready to expire. "You're starting to sound just like my wife."

Brenda laughed. "Go ahead, Carlie, I'm listening. You know I dearly love a good plan."

Jason sat, and the women looked at him pointedly. "I'm not budging. You two are plotting something against my poor brother, and I need to be here to look after his interests."

"Well, all right." Carlie leaned forward, and Jason and Brenda followed suit. "Here's want I want to do."

TYLER STARED at Jason, dressed in an elegant suit and obviously preparing to leave the house. "I thought you wanted me to help you with some work around here today."

Jason smacked his palm to his forehead theatrically. "Oh, boy. I forgot, Tyler. Bren made plans for us to go out tonight. Do you mind?"

"Well, no." Actually, Tyler had been looking forward to working with his brother. He needed some physical labor to drain him, to weary his mind enough to drive out thoughts of other things. He only hoped his disappointment didn't show.

Shoving his hands into his jeans pockets, Tyler stepped around Jason. He didn't want to return to his apartment. The mere thought was enough to make him shudder. Lately, all he could do was think of Carlie. Oh, how the mighty did fall. Flat on their faces.

And it still hurt, dammit.

Moving away was a desperate decision. He couldn't be so close to Carlie, knowing she was only minutes away, and constantly be reminded of how he had failed, both her and himself. He needed to get on with his life, but no one had ever told him how to do that.

Jason interrupted his thoughts, slapping him on the shoulder. "I have a favor to ask. If you don't have anything else pressing to do, could you go ahead and get started on a few things for me? You know how I'm already rushed for time, especially now that I've started helping with the after-school basketball program."

Tyler winced. "How are they? The kids, I mean. Little Lucy is doing all right?"

"They're all the same." Jason's answer was deliberately vague. "A few of the parents asked me to extend their thanks for your help. It was great of you to figure out a way for them to earn extra money. I hadn't realized you were doing so much."

Tyler frowned, uncomfortable with the praise, but Jason didn't give him time to argue. "I made a list of a few jobs that had to be done."

Tyler forced a smile. "I wouldn't mind helping out. I don't have anything else to do today, anyway."

Jason almost grinned. "You're sure? I'd really appreciate it."

"No problem. What's first on the list?"

Jason produced a folded piece of paper and stuck it into the front breast pocket of Tyler's flannel shirt. "I gotta run. Do me a favor first, though, will you? Carlie called the other day and said she left something in the pool house. I don't remember what. Go down and check it out, will you? Look around and see if you find anything."

Tyler didn't move a single muscle. "She's not stopping by here, is she?" He knew he sounded panicked, but to be alone with Carlie would nearly kill him. He couldn't trust himself not to act like an ass again.

Jason waved away his concern. "You don't have to worry about her dropping in." He turned away quickly. "I really do appreciate this, Tyler. Bren and I won't be home till late, so help yourself to anything you need, and..." Jason grinned suddenly. "Relax, will you? Things are never as bad as they seem."

Tyler had no answer for that. Things seemed pretty damned bad to him.

Despite himself, he was anxious to see what Carlie had left in the pool house. Her mask? Some small part of that alluring harem costume? Maybe he'd find it and keep it. As a memento. What could she say? Not a thing.

He waited till he heard Jason's car drive away, then went out the back, heading for the pool house. It seemed so achingly familiar, each step he took on the flagstone walk brought the memories closer. But instead of soft party lights to guide his way, the sun was shining brightly. The breeze chilled him, and he hunkered his shoulders forward, his head down.

The pool house door was slightly ajar, but Tyler paid no attention to that small detail. He was too overcome with memories. Odd, but knowing now that it had been Carlie, not another woman, only enhanced the memory, made it more erotic and more tantalizing.

Heat washed over him in waves as he closed the door behind him, but it wasn't from the warmth of the room. Just looking around caused his body to react, and when he spotted the couch, his thighs clenched and his stomach tightened.

"Tyler?"

He froze. He couldn't possibly be dreaming, not so vividly, not with such stark reality. He turned slowly, and felt his breath catch in his throat.

She was almost exactly as he remembered, hovering in the corner, her back to the wall. But there was no wig, and somehow he knew the mask was for effect, not concealment.

Tyler stared, his eyes so hot he could barely see. There were no shadows today. Each and every lamp had been turned on. Carlie's hair, appearing more blond than brown in the bright light, hung loose about her shoulders. It was in gentle waves, sexy and shimmering and tempting him to touch it. Her hazel eyes, brightly lit with anticipation and anxiety, stared at him, direct and unblinking.

Very slowly, not daring to breathe, he walked toward her. Reaching out, his fingers touched the mask. "May I remove it?"

Her smile quavered, dimpling her cheeks, but then vanished quickly. It was a nervous reaction, he knew, and his love for her doubled.

"If you like." Carlie held his eyes, her breathing suspended, her heart pounding erratically. She loved him so much. "Whatever you like, Tyler."

"I like you." He slipped the mask from her face, gently laying it aside. Cupping her cheeks, he smiled at her. "Do you realize how rare and special that is, Carlie? I like everything about you. I like being with you, I like looking at you, I like talking with you."

He kissed her lightly, fleetingly, on her trembling lips. "I'll never grow bored of you or try to change you."

Carlie rubbed her cheek against his palm. "Except my clothes?"

It was an attempt at humor, but Tyler didn't laugh. "You can wear any damned thing you like. I don't care."

Her eyes welled with tears, and she had to fight to keep from pressing herself against him. But they had to talk. She had to make him understand. Drawing a deep breath, she looked up at him. "I want to make you happy, Tyler. I...I love you."

He closed his eyes, then hugged her tight. "I love you, too, Carlie. So damned much."

Her smile was tremulous. "It's a little scary, isn't it?"

"No!" He held her away from him, his expression fierce. "Losing you is scary. Loving you is easy, and unbelievably exciting." Then he smiled, his hand dropping to finger the edge of her skimpy bodice. "Much like this costume of yours."

Very seriously, without any hesitation, Carlie whispered, "I want to be whatever you want me to be."

"I want you to be yourself." He pressed his face into her shoulder, inhaling her soft, feminine scent. "You're a beautiful woman, Carlie. And so special. Just be yourself for me, honey. Stop hiding."

She almost laughed out loud, she felt so relieved. Teasing Tyler with a smile, she asked, "Did Jason tell you what I lost here?"

He looked struck, having all but forgotten about his brother. He grinned. "No. What did you lose?"

She ducked her head. "I lost my heart."

"No." He tipped her chin up. "It's not lost. I have it, and I'm not giving it back."

Carlie started to say something more, but Tyler touched his fingers to her lips. "Did you wear this costume only to torment me, or do you plan on making my fantasies come true?"

"A little of both." She almost made it out of reach before Tyler grabbed her and held her close.

A long kiss followed, and Carlie was finally able

to hug herself to him. It felt so right, so perfect. Paper rattled when she leaned into his chest, and Tyler pulled away. With a suspicious look, he tugged out the note Jason had given him. Keeping Carlie close, he read the message aloud. "Women have fantasies, too, or so Bren insists. There's a large paper bag behind the couch. Have fun, kids."

Carlie laughed, then squirmed from his grasp to retrieve the bag. She looked inside, then grinning, she tossed the bag to Tyler. "Here you go."

He caught it automatically. "What is it?"

"Your pirate costume." She bobbed her eyebrows comically. "Remind me to thank your brother."

Tyler grinned wickedly as he began unbuttoning his shirt. "I'm not a man you can trifle with, sweetheart. If you want to play games, you're going to have to promise to marry me."

Carlie watched him remove his shirt, her gaze rapt. "I'll marry you, I'll choose a whole new wardrobe, I'll even get rid of my glasses. But you have to promise me something, too."

He unsnapped his jeans, then slowly shoved them down his hips. "What's that?"

"You can never stop being outrageous."

He laughed, sounding smug. "Told you you'd like it."

Carlie walked into his arms, feeling loved and in love. Happy. She didn't stop until Tyler was holding her close again. "Indeed I do, Tyler. Indeed I do."

ONE WICKED WEEKEND

Julie Elizabeth Leto

CHAPTER ONE

"If I was that sugar, I could die a happy man."

Lauren LaCroix ignored the male voice and continued to dust powdered sugar off her breast. Women from New York City did *not* overreact to innuendo, particularly the expert come-ons of men like Luc Dupre.

Unfortunately, she was no longer in New York City. She was back home in New Orleans, about to face the man who'd shattered her heart eight years ago and sent her running to lick her wounds. Well, she'd done more than that, hadn't she? She'd become a whole new woman—one Luc wouldn't be able to resist.

Lauren leveled her steeliest stare into Luc's crystal-blue gaze. Her libido jolted her, but she managed to tamp down the dueling urges to smack him or kiss him. She was going to make Luc one happy man, all right—just before she walked away.

"Gosh, Luc. If you were this sugar—" she slapped the last of the white stuff off her hands "—could I brush you off this easily?"

Luc's grin spread across his lips like sunrise on the

Mississippi—slow and easy. But his eyebrows, dark slashes that matched his long, jet hair, shot up at her retort. Lauren indulged a satisfied smile. She'd bet her entire set of Gucci luggage that he hadn't expected her to defend herself against his legendary charm. Why would he? She'd once been his willing, pliable plaything—fantasizing about marriage and home and hearth. Then he'd dumped her.

She'd been so young and helplessly in love. Luc had done her a favor by breaking her heart. If she'd stayed with him in New Orleans, she never would have found her backbone or the courage to discover the woman she really was—a woman of strength, intelligence and fire. She no longer needed a man to tell her what she wanted. She could tell him herself. Or better yet, she could show him.

Metal grated on concrete as Luc pulled out a chair and joined her, uninvited. The patio at Café du Monde was surprisingly empty for a Friday morning, and Lauren had hoped to grab a quick bite before reacquainting herself with the city, alone, for now. She had only the weekend to put together a proposal that would knock the socks off her editor. In line for a coveted promotion, Lauren knew her "Sexy City Nights" feature could give her the edge over the other candidates. But she'd been away from New Orleans so long. While finding Luc and enticing him to be her very personal tour guide had been on her agenda, she'd been unprepared for him to find her first.

Sometimes, Fate worked mysteriously, but Lauren had learned not to argue with the inevitable. Before she could ask him how he knew she was in town, he snagged a beignet from the three on her plate, took a bite, then motioned to a nearby waiter to bring him a café au lait.

"Life should be so sweet, Ren," Luc said with a drawl. "What brings you back home?"

"Business…mainly."

He nodded and munched, his expression casual, as if he knew all about her new life and her new attitude and didn't need the details. She shook her head, wondering if Luc had cornered the market on arrogance. He had no way of knowing that in the past eight years she'd finished college, worked hard, and could soon be named the features editor of a top women's magazine. She mingled with celebrities. Oversaw seven-figure budgets. Called the industry's top supermodels or fashion designers just to chat or "do lunch." She'd had no contact with him at all except for the card he'd forwarded through her Aunt Endora for her recent thirtieth birthday.

The sentiment had been simple—"Hope you've found all you've ever wanted. Luc"—but the timing piqued her curiosity, and eventually lured her home.

Still, she kept her accomplishments to herself. Maybe Endora had told him. Maybe he wouldn't be impressed. As the owner of the hottest nightclub in New Orleans, the infamous Club Carnal, he knew all the same stars and supermodels. And with his family's money, he could drop seven figures in one night playing blackjack at Harrah's and not miss a beat.

"Have you called on your aunt yet?" Luc asked.

"She knows I'm here."

Luc's lazy smile widened. The waiter brought his coffee and a short glass of ice water to undo the heat of an increasingly warm morning.

"Of course she knows you're here, *chère*. Question was, did you call her?"

"My aunt's no more psychic than you are humble."

He shook his head. "You've been away too long, Ren. There's a strange magic that works in this part of the world. This is the perfect example. I never thought I'd see you back here in a million years, but here you are, looking all glamorous. Sophisticated."

Lauren swallowed and pressed her lips firmly together, aware of the smoldering look in Luc's aquamarine gaze, of her instinctive, sensual response to his Southern speech, undisguised compliments, and intimate endearments. *Chère*. Ren. No one called her those things. No one but Luc.

She shook off the memories and finished her coffee in two swallows. She had to remain in control. This was *her* seduction, dammit. She had to set the pace.

When her editor had first suggested that she use her hometown to kick off her project, Lauren imagined herself spending the weekend only fantasizing about having incredibly erotic sex all around the city. But Lauren's ''Sexy City Nights'' feature could conceivably rock an industry that pushed the envelope every day. She had to develop a knockout mock-up, tour the sultry sites, trendy clubs, and sizzling hot spots—from the raucous French Quarter to the glitzy Central Business District—firsthand.

And watching Luc sip his coffee with utter coolness though the temperature neared eighty at nine o'clock in the morning solidified her decision to see it all, feel it all, with Luc as her personal guide. He *was* the sinful side of New Orleans—living and breathing and sexy as hell.

''So—'' Luc cupped the white mug close to his chest, forcing Lauren to note how his gray T-shirt molded over muscles tight and ripe with masculine power ''—what has enticed you back after all these years? Must be something good.''

''Oh, it is.'' She lifted her knapsack and pulled the card he'd sent her out of the side pocket. She slid it across the table without a word.

Luc chuckled and shook his head, releasing a lock of dark hair that fell across his cheek.

''I wasn't sure you even got this,'' he said. ''But you didn't have to come all the way home to thank me.''

When he slid the errant strands back behind his ear, Lauren's fingers tingled with the memory of sliding her hands into that dark mane of his, skimming his lobe with her nails, then sealing the intimacy with a soft kiss on his temple.

"That's *not* why I'm here."

He leaned forward, invading her personal space with all the musky spice and powerful presence that made him so incredibly irresistible, so undeniably dangerous. "Then why are you here? You swore you'd never set foot in this city again. I didn't believe you, but you proved me wrong. Until today."

She watched Luc assess her from the top of her newly frosted blond hair to the tips of her smart, black leather boots. He didn't hide his approval or the clear question in his eyes that asked, who are you? You most certainly aren't the mousy little twit I dumped eight years ago.

Oh no, she wasn't. Now she had an absolutely perfect plan to show him just how different she was.

"I'm here to seduce you, of course."

CHAPTER TWO

LUC WATCHED Lauren's hazel irises light with a wicked gleam. The Lauren LaCroix he'd known eight years ago, the Lauren he'd been undeniably cruel to in his youthful ignorance, had been a lot of things— kind, sweet, relatively low maintenance so far as lovers went.... But wicked? Never that. Never until now. Luc had been around enough women to recognize nefarious intentions when he saw them, but on Lauren, the effect was particularly potent.

"You've come home to seduce me? That may not be so easy."

Or it might be as simple as finding a dark, secluded corner somewhere.

She leaned her elbows on the table, diminishing the space between them to mere inches. Dressed in blue jeans and a sleeveless leather vest, she would have looked like a certified biker-chick if not for her neat blond hairstyle—slicked back from her china-doll face and clipped with an expensive silver barrette. Her newfound style was subtle, sexy, sophisticated.

He was in deep, deep trouble.

"I'll take my chances. I don't shy away from challenges anymore, Luc. I just figured while I was back in town, I'd mix a little pleasure with business.''

"Business? Your magazine?''

Her eyes widened. She hadn't mentioned the magazine to him—yet. "You know about that?''

Luc grinned sheepishly, not entirely willing to admit that he regularly checked up on her through her aunt, Endora LaCroix Deveaux, who was not only the most respected psychic medium in the French Quarter, but was also an interminable gossip and his very good friend. When Lauren's parents left to tour the country with their jazz trio, Endora had been Lauren's surrogate mother. She cared about both of them, so Luc had taken Endora's phone call this morning very seriously.

"Word gets around. You here to do a fashion shoot?''

She shook her head. "I'm here to scout out locations for a *very* special feature on New Orleans.''

Luc relaxed into his chair, unnerved yet fascinated by the woman she'd become. Endora had warned him that her niece had "found her center.'' Yeah, like an earthquake. He'd have to watch his step, or he might find himself smothered by an unexpected aftershock.

Lauren scooted her chair closer to his. The scent of her perfume chased away the smells of chicory coffee and fried beignets and lured Luc back to the past. Valentine's Day. Dinner at his family's flagship restaurant. A shiny red satin box with an expensive bottle of perfume to replace the drugstore brands she wore.

The mingled scents of exotic spices and fine essences assailed him. Did she still wear the fragrance he'd chosen for her, or was his imagination hoping for more than he deserved?

"I know you are a very busy man," she said, toying with the card he'd sent. "But if you can spare a weekend, maybe you can help me."

She opened her leather backpack again, this time retrieving a dog-eared collection of tour books, maps, local newspapers, and magazines. Post-it notes stuck out in all directions. He scanned the handwritten notations, his jaw dropping with unadulterated shock as each word, each sexual fantasy, each fetish registered in his brain.

He cleared his throat before he spoke, wondering if he didn't need to swallow another glassful of water before he could command his tongue to work.

"This is all about sex," he said, feeling somewhat idiotic for pointing out something so obvious.

She smiled slyly. Then winked. "Yup."

"Who are you working for now, *Playboy?*"

Her laugh was throaty and deep, as if she knew a secret she wasn't yet ready to share.

"I pitched a feature idea to my editor called 'Sexy City Nights.' We're devoting a full-color spread in seven issues to having sultry, erotic sex in the nation's top cities."

"That doesn't sound politically correct," he commented, not needing her snort to point out the hypocrisy of such a remark—coming from him. "Let me rephrase that."

"Don't bother," she assured him, "I know it's an edgy premise. And as you can see by my notes, the photos might be…controversial. That's why New Orleans was a natural choice for the first city. Since this is my hometown, and the feature was my idea, my editor suggested I do the, um, legwork."

"Sounds like a plum assignment," Luc answered, mentally clearing his schedule for the next two days. The idea of her exploring the sensual, sexual side of *his* city without him didn't sit well. Not one bit.

She toyed with a slip of pale yellow paper where she'd scribbled the word *tongue*. "Yes and no."

It was his turn to snort. "Name one drawback to such an assignment."

She pushed the pile of paperwork back into her knapsack, along with his card, which he noticed also had some note written on the back. "Guidebooks don't exactly point out the sultry side of a city. But I've been gone so long, I really don't know what's hot around here anymore."

Lauren slid her hand onto his knee and Luc suddenly wished he hadn't finished his coffee in such a hurry. Moisture evaporated from his mouth with the same speed as a puddle on a July afternoon. When Endora had called to tell him his former lover was back in town and most likely having beignets and coffee at Café du Monde, he'd wondered if her return wasn't a sign. Lauren had been on his mind quite a bit lately, but he figured his curiosity was just a symptom of his growing restlessness with the state of his life.

When he'd spotted her from across the sidewalk, her transformation from a somewhat shy girl into a sexy, sophisticated woman compelled him to approach her, tease her, see how she'd react to him barging into her morning. Test the waters for something more.

But now, she had a proposition in her gaze, on her pale, glossy lips, which she licked, slowly, and with the expertise of a seasoned seductress.

"You wouldn't happen to have the time to be my *personal* tour guide, would you?"

Her tone was breathy, her rhythm laced with suggestion.

"I'll make the time."

Her half smile put him on alert. This woman was up to something. Most likely revenge. He'd been cruel to her when they broke up—insensitive, arrogant, and downright mean. He didn't know that then, of course. He'd actually patted himself on the back for being so thoughtful and selfless to push her out of the nest even if she didn't want to go.

Was that why he'd come here? To apologize? Unfortunately, her sly grin and the soft play of her fingers up his thigh didn't exactly set the scene for a heartfelt admission of guilt and regret.

"You sure?" She inched closer with each word until her breath teased the shell of his ear. "You'll have to show me around town, talk to me about sex, maybe even do a little fantasizing or role playing while I decide all the best places to do it. Could make you uncomfortable, what with our past and all."

"Screw the past, Ren. There ain't a red-blooded man in this city who'd turn down an offer like that."

"Great!" With that, Lauren popped out of her chair and was halfway out of the restaurant before his head cleared enough to register her escape. Did she expect him to follow? Had his enthralled response been enough to satisfy her? Well, damn, he wanted to pay a higher price. Some good, old-fashioned torture was more than in order—and in fact, already had him hot and bothered from the back of his collar to the crotch of his jeans.

"Wait! Where are you going?"

She slowed, but didn't stop. "To my hotel." She glanced over her shoulder just before her pace quickened from a lazy saunter to a sinfully swinging strut. "You coming?"

CHAPTER THREE

EVERY FRIDAY MORNING, Endora LaCroix Deveaux held court on an old iron bench in Jackson Square, more to chat with friends than to practice her trade as a psychic medium. This morning, however, she simply watched with satisfaction as Lauren LaCroix, her wayward niece, bolted out of Café du Monde with sexy Luc Dupre tearing after her like a dog who'd just lost his favorite bone.

The man worked fast. She'd only called him an hour ago, the minute she spotted Lauren walking down Decatur Street instead of Fifth Avenue in Manhattan. Endora had dreamt that a misguided family member would return home soon...and that she'd play a role in settling whatever disquiet had sent him or her away in the first place.

Then she'd spotted her niece. Lauren had abandoned the Quarter eight years ago, after Luc had broken her heart. Now that she'd returned, Endora had no qualms over helping them reconcile.

So far, she'd only made a phone call. She suspected this had been too easy, but resolved to give the young people a chance to work things out on their own. And since Lauren, once a quiet, malleable child with no self-confidence to speak of, already had cocky Luc Dupre chasing after her, Endora surmised that Destiny had everything under control.

LAUREN SLID HER KEY into the door and shielded her trembling hands from Luc's view. He'd caught up to her just outside Jax Brewery and hailed them a cab back to her hotel in the Central Business District. She'd made the reservation on the mistaken belief she'd be more in control, less nostalgic outside the Quarter. She wanted whatever happened between them now to be on *her* terms—a cleansing of the past rather than a reenactment.

She'd tried to make Luc love her, only to be called "whipped" and "clingy." By him. By her friends. Maybe they'd been right. Then. But she would use this weekend to show him precisely how she'd changed. Not that she wanted him back—oh, no—she just wanted him to know what he'd missed.

And, she admitted to herself, she'd missed the fire that Luc's touch ignited in her—the fire that made her hands tremble now, with anticipation. When she couldn't manage to work the lock, Luc removed the thin plastic card from her hand.

"Here, let me."

She snatched the key back. "I can open a door, Luc."

"Relax, Ren."

Lauren took a deep breath and finally unlocked the door. But before she stepped inside, Luc pressed the full length of his body against her. His hard erection, his hands sliding up her bare arms, his breath skimming her sensitive skin, jolted her with a mad rush of desire. "I was just trying to help. That's why you brought me here, right?"

The moment the door closed behind them, she swung around and shoved him against the wall. Lauren LaCroix didn't operate on slow simmer anymore. Luc needed to learn that toying with her meant a quick flash of fire.

She grabbed his face and crushed her lips to his, snatching fistfuls of T-shirt to pull herself up and grind against him, sharing her delight with his body, his tongue. He didn't miss a beat, didn't question, argue, or attempt to slow the pace, but removed her vest with a succession of popping snaps. He pushed her away only long enough to take off his shirt, then lifted her into his arms, suckling her nipples through the thin lace of her bra while he carried her to the bed.

After he stripped her of her jeans, he removed his, giving her a moment to retrieve a condom from her bag and slip beneath the sheets. He quickly put it on, spreading her legs with hungry hands before he covered her body with his.

"Is this how you like it now? Hot and fast?"

"Touch me, Luc. I'm ready. Don't wait."

He did as she asked, growling with desire as he found her eager and responsive. In the past, coaxing Lauren to climax had taken patience, time. But she was older now, more experienced, more willing to surrender to the physical side of womanhood, the side Luc filled when he pushed inside her.

When he insisted on a rhythmic, measured pace, Lauren thought she'd go crazy. When he captured her gaze with his, challenging her to keep her eyes open and watch the passion as it played on his face and body, she knew she'd soon cross the edge. The minute he cried out his release, she toppled over with him, dizzy from a starburst of sensations, from the errant thought that now, she'd finally come home.

"You're not the girl I used to know," he said, rolling aside, but bracing his hand possessively across her belly.

"I warned you."

"Yes, well, I will operate with that knowledge close at hand from now on."

"What do you mean?" She sat up against the fluffy pillows and slid her leg beneath her, curling into a comfortable, relaxed position.

He remained silent, his gaze lost in the view outside her window. She watched his transparent blue eyes, his kiss-swollen lips, and the twitch in his sinfully square jaw. Luc was weighing his words. Apparently, she wasn't the only one who'd changed.

"It means I'm sorry."

Lauren didn't disguise her surprise, or her residual anger. "You mean about how you dumped me eight years ago."

"Yeah, that."

"Is that why you sent me the card? Why you approached me at Café du Monde? Guilt?"

He tempered his grin with a nonchalant shrug. "Guilt, curiosity…attraction. Do we have to label it?"

Lauren didn't answer, mulling over the gift she'd just been offered. Luc Dupre, graduate of the School of I-Am-Never-Wrong felt…guilty? The man who, apology or not, once swept her aside without a backward glance was admitting to curiosity about who she was now, even after they'd made love? Harumph. Here she was all set to exact a clean, cold act of revenge and he was apologizing for his sins of the past—with no prompting!

"No label, that's fair," she said. And probably safer. His pale blue eyes spoke silent volumes as his pupils enlarged and his irises darkened. Luc couldn't conceal his passions and so far as Lauren remembered, rarely bothered trying. He wanted her forgiveness as much as he wanted her. Again. He might get lucky on one point, at least. "But your apology better be sincere."

Because you just sank my master plan. Funny thing was, she found his maneuver clever and, God help her, endearing.

"So you accept my apology?"

"I haven't decided," she said.

With his signature-smooth grace, Luc slid her back beneath the covers. "Now, that sounds like a fascinating challenge. Then you still want me for your tour guide?"

With a narrowed gaze, Lauren considered the danger of messing with Luc beyond this one erotic encounter. Then he slid his thumbs over her nipples, blowing any reluctance out of her like candlelight in a storm. He did know the hot spots better than anyone did—and she didn't just mean those in New Orleans.

"When do we start?"

CHAPTER FOUR

"You have only two days to see all of what's hot in New Orleans, right? We don't have a moment to lose," he answered.

Lauren swallowed, her gaze riveted on Luc's long fingers as his hand inched from her breasts to her belly, then stopped. He rested there with casual comfort, as if touching her, naked, after fast, furious sex was something he did every day.

"You always were an impatient man." She playfully slapped his hand away and stood, taking the sheet with her. "The feature I'm doing is called 'Sexy City *Nights.*'" She emphasized the last word. "We've got a good eight hours of daylight before we can do serious exploring."

Luc shook his head as he pulled on his boxers. "Just admit you need some space, Lauren. Let's not undo my heartfelt apology with silly lies now, okay?"

She raised her right hand, palm out. "Nothin' but the truth. And the truth is, I need to visit the powder room."

As she walked away, Luc admitted one thing— okay, two. First, the woman had a backside built to squeeze tears from a stone-faced man. Second, without him and her family around to chart or influence her every move, Lauren had indeed bloomed into a strong-willed, independent, incredibly responsive, and fearless woman. Letting her go hadn't been his crime. His biggest blunder was never going after her.

Well, Luc Dupre never made the same mistake twice.

"Eight hours, huh?" He interrupted her retreat by throwing an arm in her path. "We could always leave the 'City Nights' part for later and focus on the 'Sexy' again."

She dodged his block with a sassy smirk. "Who says there will be an *again?*"

Her expression might have deflated the confidence of a less arrogant man. Luckily, Luc still had the echo of her climax to spur him on. "I do. No lies, remember?"

"Let's just get dressed and maybe tour some of our old haunts. Help me get my bearings." Lauren disappeared behind the bathroom door. "Sound reasonable?"

Luc lay back on the bed and folded his hands beneath his head. "That's me—good ol' reasonable Luc Dupre."

Despite her bravado, Luc suspected their unexpected, wild and passionate reunion had Lauren as emotionally and physically off-kilter as he was. And when the dizziness subsided, he intended to catch Lauren—possibly for good.

Luc led an exciting life, ran a profitable business. But no matter how he tried, he couldn't fill the emptiness inside him—the expanding void of dissatisfaction that plagued his days and haunted his nights. Even before Endora's phone call, Luc had been thinking about Lauren. Hence the card on her birthday. He'd also been obsessing over the love she'd once so freely offered—the same love he'd carelessly tossed aside.

He missed her. He wanted her back. Maybe at one time she needed to leave him to find herself, but now that she'd returned—stronger and sexier than ever— he couldn't pass up the chance to show her how he'd changed, as well. Or at least, how he could change with her in his life.

When he heard the rush of the shower, Luc wasted no time. He grabbed her knapsack and pulled out the books she'd marked with slips of paper. The places she wanted to go. The sexual images that had sprung from her fantasies—dreams he'd turn into reality. Studying them would give him the edge, the secret he needed to coax Lauren back into his bed—and back into his life.

LAUREN TURNED ON the water, needing the noise. Frenzied and disoriented, her thoughts banged in her head so loudly, she feared Luc would hear.

What the hell am I doing?

Her legs wobbled, her skin still thrumming from where he'd touched her. Never in her life had she allowed her passions to overwhelm her, rule her. She still felt high in the aftermath, her body primed. But no matter how much her mind and body wanted Luc, she had to keep her heart protected. Off-limits.

In the shower she reminded herself to be strong. Luc's touch would drive her insane with wanting. Not the wanting of sexual desire—that he'd satisfied once and would again if she allowed him. But in the past, she'd wanted more from Luc than just sex. She'd wanted his heart, his love. A future. Now she knew that was impossible.

She showered quickly, freshened her makeup, then brushed her teeth, and reclipped her hair while she forced her brain to accept hard facts. Her life was in New York City. Her job was more than just important; it was her greatest life accomplishment. She'd worked hard and was only now attaining the payoff. Nothing, not even Luc's love, would make her give up her dream.

And so far as she knew, not one member of the Dupre family had *ever* left New Orleans. Not counting Luc's club, the family owned and operated twelve restaurants, a bed-and-breakfast, and a specialty food shop. He'd rooted his life in New Orleans as firmly as she had hers in Manhattan.

But what would an affair with Luc cost her? So

long as she kept her heart out of reach and her expectations focused on the sensual, one wicked weekend with Luc would pay out with only pure pleasure. Some erotic memories. Wasn't that the very same premise as "Sexy City Nights"? Wild passion and intimate behavior amidst the bright lights and swelling crowds? Love affairs as fast and furious as an exciting city lifestyle?

Luc was stuffing a few necessities into Lauren's bag when she emerged from the bathroom.

"What are you doing?"

He slung the knapsack over his shoulder. "Just making sure you have all the things you need. We won't be back here until much, much later."

"What about my books?"

Luc chuckled at the pile he'd made on the coffee table. After reading all her notes, and stuffing a few in his pocket, he'd committed all he needed to memory.

"Who needs maps and tour guides? You have me, remember?"

"How could I forget?"

He closed the space between them in two broad steps. Without warning, he snagged her around the waist and pulled her against him.

Luc grinned. The possibilities were as endless as the nightlife in New Orleans. "If I play this right, *chère,* you won't be forgetting much about this weekend."

CHAPTER FIVE

BY THE TIME THEY REACHED Bourbon Street, Lauren was exhausted. They'd toured all their old haunts—the spot in Jackson Square where they'd met when she should have been spending the night with a friend. The shop on Royal where Luc had selected and bought her prom dress. Even the low-rent apartment she'd lived in.

Facing the memories, both good and bad, hadn't tired her. Neither had the heat. What had her muscles aching and her lungs sore was one simple thing—*not* touching Luc. Or more precisely, him not touching her.

The taste of his mouth, the feel of his rock-hard body, still resonated through her. The musky scent of his cologne clung to her clothes, haunting every breath she'd taken since. He'd meant to surprise her up against the door and take control of the seduction she'd promised at Café du Monde. But she'd turned the tables and seduced him by taking the lead—a survival tactic meant to show him he couldn't use her passions to manipulate her anymore.

How wrong she'd been. The encounter had only

stoked the lust she'd denied for years; the reality was that Luc could still make her body thrum with needs so distinctly feminine, so innately personal, that she remained ready for him. On edge. On fire.

Her arousal escalated as they toured the city. He'd been careful not to touch her or allow any contact with his hands or body. Yet, he'd stroked her with his eyes. Seduced her with words. His hot breath against her ear. His wild, irreverent laugh.

"How 'bout we sneak in here?" He pointed to a large building on the corner of Bourbon and Iberville, a place Lauren had never seen before, a place Lauren hoped was noisy and not the least intimate where she could regain her bearings. Knowing Luc, though, she didn't harbor much hope.

"Storyville?" she read off the sign.

"You want to know what's new and hot in New Orleans."

"Does your family own it?" she asked.

"No. The *other* family does."

Lauren smiled, grateful she still knew enough about the rivalry of restaurant-owning families in New Orleans to not have to grill Luc about his comment. She also wasn't surprised that he'd frequent an establishment owned by the competition. Luc Dupre hadn't become a rich man by limiting his experiences. He tried most everything once, giving him a mixture of knowledge and worldliness that had attracted Lauren when they were young and continued to now.

After a quick chat with the hostess, they were led through the Storyville Jazz Café to the Jazz Parlor, a room awash in crimson and tinged with forbidden romance. Cubes of candlelight flickered from the tables. A dozen fringed lamps glowed scarlet and amber from the polished wood bar. The concrete floor looked like softly tanned leather and the red velvet curtains, also fringed in gold, could very well have hung in the real Storyville, the red-light district of old New Orleans.

"This looks like the inside of a brothel," Lauren said.

"Yeah, great, isn't it?"

The waiter delivered two old-fashioneds in short, squat glasses. Lauren took a sip of the sweetened bourbon, allowing the icy heat to slide down her throat. Warmth infused her, relaxing muscles that had been tight with wanting all day long.

"I can use this place in my layout. Very provocative."

Luc sipped his drink, obviously not needing to look around to nod in agreement. "Photographs, right?"

"Mostly. But the text has to be sexy, too. I've been reading romance novels to find a rhythm for my words. Those women have sexy under control."

He scooted his chair closer. His breath, scented with sugar and whiskey, caressed her cheek. "What would you write?"

"Depends on the photo."

"Describe the photo to me. I'll even close my eyes."

She watched his lashes flutter down, his bottom lip nearly pouting in expectation.

"I don't know."

He licked that curved lip. "Come on, Ren. Let me help you start. You had a note on the jazz club listing in that tourist book you brought. You wrote *sweat* and *her thigh in his palm*. What was that?"

Lauren took another sip of her drink. She wasn't so surprised that he'd read her notes, but she wondered why he'd taken the time to memorize the fanciful scribbles she'd made on the plane. "Dancing."

His lids drifted closed again. "What kind of music?"

"Something…hot."

"Jazz?" he asked.

"No. Louder. Frenzied."

"Zydeco."

"Yeah."

Lauren couldn't help closing her eyes, too. It had been years, but the low country Cajun music, banged with spoons on washboards and pulled from frenetic accordions, always appealed to her. It was wild, fun, raucous and earthy.

"Dance with me."

"The band's on break," she argued, missing a grab for his arm when he darted away from the table. Two minutes later and probably a few twenties poorer, Luc returned and held out his hand. The soft jazz background music faded as the band scrambled back into place. In a flash, the five men started thrashing out a zydeco tune complete with lyrics sung in Creole French.

The room, sedately low key in the late afternoon, immediately came to life. By the time Luc dragged Lauren to the front, five couples were already swaying and hopping to the quick-paced rhythms on a spontaneous dance floor. Luc grabbed her hands and swirled her into a shuffling two-step. Years without music, years without dancing, melted away with the pressure of Luc's hands, the kick in his step, and the graceful yet masculine glide of his body.

HE TWIRLED HER AGAIN, then pressed her close. Her body celebrated the contact. Her breasts, wet with sweat beneath her leather top, tightened. Gooseflesh prickled like a thousand tiny needles, but the result was pleasure, not pain. The bourbon, the music—the man—combined to make her giddy and carefree.

The band switched gears, slowing from a furious frenzy to a lazy bop. Luc turned her to face him; a full measure of music beat past before she realized his intention.

He swayed his hips with a subtle rock. Placing her palms on his waist, he injected her with his rhythm. Hot and slow. His stare captured hers. She bit her bottom lip. Without breaking the cadence of the dance, he slid his palm down from her waist to her thigh, then hooked his hand beneath her knee and lifted her leg, pulling her forward in one insistent thrust. He held her, her thigh in his hand, his erection to her hot center, while they rocked and rolled with the music.

Though the sun hadn't set outside yet, the room soaked up the darkness to come. Lauren knew no one could see when Luc inched his fingers higher up her thigh, using the seam of her jeans as a path, touching her precisely in the spot that rocked her more than the music. A scarlet haze enveloped her, a combination of the music, the atmosphere, but mostly…Luc.

"I'm going to make you come," he promised, his whisper overriding the driving rhythm of the sultry bass.

"Not here," she begged, but her protest was too little, too late. With skilled pressure, he forced her over the edge. Her thighs clenched, but he yanked her full against him, holding her, hiding her release in the guise of the dance.

When the music ended, Lauren forced herself to look at him, fully expecting a self-satisfied smirk on his face. Instead, he kissed her. Softly.

"That wasn't fair," she chastised.

"No, it wasn't." A strand of hair escaped her clip and Luc took his time curling it back around her ear. "You'll just have to get me back, then, won't you?"

CHAPTER SIX

"WHERE TO NEXT?" Lauren's tone brimmed with impatient expectation while Luc led her across Iberville to Canal Street where he hailed a cab. They'd spent nearly two hours dancing, nibbling on barbecued shrimp and sausage bits, washing down the spiciness with tall glasses of iced tea and one last bourbon for the road. They'd swayed to rocking blues and rolled to sassy jazz, learning each other's bodies again under the guise of dance. After Luc paid the check and pulled Lauren out into the night, she was breathless and giddy. He was simply aroused, waiting for Lauren to pay him back for his trick on the dance floor.

"Somewhere to cool down," he answered.

In New Orleans, sunset didn't bring cooler temperatures. The sultry heat of the city intensified after dark and he was more than ready to get inside and turn up the heat in a more intimate setting.

He directed the cabby to make a U-turn, then gave him an address in the Warehouse Arts District, the recently renovated area just inside the Central Business District. Lauren didn't miss a thing, her nose practically pressed to the glass as they wove toward his home away from home.

Club Carnal.

He checked his watch, glad they could sneak in well before the club opened at 10:00 p.m. Just before eight o'clock. They'd arrived even before his manager or the waitstaff.

Luc wondered if Lauren would remember the significance of coming here. When they pulled up in front of the boxy white building with the sleek, brushed-steel entrance her bright face wilted to a deep frown.

"This is your club," she said simply, but emotion washed her words with a sheen of resentment.

"One of the hottest hangouts in New Orleans."

She opened the door and pushed herself out while he paid the fare. By the time the cab pulled away from the curb, Lauren stood, arms crossed and legs stiff, while she looked up at the business that had been the impetus for their breakup.

Her eyes flashed with anger when he reached to take her elbow. "Is this supposed to be a joke?"

"No joke, Ren. I thought you might like to see what I did with the place. Besides, we can't run from the past."

"You said you were sorry," she reminded him, but he knew that a few simple yet heartfelt words weren't really enough to undo the hurt between them. Especially since she still hadn't officially accepted his apology.

At Storyville, they'd danced as they had when they were first together—carefree and passionate and with nothing but the moment to live for, nothing but the here-and-now to milk for all its excitement and fire.

In this building, their past had all come to an end. But Luc wanted to use this same setting to burn past the hurt and rekindle what was once so precious and rare, it had scared the living hell out of him. He wanted Lauren back in his life and he could think of no better place to tell her. Show her.

"Come inside with me. Let me apologize again. The right way."

Lauren bit her lip, rolling the pink skin beneath her teeth.

"You're not afraid, are you?" he asked, aware this was a cheap and childish ruse, but not caring so long as it worked.

She rolled her eyes and marched forward. "You know, that trick worked much better when I was sixteen."

"Worked damned good now, too."

She slapped his shoulder while he unlocked the door. Humor danced in her eyes—humor and curiosity and a hearty dash of her new, I'll-show-you impertinence that truly fascinated him. What had happened to imbue her with such brazen strength? Would he destroy that part of her, without meaning to, as he had in the past? Or was her strength and courage now so woven into her that nothing and no one could break it? He hoped that was the case. He'd soon find out.

A former textile warehouse, Club Carnal had been gutted from the fourth floor down to create a cavernous, yet open space. Sensual, erotic murals adorned the walls, highlighted by neon now as dimmed as the lights. Once he locked the door behind them, he grabbed Lauren's hand, pulled her into an elevator and swiped a key card that gave him exclusive access to his fourth-floor office.

"Nice elevator," she said. "Think you'll actually let me see the club?"

Luc swallowed his response until the doors slid open at his office. He took a deep breath, wondering when the last time was that he'd allowed anyone in his sanctuary. His club manager? Probably once a week, less if possible. Mainly, this room, narrow but long and featuring a full bank of tilted windows that allowed him to watch the action below, was Luc's escape from the world of trends and hip music and fashion that he made his living from.

He swept his hand toward the windows. "Look your fill."

Lauren walked slowly, checking out the lush leather furniture, paneled walls, and thick plum carpet of his domain. A chamois lampshade gilded the room with candlelit ambience, making the textures richer, the fabrics and finishes resonant with the state of his heart—dark emptiness surrounded by the illusion of light.

"I can't see anything." She leaned forward on the sill that jutted from beneath the windows.

Luc trapped her with his body, his chest pressed to her back, the evidence of his need snug against the gentle slope of her derriere. Here in the amber darkness, he wanted to do nothing but touch her again, but flipped a switch to his left instead, biding his time. Bright pinks, cool blues, and deep purples sputtered and glowed to neon life. Another switch and a bank of floating disco balls spun from the ceiling, their tiny sparks of laser color flashing into his office as they dipped up and down like yo-yos. Then, he turned on the music. Saxophone jazz. Wailing with want, vibrating with vital need—playing the very music that seared his soul.

"Very slick," she said, her tone devoid of inflection, so he couldn't tell if she meant her words as a compliment or a criticism. And he didn't care.

"Like your skin."

He slipped his hand around her waist, beneath the gap that separated her leather vest from her skin. She leaned back into him, rested her head against his chest.

"Dancing does that to me. Is that why you brought me here? So I can return that favor you gave me at Storyville?" Lauren smiled despite herself.

"You repaid that favor just by coming inside with

me. You know, the last time I brought you here, I wanted to make love to you. You were insulted.''

"It was a musty, abandoned warehouse, then. You'd just convinced your father to front you the money to buy it and if I recall, you only wanted to christen the space appropriately. Didn't seem to matter much who your lover was.''

"That's not true, but I understand why you thought that. I wasn't good at expressing my feelings back then.''

"And I wasn't good at being spontaneous.'' She slid one hand along the side of his thigh, slipped the other back to cradle his neck and pull him closer so that not a wisp of air-conditioned breeze could slip between them.

"You've changed,'' he said.

"Yes, I have, Luc. In more ways than you'd imagine. Close your eyes. Let me show you.''

CHAPTER SEVEN

LIKE A SECOND LAYER of skin, Luc pressed against her. His muscles rigid, his scent musky and male and aroused. Lauren had wanted to make love to him in his club eight years ago, had craved the freedom, the total trust such a rendezvous symbolized. She'd longed to let herself go, safe in the knowledge that he'd cherish her, protect the secrets he learned when she revealed the full capacity of her body, heart and soul.

But life had taught her not to trust someone who kept his heart under lock and key. So she'd refused. Soon after, he'd said goodbye.

He'd called her a coward. A prude. According to him, she'd never be anything more than a reflection of the man who owned her, and not even that if she didn't learn to open herself up to new adventures.

She'd changed, all right. Thanks to him.

"I already see how different you are, Ren. You're all spit and sass now. Completely unafraid." With legerdemain skill, Luc released the lowest button on her vest. A trill of electric need sizzled up her spine.

"No woman with sense is completely unafraid. I just choose not to let fear keep me down anymore."

"I never meant to hurt you then."

"But you did. A few orgasms and an apology can't erase that."

"Then I'll try something new. How about more honesty? Lauren, you didn't come home because of some article. Not entirely. You also came to teach me a lesson, didn't you? To show me what I missed when I let you go. Well, you know what? You're right. And I've known it for a very long time."

"So why didn't you come after me?"

"I'm not that quick a learner. By the time I realized what I'd lost, you were long gone...in New York, discovering the real Lauren LaCroix." He released the second clasp on her vest and splayed his palm completely against her belly.

She closed her eyes and reveled in the sensations of his touch. Hot, but gentle. Smooth, but honest. Like his words. He'd nailed her motives dead on, and still he wanted her. Just as she wanted him.

"I'm just a woman who wants to make love with you. For now. I'm not staying, Luc. I can't."

Luc spun her around, tipping her chin up so their gazes locked. "I'm not asking you to stay. But when we make love, here, now...let's do it right. In the hotel room was exciting, but too fast. I want to savor you, Lauren. Make this last. Really last."

She tried to laugh to deny his underlying meaning,

but the sound came out more like a strangled squeak. She cleared her throat. ''You're a man of many passions, Luc. You get bored easily.''

His grin tilted higher on one side than the other, just as it always did when he was caught red-handed. ''But now, you're a woman of many passions. Used to be, your only passion was me.''

''No challenge in that, huh?''

''None at all. And I like a challenge. Live for them, actually.''

She popped the next three buttons on her vest herself, revealing more and more flesh. She remembered to breathe only after he stopped her from removing the vest by capturing her hands and pressing a sweet, soft kiss on each set of knuckles.

''I'm not being much of a challenge, am I?''

He smoothed the soft back of her hand across his stubbled cheek. Like a match head to flint, a spark of awareness flared and burned until her nipples tightened and her mouth dried. ''You have no idea,'' he answered. ''None at all.''

Luc fully understood the challenge, even if Lauren didn't. Simple desire was easy, chemical—and sating that need required no more than a physical act. But he wanted more with Lauren. She was a woman of layers, of depth, but neither of them had been mature enough to see that until they'd parted. She'd learned about herself on her own in the big city. And in one day in the Big Easy, she'd proved what he'd long suspected—Lauren, fully developed, independent and free, was his missing other half.

But he couldn't tell her. The words sounded sappy. Rehearsed. Insincere. How could he know something so intimate after less than a day with her? But he could show her.

Yeah, he could show her. Right here. Now.

He pressed her hands onto the ledge beneath the window, then pulled off his shirt and unzipped his jeans. Only after he was half undressed did he slide Lauren's vest off her body.

His breath caught. "You're so beautiful."

With slightly trembling fingers, he traced her bare breasts, her slim rib cage, her curved waist and belly. Familiar, but new. Comfortable, yet utterly dangerous.

She arched her back. Pinpoints of light from the spinning mirrored balls danced across her flesh, adding a kaleidoscope of color to her flushed and dampened skin. He couldn't stop the urge to taste her, so he did. And she cooed and groaned in wild response.

The rest of their clothes seemed to melt away. He carried her to the leather couch in the corner. He kissed her from her temples to her toes, pleasing her with his hands and teeth and tongue.

Then she returned the favor. By the time he donned the condom he'd pulled from his wallet, nothing existed in the office but Lauren and Luc and their mutual need. He clasped her hands when he slipped inside her, and an explosion of pure wonder rocked him long before they reached their climax.

"Lauren," he gasped.

"How do I feel?"

He shifted, thrusting gently, cautiously, trying with concentrated desperation not to go too quickly, take too much, too soon. For all he knew, this time, here, now, in the shadow of where it had all ended, would be his last chance. To show her. To love her.

"Like heaven, *chère*. Pure heaven."

"Take me there, Luc, please."

So he did. And when she shouted his name in divine delight, he knew he could never let her go, weekend deal or not.

THEY DIDN'T RUSH TO DRESS, and after Luc explained that the windows had a mirrored coating that allowed them to see out into the club while no one could see in, Lauren rolled off the couch and explored. More lights were on downstairs as the waitstaff readied the club. The music changed to retro disco. Lauren couldn't help moving to the beat. And doing so while naked, while Luc watched, primed her for sex all over again.

Yet she grabbed a photo off his desk instead of revisiting him on the couch.

"This recent?"

The brass frame contained a picture of Luc and his

parents, flanked on each side by his sisters and their husbands.

"Last year, at the Club Carnal fifth anniversary."

"Five years? Took you a while to get going. You bought the building before I left."

"Had to do things my way, on my own dime. Investors don't come easy, even with the Dupre name."

She replaced the photo, then returned to the window overlooking the club. They'd both made great strides in eight years. They'd made their own way on their own terms. When they made love on the couch, Lauren had sensed an inner strength in Luc that hadn't been there before, or at least, one she hadn't had the ability to see.

"You must be very proud."

He joined her at the window and wrapped his arms around her waist. "I am. But now, it's time for me to move on."

CHAPTER EIGHT

"MOVE ON? TO WHAT?"

Lauren tried to turn around, but he held her close in his arms, steadying her by nuzzling her neck.

"To something new. Something exciting. Unexpected. New York City, maybe."

She fought out of his embrace, retreating a few paces while scrambling to retrieve the nearest clothing, his discarded T-shirt.

"What are you talking about, Luc? New Orleans is your home. It's part of who you are."

He leaned one naked hip onto the ledge. "Then it'll come with me wherever I go, won't it? But you won't. You'll only be a part of my life if I become a part of yours. I'd like to do that, Ren."

She yanked the shirt over her head, suddenly dizzy as Luc's singular scent surrounded her, warmed her.

"Luc, we haven't seen each other in eight years before today, yet you want to move your entire life just to be with me? On the off chance—and it's a *very* off chance—that we might make some sort of relationship work?"

Luc shook his head as he tugged on his jeans.

"Okay, there are so many mistakes in that statement, I'm not sure where to start. First, don't for one minute think that I haven't been getting regular updates on you from your aunt. And I'm willing to bet the reverse is true, too."

She captured her bottom lip with her teeth. Endora had indeed made it a point to keep Lauren abreast of Luc's activities, as had many of her friends in the modeling world. She hadn't always been happy with what she heard, but she'd always been interested.

"Second." He moved on, grinning when her silence admitted the truth. "I don't want to relocate just for you, although frankly, you're my inspiration. Club Carnal was the first thing I did on my own. My father fronted me the money so I wouldn't lose the building, but I paid him back within six months. My family taught me all I know, but they had no say in what I did here and I still made it work. You of all people must understand how wonderful that feeling is."

Yeah, she knew. Though Endora had paid her tuition and housing for her first year at college, she'd accomplished everything else on her own. Her mother and father enjoyed playing the music circuit more than parenting and after Lauren left New Orleans, she had only seen them three times.

She'd chosen New York, self-banished from the only family she had left—Endora and her daughters—and still, she'd survived the lonely holidays. The empty celebrations of good grades, scholarships, and eventually, promotions.

She might never have managed to come home if not for the anchoring knowledge that she'd done it all herself. She might never have managed to face Luc again.

And now he called her his inspiration.

The full force of that statement sent her wandering back to the couch. She plopped down, numb until he took her hand in his.

"And third…"

"There's more?" She didn't think she could take it and bowed her head, trying to summon up the gumption to hear what she knew was the honest truth from Luc Dupre.

He laughed, removed the clip that dangled from her hair and smoothed his fingers through the frosted strands. "The inspiration thing hit you pretty hard, didn't it?"

"You never admired me before, Luc." She looked up. "You wanted me. You liked me. Sometimes I think you even pitied me, what with my parents having nothing and hardly being around."

"You learned to be around for yourself. That's what I need to do now. But being the creature of habit I am, I prefer to have someone familiar with me. I prefer to have you."

"But I'm not familiar! I'm someone entirely new now, Luc."

He pulled her into his arms. "You don't think I know that, too? That'll be the fun part. Getting to know each other again. I figure I'll sell the club, move to New York, check out the industry, maybe open something new there. Something bigger. Better. Even hipper than Club Carnal. Your magazine will be begging me for an interview," he teased.

"At least I'll have an inside track," she said.

He yanked her onto his lap. "Definitely. Definitely *inside* and definitely with some serious begging involved."

She threw her head back and sighed. "I can't believe this is happening! I come home to put together a magazine layout and I end up with a lover."

"More than that." He shifted her so they were eye to eye. The sincerity and honest, open vulnerability in his gaze tore her heart wide open. "A lover who loves you. I always have loved you, Ren. Even when we broke up, you were still a part of me. That scared me more than anything. You needed me so much then, and I needed you, too. But I wasn't ready to admit it. Now I am. Are you?"

She squeezed her eyes shut and forced herself to take deep but even breaths while her mind swirled with a storm of passion, love, fear and mistrust. If she let him back into her heart, he'd have to uproot his entire life. He'd already laid his emotions on the table. He'd put himself at risk for hurt much more than she ever had—more than she ever could again.

"I've become quite an adventurer, Luc. And as much as I tried over all these years, I never stopped loving you, either. I want you to come back to New York with me and share my new life. Make it new all over again."

A kiss, deep and long and intense, sealed the deal. They made love again, then talked and planned and kissed and teased until Luc scrambled to his desk to find what she was sure was another stash of condoms. After hearing him swear for a good five minutes, Lauren laughed and dressed.

"Where are you going?" he asked.

She found her hair clip on the floor and shoved it into her pocket. She didn't care if she looked like a woman who'd just been made love to. She checked her reflection in the window and decided the look suited her just fine.

"I didn't come to New Orleans to hear you curse at your desk, Luc. There are plenty of drugstores in this town. And since you still owe me a nighttime tour, why don't we find one and get started?"

Luc had never dressed so fast in his life. Except for maybe this morning when Endora had called to tell him Lauren was back in town. Before he left for New York, he was going to throw that woman one hell of a party.

"Still interested in all the sexiest places to make love in New Orleans, I see," he teased, strutting over to the elevator to push the down arrow, brimming over with joy at luring Lauren back into his life again.

She sauntered with a sassy bravado that had his swagger beat. "More interested than before, frankly. I want to experience some seriously sexy city nights in our last two days here, Luc Dupre."

"*Chère,* if I do my job right, you're going to have sexy city nights for the rest of your life."

Indulge in summer savings!

Enjoy the lazy days of summer with a brand-new *sizzling* Silhouette Desire or Harlequin Temptation book.

V *Silhouette*

Desire

◆ HARLEQUIN®

Temptation

SAVE $1.00
off your purchase of any
Silhouette Desire® or
Harlequin Temptation® title

RETAILER: Harlequin Enterprises Ltd. will pay face value of this coupon plus 8¢ if submitted by customer for this product only. Any other use constitutes fraud. Coupon is nonassignable. Void if taxed, prohibited or restricted by law. Void if copied. Consumer must pay any government taxes. Valid in the U.S. only. For reimbursement submit coupons and proof of sales to: Harlequin Enterprises Ltd., P.O. Box 880478, El Paso, TX 88588-0478, U.S.A. Cash value 1/100¢. Limit one coupon per purchase.

Coupon expires September 30, 2003.
Redeemable at participating retail outlets in U.S. only.

110579

5 65373 00076 2   (8100) 0 11057

Indulge in summer savings!

Enjoy the lazy days of summer with a brand-new *sizzling* Silhouette Desire or Harlequin Temptation book.

Silhouette

Desire

HARLEQUIN®

Temptation.

SAVE $1.00 off your purchase of any Silhouette Desire® or Harlequin Temptation® title

Coupon expires September 30, 2003.
Redeemable at participating retail outlets in Canada only.

52605228

Treat yourself to the ultimate summer delight and save $10.00!

Indulge in your own custom-flavored ice cream creations at home with the

BLACK&DECKER

Arctic Twister™

It's easy to use!

Just layer store-bought ice cream or frozen yogurt with your favorite candy, nuts, fruit, cookies or cereal for a delicious, one-of-a-kind snack!

It's easy to clean up!

Removable parts are dishwasher safe.

It's delicious fun that will delight all of your friends and family!

Perfect for parties, snacks, gift-giving and escaping the summer heat!

Turn the page to SAVE $10.00 off your own Black and Decker® Arctic Twister™ Ice Cream Mixer!

Indulge yourself with special summer savings–

Log on to our special promotional site at

www.Summersaving.com

You'll get

$10.00 OFF

your online order for the
Black and Decker®
Arctic Twister™ Ice Cream Mixer

as well as

**Special Savings on
other select Black and Decker®
household products, such as fans,
blenders, irons and toaster ovens.**

Log on to make your summer a breeze!

BLACK&DECKER®

Offer expires: 9/30/03.

© 2003 Applica Consumer Products, Inc. Black and Decker® is
a trademark of The Black and Decker® Corporation, Towsan,
Maryland, U.S.A.

Take a break from life
this summer with Treasures...

one of Nestlé® Signatures™
luscious little chocolates.

Nestlé Signatures. A sweet break from life.

Visit us at nestlesignatures.com

There is no easier way for you to own a cellular phone.

TracFone is simple and convenient wireless. You pay as you go. With TracFone you buy the phone and prepay for your minutes as you need them by purchasing TracFone Prepaid Wireless Airtime cards available at over 60,000 retailers nationwide. Your TracFone tracks how much airtime you use and how much is left by displaying the exact airtime balance on the phone, so you control your costs. No more monthly surprises. There are no phone bills!

Every TracFone contains the Airtime Balance Display that shows you how much airtime you use and how much is left.

 minutes never expire with active service

 largest digital coverage area in the U.S.

$30 Mail-In Rebate

Name_____

Address_____

City_____

State_____ Zip Code_____

Day phone (_____)_____

E-mail_____

Phone Serial Number (ESN#)_____

$30 rebate or $39.99 (150 unit) prepaid wireless airtime card on the purchase of any digital TracFone wireless phone.
Please select one category ___$30.00 Rebate or ___$39.99 Wireless Airtime Card (150 units)
Mail your original dated cash register receipt, the UPC label off the TracFone package along with this completed original form to:
TracFone $30 Rebate Offer
Dept OTCF00032/33 • P.O. Box 8016
Walled Lake, MI 48391-8016

To obtain the ESN# remove battery from the cellular phone and locate the number on the back of the phone.

ADDITIONAL TERMS:
1) 90 days of uninterrupted service is required for qualification plus allow 3 to 6 weeks for processing. 2) Offer limited to U.S.A. ONLY, except where prohibited, taxed or licensed. 3) Valid for new activations only. 4) Limit one Rebate per phone. 5) Duplicate requests will not be acknowledged. 6) Not valid in conjunction with any other coupon, promotion or offer. 7) Not responsible for lost, stolen or illegible submissions. 8) Republication of this offer violates copyright statutes. 9) Photocopies of proof of purchase will not be accepted. 10) Void where prohibited. 11) If no selection is made, you will receive OUR BEST VALUE, the $39.99 airtime card. 12) Offer valid only for TracFones purchased between March and December 2003. **Must be postmarked by March 31st, 2004.**

nationwide prepaid wireless

NCPTRACCOUP2

reflect
TRUE CUSTOM BEAUTY

Indulge in a Custom Lipstick at a special price!

Try yours for only $10 ($17 value)

Your lips have never been so kissable. Create your ultimate lipstick with a formula and shade perfect for you—because you help create it!

To redeem this offer, simply:

1. Visit www.reflect.com.
2. **Create a custom LIPSTICK** and add it to your shopping bag.
3. **Enter the following code** in the promotion/gift certificate box during checkout: **KISSMYLIPS**

The discount will automatically be applied.

All of our products are unconditionally guaranteed. Simply contact our customer service representatives. Experience the difference of custom beauty—beauty products made for you.

Offer may be used only once per customer and may not be combined with any other offer. Offer good only for the product indicated. Offer carries no cash value. Offer expires 07/31/04.

NCPREFLCOUP1

reflect
TRUE CUSTOM BEAUTY

Special offer on Custom Mascara!

Try yours for $10 ($16.50 value)

Go ahead: cry at all the good parts.
Now your mascara will stay in place—even when
you're swept away by the story! Create a waterproof
(or regular) mascara customized perfectly for your
lashes, with the brush style you prefer.

To redeem this offer, simply:

1. Visit www.reflect.com.
2. **Create a custom MASCARA** and **add it to your shopping bag.**
3. **Enter the following code** in the promotion/gift certificate box during checkout: **LOVECRY**

The discount will automatically be applied.

All of our products are unconditionally guaranteed. Simply contact our customer service representatives. Experience the difference of custom beauty—beauty products made for you.

Offer may be used only once per customer and may not be combined with any other offer. Offer good only for the product indicated. Offer carries no cash value. Offer expires 07/31/04.

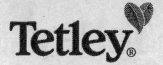

Tetley®

Let Tetley Iced Tea
Quench Your Passion!

Escape the steamy days of summer in style. Kick back and cool off with your favorite Harlequin or Silhouette romance and a thirst-quenching Tetley Iced Tea.

Visit us at www.tetleyusa.com.

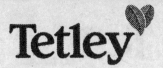

Tetley

Let Tetley Iced Tea Recipes
Quench Your Passion!

Escape the steamy days of summer in style. Kick back and cool off with your favorite Harlequin or Silhouette romance and a thirst-quenching Tetley Iced Tea. Visit **www.tetley.ca today for iced tea recipes.**

For a Different Kind of Love Story, Experience Le Petit Écolier.

LU's beloved Little Schoolboy has won hearts the world over.

Whatever your chocolate mood, there is a luscious Petit Écolier for you: Choose Milk, Milk Hazelnut, Dark or Extra Dark Chocolate.

Or, try any of these delicious varieties: PIM's (Orange, Raspberry and Orchard Pear), Chocolatier, Petit Beurre, Bastogne, and Fondant.

absoLUtely delicious.

Available in the specialty cookie aisle of your supermarket.

For a Different Kind of Love Story, Experience Le Petit Écolier.

LU's beloved Little Schoolboy has won hearts the world over.

Whatever your chocolate mood, there is a luscious Petit Écolier for you: Choose Milk, Milk Hazelnut, Dark or Extra Dark Chocolate.

Or, try any of these delicious varieties: PIM's (Orange, Raspberry and Orchard Pear), Chocolatier, Petit Beurre, Bastogne, and Fondant.

absoLUtely delicious.

Available in the specialty cookie aisle of your supermarket.

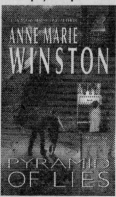

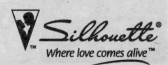